DIVIDED NATION, UNITED HEARTS

Visit us at www.boldstrokesbooks.com

By the Author

In Medias Res

Rum Spring

Lucky Loser

Month of Sundays

Murphy's Law

The War Within

Love's Bounty

Break Point

24/7

Divided Nation, United Hearts

Writing as Mason Dixon:

Date with Destiny

Charm City

21 Questions

DIVIDED NATION, UNITED HEARTS

by

Yolanda Wallace

2017

DIVIDED NATION, UNITED HEARTS

ISBN 13: 978-1-62639-847-4

This Trade Paperback Original Is Published By
Bold Strokes Books, Inc.
P.O. Box 249
Valley Falls, NY 12185

First Edition: March 2017

Credits
Editor: Cindy Cresap
Production Design: Susan Ramundo
Cover Design By Melody Pond

Acknowledgments

Living in Georgia, it's practically impossible to escape reminders of the Civil War. There are monuments, statues, and fancifully dressed re-enactors everywhere I look—and the South lost the war. Imagine what the architecture in downtown Savannah would look like if the North had surrendered at Appomattox Court House in April 1865 instead of the other way around. What is harder to find than the memorials to a conflict nearly two centuries old, however, are stories like the one that fills these pages. Stories of the various roles women played during the War Between the States. Countless books have been written about the thousands of men who put their lives on the line to fight on both sides of the war, but that doesn't hold true for the many women who felt compelled to take the same risk. I hope I've done them justice. And I fervently hope, given the divisiveness of the recent presidential campaign and its unexpected election results, that history doesn't soon repeat itself.

My thanks, as always, to the usual list of suspects: Radclyffe, my editor Cindy Cresap, and the rest of the team at Bold Strokes Books for making the writing process so much fun. Thanks to my wife Dita for continuing to put up with my frequent flights of fancy. And thank you to the readers tor taking those flights with me.

Dedication

To Dita,
Nothing can divide us.

CHAPTER ONE

February 1862
Philadelphia, Pennsylvania

Wilhelmina Fredericks reminded herself to breathe as she listened to the black man with the thick shock of coarse white hair speak so eloquently about a subject that had divided an entire nation in two.

"I prayed for freedom for twenty years," Frederick Douglass said, "but received no answer until I prayed with my legs."

Drawn in by the force of Douglass's commanding presence, Wilhelmina leaned forward in her seat. The lecture hall was filled with people who had come to hear the former slave and famed abolitionist speak. Powerful men whose riches funded businesses across the Northeast, and the well-dressed women who bore both their children and their last names. Like the rest of the audience, Wilhelmina hung on Douglass's every word.

"The white man's happiness cannot be purchased by the black man's misery." Douglass's long fingers clutched the lapels of his coat as he stood at the polished oak lectern. His dark brown eyes scanned the room, taking in the faces of his all-white audience.

Wilhelmina admired his bravery. His willingness to speak his mind despite the rabid opposition he often faced. She had heard he was nearly killed during a lecture tour nearly twenty years before when he was chased and beaten by an angry mob before being rescued by a family of pacifists who offered him shelter. Wilhelmina wished she had a modicum of his courage. How brave it was to fight for what you felt was right when so many around you tried to convince you that you were wrong. Tried to beat into your mind with whips and with words that you did not deserve the freedoms and opportunities granted to others simply based on the color of your skin. She had been denied opportunities, too. Not because of her race, but her sex. Oh, how she wished she had the luxuries—and the freedom—her brother was afforded simply by the happy circumstance of being born male. Then she could have both a mind and a voice of her own without being looked down upon for daring to express her opinions. Or her desires.

"Those who profess to favor freedom and yet depreciate agitation are people who want crops without plowing the ground," Douglass said. "They want rain without thunder and lightning. They want the ocean without the roar of its many waters. The struggle may be a moral one, or it may be a physical one, or it may be both. But it must be a struggle. Power concedes nothing without a demand. It never did and it never will."

Wilhelmina felt galvanized as Douglass continued to speak. Her father, Martin Fredericks, was one of the richest and most powerful men in the country. Though he frequently invited politicians into his stately home in one of the oldest neighborhoods in his native Philadelphia in the hopes of currying their favor for potential business deals, he privately derided politics as a dirty business unfit for women or children. All the more reason for Wilhelmina to experience this auspicious occasion in person rather than hearing about it secondhand. She wanted to hear the unvarnished truth about the state of the nation, not the whitewashed version her father thought fit for her and her mother's delicate ears.

She suspected her father would have been bored to tears by tonight's event—he usually was if an opportunity to make even more money seemed an unlikely occurrence—but she was inspired by every word that fell from Douglass's lips. She had never heard anyone speak so passionately or so persuasively about the divisive issue of slavery or the civil war its defenders and opponents were currently waging on battlefields on both sides of the Mason-Dixon Line.

"Without a struggle, there is no progress," Douglass said as he reached the end of his oratory. "Our destiny is largely in our hands."

Wilhelmina applauded wildly as she rose to her feet. She wanted to join the rest of the well-wishers as they surged forward to shake Douglass's hand or simply bask in his presence, but she didn't dare. Her disguise had managed to get her a seat in the predominantly male audience, but she feared it might not stand up to closer inspection. What would she do if she were found out? Her father had business interests in both the North and the South so he tried to remain neutral about the outcome of the war. He would never allow her to go anywhere without an escort if he discovered she had attended an event sure to draw the ire of his slave-holding cronies in Virginia, Georgia, and the Carolinas. If sufficiently angered, he might not even allow her to leave the house. She couldn't risk losing what few liberties she had. If she did, nights like this one would become a thing of the past.

She made her way to the door as quickly as the crush of people in her way would allow. Her long brown hair was pinned under, parted on one side, and slicked down with oil to mimic the most popular men's hairstyle of the day. She covered her head with a black stovepipe hat to prevent any stray locks from falling out of place. Making sure to meet men's eyes as she passed them instead of keeping her gaze directed at the ground as she would if she were sporting her normal attire, she headed outside and hailed a carriage.

"Where to, young sir?" the driver asked after she climbed into the back of the horse-drawn conveyance.

Taking care to pitch her voice into an even deeper register than her usual alto, Wilhelmina recited an address almost as familiar to her as her own. She settled into her seat after the driver slapped his leather reins across his horse's broad hindquarters.

"Here we are," the driver said after he stopped the carriage in front of a mansion in North Philadelphia.

"Thank you." Wilhelmina climbed out of the carriage and paid the fare, making sure to provide a generous tip as she did so.

The driver's eyes widened after he took a look at the extra coins in his hand. "Any time, young sir," he said, tipping his cap. "Any time."

Wilhelmina waited for him to leave before she approached the house. Gas lamps burned all along the street, but the rooms inside the cavernous house were dark. Wilhelmina picked up a pebble and carefully threw it at a window on the second floor. When she didn't receive a response, she tried again, using a bit more effort this time. She held her breath, hoping the fragile glass window wouldn't shatter from the combined pressures of the cold weather and the force of the rock's impact. A few minutes later, the heavy brocade curtains parted, and the face of Elizabeth Reynolds, Wilhelmina's oldest and dearest friend, peered through them.

Libby was obviously dressed for bed. For propriety's sake, she had pulled on a wool robe to cover her cotton nightgown. A white sleeping cap sat snugly on her head, but a few unruly blond curls had managed to find their way free. Wilhelmina had never seen her look more beautiful, but Libby clearly had no idea who she was.

"What is the meaning of this?" Libby asked in a fierce whisper after she raised the window high enough to stick her head through the opening. "If you would like the pleasure of making my acquaintance, kind sir, there are rules you must follow. Rules that don't include you attempting to break into my bed chamber at such an ungodly hour."

"Please don't take offense, madam." Wilhelmina removed her hat and bowed at the waist like a lovesick beau pleading for an audience with his intended. "I would have filled out a calling card, but I didn't want to risk having mine getting lost in the shuffle."

Libby gasped and covered her mouth with her hands. "Wilhelmina?" She stuck her head farther out the window. "My God, it is you. Why on earth are you dressed that way?"

"Let me in and I shall tell you."

Libby held a finger to her lips and patted the air with her hands, pleading for Wilhelmina to keep her voice down. "I'll come fetch you, but we must be discreet. We simply cannot let anyone see you in that god-awful attire. How would we possibly explain it?" she asked as she slid the window shut.

"How indeed?"

Wilhelmina grinned as she climbed the front steps. Her reasons for coming here were twofold: she couldn't risk going home dressed as a man, and she couldn't go to sleep until she shared the events of this day with someone. Not just anyone. Libby. The woman she had known since she was a child and had loved for nearly as long.

Libby opened the door, pulled her inside, and ushered her upstairs. "What were you thinking?" Libby asked after they were safely behind closed doors.

Wilhelmina tossed her hat, gloves, and overcoat in a nearby chair and began to remove the many pins that held her hair in place. Once free, the locks fell well past her shoulders. She missed the refreshing feel of the night air on the back of her neck. She also missed the feeling of independence she had gained by donning her disguise.

"I wanted to hear Frederick Douglass speak," she said, raking her fingers through her hair to tame the tangles, "and I couldn't afford to have any of my father's business associates recognize me. One of our most trusted maids helped me get dressed and promised to come up with a good story to explain my absence at dinner. As long as I'm back in my bed before morning, my family will never know I left the house."

"What a scandal." Libby's bright blue eyes threatened to pop out of her head. Wilhelmina felt a secret thrill for being the source of Libby's obvious titillation. "You can stay with me tonight and borrow one of my dresses for your trip home in the morning. But first you must tell me all about your adventure. After you change out of those clothes into something more appropriate, of course."

Libby rummaged in a dresser drawer, pulled out a nightgown, and turned her back while Wilhelmina undressed.

Wilhelmina removed the waistcoat, dress shirt, and trousers she had borrowed from her brother. Martin Jr. was such a clotheshorse he probably wouldn't even notice the articles were missing. She paused as she pulled her chemise over her head, wishing Libby would turn and look at her. Wishing Libby would see her standing naked before her. Both her body and her heart were Libby's for the taking. To claim them, all Libby had to do was turn around. Alas, Libby continued to face the wall, waiting to know that she was decent—and to hear her tale.

Wilhelmina pulled Libby's nightgown over her head and climbed into the large four-poster bed. Both the silk nightgown she wore and the cotton sheets she lay between smelled of the rosewater perfume Libby dabbed behind each ear twice a day. Once before breakfast and once before retiring for the night. Wilhelmina pulled the covers up to her chin. Her head swam as Libby's scent permeated her senses.

"Was it everything you thought it would be?" Libby asked.

"It was even better."

Libby crawled into bed and wriggled close to her, making Wilhelmina's head swim even more. "You simply must tell me all about it."

Libby's eyes shone even brighter than the flames dancing in the fireplace across the room. Wilhelmina's heart skittered at the sight.

She began to recite Frederick Douglass's impassioned speech practically word for word, but Libby grew bored within minutes. Libby didn't want to know what was said. She wanted to know who had been in attendance and what everyone was wearing. Wilhelmina did her best to provide the requested details, but she had been more interested in the man on stage than the people in the audience.

"I thank the heavens you are safe." Libby took Wilhelmina's hands in hers and kissed them fervently. Wilhelmina wished Libby would kiss her lips that way, but Libby saved such kisses for Stephen Andrews, the junior business associate who had recently asked her to become his wife. "Anything could have happened to you alone on the streets at night. Only you would take such a risk."

"The risk I took tonight is nothing compared to the one I intend to take next."

Libby smiled indulgently. "What caper are you planning to pull off this time?"

Wilhelmina pushed herself into a seated position. She had come to a decision during the carriage ride from the lecture hall. She expected few people to agree with her, but she had always been able to count on Libby's support and prayed that wasn't about to change.

"After listening to such a persuasive speech, I feel I must do my part to help the war effort."

"That's easily accomplished," Libby said. "Mother is a member of the local ladies' aid society. She's always saying she could use more volunteers. I'm certain she would love it if you and I gave her a helping hand from time to time. It would also serve as good practice so we won't begin our lives as married women unprepared."

Wilhelmina shook her head. "I don't want to learn how to can fruit, darn socks, or launder uniforms. You know that kind of work isn't for me. Neither is marriage, for that matter."

Libby laughed and took one of Wilhelmina's large hands in her dainty ones. "I've always said you would make someone a better husband than you would a wife. You're as tall as most men and nearly as obstinate when you set your mind to something. Tonight, it's obvious you don't lack for courage either."

"That is why I intend to fight."

Libby laughed again. This time, a hint of nervousness mingled with the mirth. She pressed Wilhelmina's palm to her cheek. Wilhelmina felt the warmth of Libby's skin. Longed to taste it with her lips and tongue.

"Don't be silly, Wil. You know women aren't allowed to join the military. A good thing, too. I would faint if I saw all that blood and gore. The most you could hope for is to be a nurse, but you wouldn't be given a gun or permitted to fight."

Wilhelmina brushed a lock of blond hair off Libby's forehead. "Who said I intend to enlist as a woman?"

Libby's mouth fell open in shock. "Surely you jest."

"Quite the contrary. In fact, I have never been more serious."

"Do you honestly think you could get away with such a ruse?"

"I pulled the wool over everyone's eyes in the lecture hall tonight, didn't I? Not to mention I even managed to fool you, my lifelong friend."

Libby's cheeks colored at the reminder she had believed Wilhelmina to be a stranger when she spied her standing beneath her window.

"Yes, but that was from a distance. Do you think you could stay hidden in close quarters for months, maybe years at a time with hundreds of men and convince them that you're one as well?" Their conversation was already hushed due to the lateness of the hour and the topic of their discourse. Shuddering with distaste, Libby lowered her voice even more. "How do you plan to perform life's most basic functions surrounded by an army of men without revealing your true sex?"

Wilhelmina had asked herself the same question during the carriage ride. She couldn't bathe or relieve herself without exposing part of her body. How could she manage to do either without giving herself away? Either in the barracks, in camp, or on the battlefield, privacy would be an even more precious commodity than peace.

"I don't know how long I can keep up the pretense, Libby, but I feel compelled to try. I want to do my part, and—no offense to your mother or the ladies who have volunteered to help her provide supplies to the troops—I want to do it where it counts the most. On the battlefield, not the home front."

Libby fixed her with an appraising stare. "I never imagined you with a rifle in your hands, Wil."

"Neither did I. Until tonight. Now I can't imagine anything else. I can sit on the sidelines no longer. I must join the fight."

"I admire your courage, but how do you plan to accomplish your task? What you're proposing is impossible."

"Not impossible. Improbable. Those are two entirely different beasts." Wilhelmina didn't know if she would be able to pull the trigger the first time she had to aim a gun at someone or if she could hold her nerve the first time one was trained in her direction, but she had to try. "I shall cut my hair, change my appearance, and sign up in a city where no one knows me."

"But what about…" Libby's voice trailed off and her cheeks colored. "You know." She waved her hand in the general direction of Wilhelmina's body.

Wilhelmina spoke to save Libby further embarrassment. "My breasts are small enough that I won't have to bind them too tightly, and I haven't had the monthly curse since I was fifteen. The doctor in charge of my care said I am barren."

"Is that why your father has created such a large dowry for you?"

"Yes." Wilhelmina lowered her head. Speaking of her marriage prospects always made her feel more like a piece of property than a person. "But few men are willing to marry a woman who cannot bear them children. The ones who have remained in the running for my hand seem to care more about my father's money than they do about me."

Libby nodded sympathetically. "I feel lucky in that regard. Stephen cares for me, not my family name or my father's riches. He wants to make his fortune on his own, not inherit it from his wife. One day, I hope you will meet a man who feels the same way about you."

Libby caressed Wilhelmina's cheek. Wilhelmina closed her eyes and enjoyed the sensation. How she wished she could tell Libby the secret she had long carried—that the only person she wanted to marry was her—but she knew Libby wouldn't understand. Libby's heart belonged to Stephen and always would. Wilhelmina's, on the other hand, seemed destined to go unclaimed.

"And what of your parents?" Libby asked. "Do you plan to tell them what you have in mind?"

"I shall leave them a note explaining my absence, though it hardly seems necessary. I have always been an afterthought in their eyes. My brother has always been Father's favorite, and my sister has always had Mother's good graces. I doubt anyone will even know I'm gone."

"I shall know." Tears welled in Libby's eyes as she held Wilhelmina's face in her hands. "Though the cause is just, are you truly willing to risk your life in order to see it through?"

"I am." Wilhelmina's heart ached for the concern she heard in Libby's voice. She hadn't meant to cause her pain. She swallowed around the lump in her throat. "Will you keep my secret?"

"Of course, you ninny. Haven't I always? I would try to talk you out of this silly notion, but I know it's impossible to talk you out of anything once you have made up your mind." Libby blinked away her tears. "Write to me every single day so I'll know you're safe. Because if you don't, I shall find you and drag you home by the ear. Is that understood?"

Wilhelmina placed her hand to her head in a mock salute. "Yes, ma'am."

Libby's joyous peal of laughter helped lift some of the burden on Wilhelmina's heart. She didn't look forward to leaving her family and friends behind and putting her fate in the hands of strangers, but Frederick Douglass's words had inspired her to do everything she could to make freedom a reality rather than a dream. Not just for the thousands of men, women, and children in bondage but for herself as well.

"Kiss me, Libby."

Libby frowned. "Whatever for?"

Wilhelmina ran a finger over the furrows in Libby's brow. "Because tonight might be the last time we see each other in this life."

"Don't speak that way."

"Don't speak the truth, you mean?"

"No." Libby pulled away. "Don't speak like one of those women who take comfort in the arms of other women." She looked at Wilhelmina as if seeing her for the first time. As if seeing a stranger. "You're not like those women, are you?" she asked hesitantly.

"I take comfort where I can find it. Surely you don't take issue with that," Wilhelmina said. Fearing the chance she was about to take might never come again, she tossed reason aside. "I won't deny that I love you, Libby. I always have."

Confusion radiated from Libby's eyes. Confusion and something darker. "You have feelings for me? You're—"

Wilhelmina smiled to ease Libby's mind. Smiled even though she felt like crying in despair.

Libby's relieved laughter filled the room. "You're teasing me again. You were teasing me the whole time, weren't you? There."

She pressed her lips to Wilhelmina's. The moment was brief, but for Wilhelmina, it seemed to last a lifetime. "There's your kiss. Now hold me close, cease your jokes, and promise me you won't speak of such foolishness again."

"I promise."

As she held Libby in her arms, Wilhelmina wondered if the joke was on her.

CHAPTER TWO

February 1862
Shiloh, Tennessee

Clara Summers was an early riser. Not by choice but by necessity. Though her family's farm was small, it couldn't run itself. Clara needed to get out of bed well before the sun rose in order to make sure all the tasks that needed to be accomplished were taken care of before the end of the day.

Since her mother died of the consumption back in 1857 and her father and older brother left to join up with the 4th Tennessee Infantry Regiment five months after the war began, the responsibility of running the farm had fallen squarely on Clara's shoulders. Not like she had any say in the matter. Despite what her father had said before he and Solomon rode away last fall, her little brothers were too young to be the men of the house. Abram was only thirteen and Percival was about to turn ten. If she didn't bear the load, who would?

She shimmied out of her nightgown two hours before dawn and splashed some water from the washbasin on her face to wipe the sleep from her eyes. She dipped a bar of lye soap into the water and ran it over her arms and legs. After she rinsed off the thin layer of suds, she dried her skin with a threadbare cotton cloth and reached for her work dress. The dress bore more patches than original material, but she refused to part with it because it was the last article of clothing her mother had sewn for her before her untimely passing.

After Clara laced up her thin-soled shoes, she tied a kerchief around her head to keep her hair from falling in her eyes while she fed the hogs and milked the cows. She had inherited her red hair from her mother, whose people immigrated from Belfast years ago. She hadn't inherited her mother's Irish brogue, but she had been cursed with her notoriously short temper. When she was in a mood, the men in her family knew to give her a wide berth. Despite the seemingly endless list of chores that stretched before her, she had awakened in a good mood today and hoped to make it last.

She put some leftover biscuits in the potbellied stove to warm while she fried some eggs and sausage in a cast iron skillet. Abram and Percy stumbled in the kitchen still half-asleep as she spooned the food onto three chipped plates. She gave her brothers the lion's share of the victuals and left only the bare minimum for herself. Nothing unusual. She was used to going without. Abram and Percy were growing so fast they would eat her out of house and home if they had the chance. Abram was already almost as tall as she was, and Percy was even with her shoulder. By next year, both would be looking down at her instead of looking up. But next year was a long way away. And unless the war ended much sooner than anyone expected it to, Clara would have to make all the decisions. Because the men of the house were still just boys.

She worried for Papa's and Solomon's safety, but in a way, she was glad they were gone. She felt silenced when they were home. Their loud voices always combined to drown hers out. They were good men at their core and Clara was proud to call them family, but they felt it was their duty to tell the women in their lives what to think and how to feel. Clara had never been allowed to have ideas or opinions of her own. Until now. She prayed every night for the war to end, but she wasn't looking forward to losing her newfound freedom. How could she go back to being quiet now that she had learned to speak up for herself?

"Slow down," she said as Percy shoveled food into his mouth like he hadn't eaten in days.

Abram snickered. "If he chokes to death, we'll have one less mouth to feed."

Clara cuffed his ear. "Apologize to your brother."

Abram glared at her and didn't make a move to comply with her wishes. Like most Southern men, Abram hated being told what to do. That was the main reason the Yankees and the Confederates were at odds now. Clara's family had never owned slaves, and her father derided most slave owners as "lazy no-accounts who would rather sip mint juleps on their front porches rather than getting their hands dirty in their fields," yet he had not hesitated to take up arms to defend their right to do so. Clara didn't care who won the fight. She just wanted Papa and Solomon to come home safe.

"Do you want me to get the strap, Abram?"

Abram eyed the leather strap hanging from a hook near the fireplace. Clara couldn't count the number of times their father had used the strap to mete out discipline. "Spare the rod and spoil the child," he said each time he smacked the strap against someone's hide. Eventually, simply the threat of its use was enough to keep everyone in line. Usually. Abram couldn't seem to stop himself from testing the limits of Papa's patience from time to time. Clara knew it was all a part of growing up, but she wished Abram would hurry up and get this part over with. Patience was a virtue she didn't possess.

"You may be the oldest one left," Abram said resentfully, "but you ain't Papa."

Clara gathered the empty plates and set them in the sink. Carefully so Abram wouldn't see how much his comment rattled her. She knew she wasn't Papa. She wasn't Mama, either. But she was doing the best she could. Why couldn't anyone see or appreciate that? She stood up straight and threw her shoulders back. She couldn't fall apart now. Not when her family needed her most. "Until Papa and Solomon come back," she said firmly, "whatever I say goes."

Abram grabbed two biscuits from the larder. He finished the first in two big bites and held the other in his grubby fist. He looked at her as if sizing her up to see how far he could go. "When he left, Papa said I should do the providing, not you."

Clara washed and dried the dishes, then set them on the counter so they could be reused during the midday meal. Abram was trying to start a fight, but she wanted no part of it. She tried not to let his words hurt her. She knew he was scared about the war and worried about whether Papa and Solomon would make it home under their own power or lying toes-up in a pine box. She shared his fears, but she couldn't afford to let him see her uncertainty. She had to be strong for all three of them, not just herself.

"You'll be running your own house soon enough, brother. Why the rush?" she asked with a smile. "Is Mary Bragg pressuring you to propose?"

Abram's face reddened and he shoved his hands in the pockets of his overalls as he pawed at the floor with the toe of his boot. He had finally reached an age where girls were objects of fascination rather than nuisances, though he tried his best not to let it show. Except when Mary Bragg was around. Then his tied tongue and blushing cheeks made his interest apparent. His shaggy strawberry blond hair shielded his face as he stared at the floor. "I'm as much of a mind to marry Mary Bragg as you are to walk down the aisle with Jedediah Ogletree."

Clara clenched her teeth to keep from saying something she might regret. Jedediah was the son of one of the richest landowners in Shiloh. He had set his cap for her long ago, but she didn't feel any of the ardor for him he claimed to feel for her. All the women she knew said she should feel honored by his attention. Instead, she felt smothered. She couldn't breathe when he tried to sweet-talk her. All she wanted to do was get away from him, not move closer. But she didn't know how to explain how she felt without making it seem like she was putting on airs or playing silly games in order to fan the flames of Jedediah's interest. She wanted to live her life on her own terms, not have some man dictate her every move. Not her father, not her brother, and especially not Jedediah Ogletree.

"He doesn't want me," she said firmly. She wanted to put the subject to rest once and for all so she wouldn't have to address it again. She had a hard enough time trying to convince Jedediah she wasn't interested in him. Why did she have to sway everyone else, too? "He and his father want to get their hands on the deed to Papa's land. He thinks he can use me to get it, but he's got another think coming. I wasn't put on this earth to be any man's property—or a means to him acquiring more."

Abram looked up and met her eye. "But don't you want to get married one day?" he asked earnestly.

"How can I when I've got Papa, you, and your brothers to take care of?" As the only daughter, it was her lot in life to look after her family until the end of her days. She could do that as a married woman or as an old maid. Given a choice, she preferred the option that didn't shackle her to a man she didn't love. "Now get out of here and go rustle up some fresh meat for supper. I've stretched the squirrel stew about as far as I can take it." She'd added in a few more vegetables each day to make it last, but at this point the meat was little more than a memory. They had pork in the smokehouse, but she didn't want to burn through their reserves too fast. This winter—and this war—might be a long one.

Abram grinned, reveling in the chance to be a child instead of the man he longed to be. "I'll bring back the biggest raccoon you've ever seen. Just you wait and see." He reached for the shotgun over the mantle and ran for the door.

"Take your brother with you."

Abram skidded to a stop. His shoulders drooped, along with his spirits. "Do I have to?"

Papa and Solomon had taught Abram to hunt as soon as he was old enough to hold a rifle. Everyone in Shiloh called Solomon the best shot in the county, but Abram might be even better. If he aimed at something, he was bound to hit it right between the eyes. Percy, on the other hand, lacked his brothers' hunting ability. Too enthusiastic to be stealthy, he usually scared the prey away before he could get close enough to raise his gun, let alone fire it.

"Mrs. Turtledove said she saw a group of Union soldiers tromping through her woods last week," Clara said. "According to her, two of them raided her smokehouse and three stole all the pigs from her pen. She's been known to tell a tall tale every now and then, especially when she's had a few sips of moonshine from Myron Chamblee's still. But in case she's telling the truth this time, I don't want either of you going off by yourselves."

"You let one of those Yankees come at me." Abram raised the shotgun to his shoulder and fired off an imaginary shot. "I'll kill him dead before he can even think twice."

Clara shivered as if someone had walked over her grave. "There's been too much killing in this war already. We don't need you adding to the tally. Now go on. Get."

She gave Abram and Percy a smack on their backsides and shooed them out the door. Once they were gone, she allowed herself a few minutes to enjoy the brief moment of peace and quiet before she headed outside to slop the hogs.

She was a country girl through and through. She was born in this rural part of Tennessee and, God willing, she would one day die here. Some of the people she had grown up with had been seduced by the lure of the big city and had abandoned the simple small-town life for the thrills Memphis and Nashville had to offer, but she preferred to be serenaded by the chirping of crickets and the croaking of bullfrogs rather than a lovelorn singer in a smoke-filled saloon. Lately, however, the quiet she had come to know and love was interrupted more and more often by the sound of gunfire as Union soldiers pushed farther and farther south and Confederate troops tried to hold them off.

She had heard tales of some people treating a few of the more pitched battles like entertainment. They packed picnic lunches and watched from the sidelines as men in blue and gray uniforms attacked each other with bullets, cannonballs, and bayonets. She had urged Abram and Percy to run the other way if they heard gunfire, but she doubted they would be able to resist the spectacle. She couldn't blame them for being curious—the War Between the States was the most exciting thing that had happened around these parts in years—but she wanted them to be safe. That meant keeping them out of the line of fire, not sprawled on their bellies watching men try to kill each other.

She tossed table scraps in the feed trough in the hog pen and prayed that the gunshots she heard in the distance came from Abram's rifle instead of a Yankee soldier's.

After the hogs were fed, the rooster began to crow. Clara tossed handfuls of crushed corn on the ground and called, "Here, chick, chickie," to coax the rest of the birds from the coop.

The chickens crowded around her feet and began to peck at the food she had scattered for them. While they ate, she gathered the eggs the hens had laid and secured them in the pockets of her dress. She looked down when she felt the barn cat who kept the rats from making a home in the hayloft rubbing against her legs.

Abram had named the now six-year-old cat Jack, short for jack-o'-lantern, because his coarse fur was as orange as a pumpkin. Mama had taken issue with his reasoning. In Ireland, where Halloween was invented, rutabagas and turnips were used to carve jack-o'-lanterns, she said, not pumpkins. But Abram hadn't been able to come up with any good names out of those choices so Jack had stuck.

"Morning, Jack."

Jack purred in response and trotted toward the barn as if showing Clara the way. Gertie, one of the family's dairy cows, lowed when she saw them approach.

"I'm coming, girl."

Clara could tell by looking that Gertie's sizeable udder was full. She sat on a stool and began to ease the painful pressure. Fresh milk—enough to make at least two pounds of butter—streamed into the bucket at her feet. When Gertie lowed again, it sounded more like a sigh of relief.

Clara was taking the milk and eggs to the house when she heard the clip-clop of an approaching horse's hooves. She didn't need to turn around to know who her visitor was.

Most of the poor men in Shiloh and the neighboring counties had gone off to war, but the rich ones had stayed behind. Jedediah Ogletree included. He had become a member of the local defense troop to save face, but his primary duty appeared to be showering Clara with unwanted attention rather than patrolling the area to prevent a Yankee invasion. He showed up at the same time each morning, whether Clara wanted him to or not.

"Good morning, Clara," he said, tipping his hat.

"Good morning, Jedediah," she said without breaking stride.

"Whoa, now." Jedediah jumped down off his chestnut stallion and circled in front of her. He used the reins to trap her on one side and placed his hand on his horse's sizeable haunches to trap her on the other. "Where are you off to in such a hurry?"

"Do you see anyone else around here who's going to churn the butter, clean the house, cook the meals, or tend the fields? The men are gone."

"I'm still here. If you need me to show you how much of a man I am, I will gladly oblige." He reached to caress her cheek. She tried to pull away but couldn't go far with his horse pressed against her back. "Still acting bashful, I see. Your apparent reluctance only heightens my anticipation for your eventual capitulation."

Even though she didn't know all the fancy words Jedediah had used, Clara understood enough of them to gather his meaning.

"I don't love you, Jed. How many times do I have to say it before it sinks into that thick head of yours?"

She tried to push him away, but her efforts didn't budge him in the slightest.

"I'm not asking you to love me. I'm asking for your hand in marriage. I can have one without the other. You do realize that, don't you?"

"Why would I want to marry someone I don't love?"

"Don't be childish, Clara. You don't need love in order to survive, but you do need a man at your side. I'm offering to stand beside yours. Use your head. There aren't very many prospects around here and you're looking at the best of the lot. No one else in Hardin County can give you what I can, and you know it. Stop pretending you don't want what I can give you and say yes."

Clara stood her ground. "I don't want you, your money, or your land."

"Then what do you want? Tell me. I'm listening."

She leaped at the rare opportunity to speak her mind, though she suspected he was only humoring her rather than truly listening to what she had to say.

"I want someone who loves me with his whole heart and soul, not someone who simply wants a companion so he doesn't have to go through life alone. I want someone who wants me for me, not for what he can get from marrying me. I want someone who treats me like an equal, not someone who acts like I'm less than he is. I want someone who wants me to be a helpmate, not a—"

He didn't see her point or give her a chance to finish making it.

"If you need my help around here, Clara, all you have to do is ask."

Clara could use the help—Abram and Percy should be going to school instead of foraging for food or trying to keep the farm going—but she would rather watch the crops rot on their vines than be beholden to Jedediah Ogletree for anything. He wasn't the kind of man who did someone a favor without expecting something in return. And she wasn't willing to sacrifice her dignity or her honor in order to pay him for services rendered.

"Work, work, work. It's all you do." Jedediah tightened the reins in his fist so she couldn't pry them from his fingers and make her escape. "If you were my wife, you would never have to work another day in your life. You would have servants to tend to your every need, and your dresses would be made of the finest silk."

She shrank under his gaze as he eyed the patches on her cotton frock. Shame, thick and hot, welled inside her. Though she and her family had never had much, they had never wanted for anything. She hated Jedediah's suggestion that her life was somehow inadequate because she couldn't afford to buy some fancy dress she had no use for.

"I don't need servants," she said defensively. "I can look after myself."

"A pretty little thing like you shouldn't have to work so hard. You should be sipping tea on the veranda while someone caters to your every whim."

A life of leisure might appeal to some women. To Clara, it sounded like a fate worse than death. Tending to the crops and looking after the animals was hard work, but she felt a tremendous sense of satisfaction come harvest time when her family was able to reap what she had helped to sow.

"Are you sure you don't want to reconsider my proposal?" Jedediah asked. "I could have any woman in the county. Maybe even the whole state. Yet I chose you."

Jedediah drew himself up tall, obviously thinking his popularity with women was due to his good looks rather than his financial and social standing. Clara was willing to admit he was good-looking. He had thick, wavy brown hair, a well-groomed mustache, and a handsome face, but she wasn't attracted to him. His words were warm, but something in his eyes left her cold. When he smiled at her, she didn't feel on fire inside like her mother said she would when she met the man she was supposed to marry. That meant only one thing: Jedediah wasn't the man for her, no matter how hard he tried to convince her otherwise.

"Why do you want me?" she asked. "Because I'm the prettiest girl you've ever seen in your whole life and you just can't live without me, or because my family's property stands between your daddy's farm and the river? If you had direct access to it, you'd have plenty of fresh water to dampen your fields without having to worry about sitting around praying for rain during an especially long dry spell."

Jedediah's gaze drifted toward the Tennessee River and surrounding land. They were the true objects of his affection, not her.

"I want you because I don't like to take no for an answer. And I'm willing to wait as long as I have to until I hear you say yes."

His answer made her sound like a prize to be won rather than a woman to be won over. Clara looked him in the eye so he wouldn't miss her meaning.

"In that case, you're going to be waiting a long time." She ducked under his arm before he could try to take what wasn't his. "If you'll excuse me, I don't have time for idle chatter. I have work to do. Good day."

"Don't work too hard." As he tipped his hat to her, the smile on his face bordered on cruel. "I'll be seeing you."

Jedediah's words sounded more like a threat than a promise. Clara picked up her pace, hoping she wouldn't end up becoming a casualty in a war she hadn't signed up to fight.

CHAPTER THREE

Wilhelmina felt tears roll down her cheeks as Rose Collins, the chambermaid who had become more of a trusted friend over the past few years than an employee, cut her hair with a pair of shears.

"It isn't too late to change your mind, lass," Rose said in her distinctive Scottish burr. She loosened her grip on what remained of Wilhelmina's hair, but Wilhelmina felt a slight tug as Rose leaned back to get a better look at her. "I haven't cut too much off yet. You could wear your hair pinned under until it grows back. It might take a few months, but no one would ever be the wiser."

"No, I beseech you to keep going." Wilhelmina dried her tears and turned in her chair so she could look Rose in the eye. "I assure you I'm not crying because I'm heartsick over my decision. I'm crying because I have never felt such peace."

Rose put her lye-reddened hands on her ample hips and shook her head in amazement as she regarded the growing pile of hair on the floor. She had already shorn a good three inches and had at least six more to go before Wilhelmina's appearance would sufficiently change to allow her to pass for a man.

"You've always been a strange one, you have," Rose said, giving Wilhelmina's chin a gentle tug. "No wonder ye and I get along so well."

Wilhelmina smiled at the atypical show of affection. Rose didn't normally resort to sentimentality. Her occasionally brusque manner had struck fear in the hearts of the rest of the maids and butlers when she joined the staff ten years ago. Her thick brogue could be impenetrable at times, especially when she was in a lather over a real or perceived slight, but she and Wilhelmina had always been fast friends. Wilhelmina felt an affinity for her she had never experienced with anyone else. Partly because she sensed in Rose a kindred spirit.

Rose had never come right out and said the words, obviously, but Wilhelmina suspected they had more in common than their shared love of a good game of chess. Once, when she had come home unexpectedly early from a party that had bored her to tears, she had discovered Rose crying in her room while holding the picture of a beautiful brunette she kept on the nightstand next to her bed. When asked, Rose had said the woman was a dear friend she had left behind when she sailed from Aberdeen to Philadelphia, but the wistful tone in her voice had hinted that the full story was being left unsaid.

"Where is she now?" Wilhelmina had asked.

Rose had blown her nose with a resounding honk that had sounded like a hoarse goose attempting to clear its throat. "Back in Aberdeen married to a whiskey-loving Highlander with three bairns tugging at the hem of her dress."

Wilhelmina had thought of her unsettled feelings regarding Libby's courtship with Stephen Andrews as she took Rose into her arms to try to offer a modicum of comfort. "I understand."

"Yes, child," Rose had said with a sad but knowing smile, "I think you do."

Until she asked Libby to kiss her, that night with Rose was the closest Wilhelmina had ever come to revealing her secret. Knowing someone else shared her desires made her feel a little less alone. Now she was about to leave Rose behind. Would Rose understand her decision to join the Union Army as well as she understood what it was like to fall in love with another woman? Probably not, but she had pledged her support, and Wilhelmina needed as many people on her side as she could get.

"There now," Rose said after she finished trimming Wilhelmina's hair. She looked at Wilhelmina long and hard. "You make a right handsome fella if I say so myself."

"You think so?" Wilhelmina regarded her visage in the mirror, surprised by the powerful resemblance she now bore to her brother. If she had the wispy moustache Marty had been trying to grow since he was sixteen, they could have passed for twins.

Rose brushed stray hairs off Wilhelmina's shoulders. "I think you could give young Martin a run for his money if you set your mind to it," she said with a hint of pride. "But perhaps you're too pretty for your own good. You don't want people to take one look at you and think you're too weak to stand up for yourself. If you like, I could give you a scar to roughen up your looks a bit so the men you come across will think twice about trying to lure you into a fight. Right along here, say?" She ran the handle of the brush in her hand along Wilhelmina's cheek. "One flick with a sharp knife and it will be over before you know it."

Wilhelmina shook her head, not wanting to imagine the pain or the vast amounts of blood such a wound would leave behind. "A scar might make me too memorable. It is my aim to go unnoticed, not to be remembered."

Rose began to pack a haversack with supplies: three pairs of socks, two pairs of underwear, a razor, and a bottle of cologne appropriated from Marty's possessions, along with a pencil, several sheets of writing paper, and a small Bible. Wilhelmina had never been especially religious, but she suspected what little faith she had would be sorely tested over the coming months.

"I'm sure you'll be wanting this, too." Rose held up a sepia-colored tintype of Libby that Wilhelmina normally kept secured between the pages of her favorite book. Wilhelmina blushed as Rose slipped the tintype into the inside pocket of her suit jacket. "Keep it close to your heart so you'll keep her safe."

Wilhelmina tried to reply, but her throat was too constricted from emotion to allow her to speak.

Rose brushed her hands over the lapels of Marty's suit, which she had taken the time to alter so that it better fit Wilhelmina's slightly narrower shoulders and waist. "You keep yourself safe, too, you hear? If anything ever happened to you, I'd—" She turned away as tears filled her eyes.

"I'll be fine," Wilhelmina choked out as she held Rose's quaking shoulders in her hands. "Thank you for all you've done for me." She turned Rose around, forcing her to face her. "I have one more favor to ask of you."

Rose blew her nose and put on a brave face. "What do you need me to do for ye?"

Wilhelmina pressed a letter into Rose's hands. "Leave this for my father to find, but make sure he doesn't discover it until long after I am gone. I need several hours' lead in case he sends someone after me."

Rose nodded solemnly. "I will." She blew her nose again as she secured the letter in the pocket of her dress. Then she reached for a broom and began sweeping up the hair that had fallen on the floor. "Go while my back is turned," she said. "I can't bear to watch you leave."

"Thank you, Rose. For everything."

Wilhelmina kissed her on the cheek, then slipped out of the room, down the stairs, and out the front door. She took a carriage to the train station and used some of the money she had "borrowed" from her brother's wallet to buy a ticket to Pittsburgh. She used even more of her meager savings to rent a room for the night. She counted what remained of her money after she locked the door behind her. She didn't have enough to purchase a train ticket home. What would she do if the men at the enlistment office saw through her disguise?

"This ruse has to be successful," she said, starting to question her decision. "I've gone too far to turn back now."

She put the money back in its hiding place in her haversack and undressed for bed. Unable to sleep, she stared at the ceiling as the sounds of a lady of the evening enthusiastically entertaining a client leeched through the thin walls.

Not for the first time, Wilhelmina wondered what it was like to feel a woman's touch on her bare skin. To hear a woman whisper her name as she neared the precipice and Wilhelmina took the journey with her. A lump formed in her throat as she realized she might never be able to experience all the things most people took for granted. The one thing she wanted to experience most: a woman's love.

After her neighbors' sounds of pleasure finally reached a crescendo, she closed her eyes and fell into a fitful sleep. She rose early the next day, bathed, dressed, and followed the signs plastered to walls and lampposts directing able-bodied men to places where they could enlist. After she reached her destination, she blew on her hands to warm them as she stood in line with the fifty-odd men waiting for a chance to shore up the ranks of the 77th Pennsylvania Volunteer Infantry. Winters in the North were nearly unbearable. She hoped the temperatures down South would prove more palatable since she and the other members of her regiment would be living outside for the foreseeable future with nothing but canvas tents for shelter and the heat from small campfires, thin blankets, and their thick wool uniforms for warmth.

The 77th was organized the preceding October for a three-year enlistment. The men under Colonel Frederick Stumbaugh's command left Pennsylvania for Louisville, Kentucky, on October 18, 1861, and were currently camped out in Munfordville, Kentucky, where the new recruits would join them after they filled out their enlistment papers and completed two weeks of training.

Wilhelmina heard the snickers as she drew closer to the table manned by two soldiers in charge of reviewing and stamping the men's enlistment paperwork.

"I know the Rebs have said they're willing to fight to the last man if they have to," one man said as he stroked his luxurious mutton chop whiskers, "but is the Union so desperate to win this war that the officials in charge are willing to sign up boys to fill its rolls?"

Wilhelmina kept her eyes trained on the soldiers seated at the table while volunteers in both lines turned to gauge her reaction to what the man had said. She had broad shoulders and large hands for a woman. To these men, however, she must look like an undeveloped youth.

"In the immortal words of President Lincoln," said a man with the voice of an orator and the carriage of someone used to being a leader rather than a follower, "we can complain because rose bushes have thorns or rejoice that thorn bushes have roses."

The man with the whiskers paused mid-stroke. "What in heaven's name is that supposed to mean?"

The second man took a puff on the pipe clenched between his teeth. "Words can mean whatever we wish them to. In this case, I choose to believe it is better not to make a mockery of this young man for his tender years but to commend him for doing what some men allegedly older and wiser have refused to do."

Murmurs of "Quite right" and "Hear, hear," sounded up and down the lines. Stripped of his bluster, the man with the whiskers grew quiet. Wilhelmina nodded her thanks to the man with the deep voice. In response, he blew out a thick plume of smoke and stuck out his hand.

"Erwin Weekley, late of Warren, Pennsylvania, and apparently destined for climes farther south. Who might you be?"

"Wil Fredericks, sir," Wilhelmina said, reminding herself to abbreviate her first name rather than using the full version of it. "From Philadelphia. It's a pleasure to meet you."

"That's a good grip you have there, young Wil," Erwin said with an amused chuckle. "What do you do back in Philadelphia, forge steel with your bare hands?"

"No, sir. Mostly, I read all the books and newspapers I can get my hands on." Which was no easy feat, considering her father felt there was no need for women to be educated in the ways of the world once they had completed their obligatory schooling.

"You forged your mind instead of steel. An equally worthy endeavor."

"If I may ask, how do you make your living, sir?"

As well read as he seemed to be, she thought he might be a teacher or a philosopher or some other profession that required deep thought.

"I have been in the lumber industry for thirty years now," Erwin said. "We used to use the Allegheny to float lumber from Warren to Pittsburgh. Sometimes, you couldn't see the water for all the logs covering the surface." He paused to shake his head. "But forests eventually grow thin and so do the profits. For the past few years, I've been taking odd jobs wherever I could find them. Now I'm here signing up for the oddest job of all."

The man with the mutton chop whiskers snorted a derisive laugh. "It's good to hear some men's sense of duty comes with a price tag attached."

Wilhelmina felt her temper flare, but Erwin's expression remained calm as he eyed the man up and down. "Pardon me, but I don't think I caught your name, sir."

"That's because I didn't give it," the man said with a smirk. "Normally, my reputation precedes me. I am Maynard Harrison from Altoona." He briefly doffed his hat, then screwed it back into place. "I was a surveyor for the Pennsylvania Railroad until this fracas began. When it's over, I shall have my work cut out for me reversing all the damage the Rebs have inflicted. They use rail lines to transport their food, supplies, and soldiers, but destroy ours to prevent us from doing the same. I fear what this country will look like when the war ends. I fear there may be nothing salvageable left."

"Without a doubt, there will be scars on both sides," Erwin said, "and not just on the land."

Wilhelmina thought of the wounded veterans she had seen haunting the streets of Philadelphia. Some were missing an arm or leg. Others were forced to live the rest of their lives with features ruined by the ravages of war. For the rest, their scars were on the inside. Hidden from view but just as painful.

Her courage wavered, as did her belief in herself. Was she doing the right thing, or was she simply a foolish girl embarking on a regrettable folly that might cost her her life?

Erwin seemed to read her thoughts. "No one will think any less of you if you decide this life isn't for you, young Wil," he said gently.

"I appreciate the sentiment, Mr. Weekley, but the life I shall be fighting for is markedly better than the one I left behind."

Erwin's face was dark and leathery from years spent working in the elements. The deeply etched lines in his cheeks framed his mouth as he smiled. "I am certain we could all say the same."

When Wilhelmina finally reached the front of the line, the soldier seated in front of her kept his hands in his lap instead of reaching for the pen resting in a bottle of black ink on the tabletop.

"You have to be eighteen to enlist," the soldier said. "How old are you?"

"Nineteen," she said truthfully.

He cast a skeptical look at her smooth cheeks. "Nineteen? Subtract three or four years from that number, and I might believe you."

Wilhelmina felt the initial stirrings of panic. If the man sent her away, she didn't have enough money to purchase a train ticket home. She could stay here and work, but she'd need to find a boarding house or a room for rent. Both required money, and her supply was rapidly dwindling. This desperate gambit had to work. Because if it didn't, she would have to contact her father and beg for his help. Given the circumstances, she doubted he would be feeling especially generous toward her for a while. If ever again.

"I've always been told I look young for my age, sir, but I was born on the third of June in 1842, which makes me closer to twenty than nineteen and well above the legal age to—"

The soldier held up a hand to stop her. "If you're that eager to join, boy, I won't stand in your way, no matter what your age."

He finally reached for his pen and asked her to provide more information. She gave him her new name but left her date of birth and city of origin the same. He didn't ask for her home address so she didn't provide it. She wanted her family to be notified if she was injured or killed while attempting to fulfill her duty, but with thousands of men already missing or presumed dead, she doubted the army had enough time or resources to contact each man's family. Why would hers be any different?

Her father could use his influence to find her if he chose, but she didn't know if he would attempt to do so. Calling attention to her actions would cause the kind of scandal he had always tried to avoid. He read the gossip columns religiously but always made sure his name didn't appear in them. He might make a few discreet inquiries at her mother's urging, but Wilhelmina doubted he would make a concerted effort to locate her. Not with Martin Jr., his namesake and heir, safely ensconced far from the front lines and her sister busy fending off a long line of suitors eager to stake their claim on her beauty and a share of her father's fortune.

After Wilhelmina signed her name on the roll, the soldier seated at the table directed her to the infirmary so the chief physician on staff could conduct a physical. Wilhelmina's steps faltered as she neared the designated area. How closely would the doctor examine her? Would she be expected to disrobe? If so, how would she explain the strips of muslin she had used to bind her breasts? How would she explain what was underneath? If it reached that point, she reasoned, words wouldn't be necessary.

The doctor, a middle-aged man with a receding hairline and the wide eyes of someone with a taste for laudanum, barely looked at her as he barked commands.

"Look straight ahead."

She tried not to blink as he waved a lit candle in front of her eyes.

"Take a deep breath."

He pressed a stethoscope to her chest and listened for a second or two before moving on to the next task.

"Open your mouth."

She opened her mouth wide as he peered at her teeth.

"No cavities or impactions," he said, almost managing to sound impressed. "You'll do. Welcome to the Seventy-seventh Pennsylvania Volunteer Infantry." He jerked a thumb toward the door. "Go see the supply sergeant for your uniform and rifle. Next!"

Wilhelmina ceded her place to the next man in line and stumbled out of the room, still not quite sure how she had managed to make it this far. But made it she had. Now she had to prove she had what it took to stay.

The supply sergeant was housed in an adjacent building. Wilhelmina expected him to take detailed measurements before he provided her with a uniform and boots, but he had been performing the task so long he was able to guess her correct sizes simply by looking at her. He issued her a rifle and ammunition, along with a dark blue uniform coat, a pair of sky blue uniform trousers, a black felt hat, a pair of heavy black brogans, a pair of wool socks, and a pair of cotton underwear.

As she carried her new belongings to the temporary barracks that would be her home for the next fortnight, she was grateful Rose had packed spare socks and undergarments in her haversack since the Army issued one only pair of each per year.

After she found a secluded place to change, she exchanged her civilian clothes for her uniform and rushed to join the other volunteers for training—rigorous calisthenics meant to build endurance and drills designed to instill the actions soldiers could use to kill their enemies from a distance or up close via hand-to-hand combat.

Wilhelmina struggled to keep up with her peers during the exercises and to refrain from bursting into tears when an angry drill sergeant barked disparaging words in her direction after she had difficulty mastering the bayonet.

"You're as weak as dishwater, boy, and your hands are as soft as a girl's," he said after her quivering muscles didn't allow her to attack with the proper gusto. "Your life of leisure has provided poor preparation for the life you've signed up to lead."

He spat a line of tobacco juice on the ground and grabbed her by the back of her collar. She felt like a wayward kitten being carried home by its mother. He pointed at the sack the new members of her regiment were using for target practice. Sand spilled from dozens of holes in the thick burlap covering, but her feeble thrusts had barely left a mark.

"That isn't a bag of sand hanging there, boy. It's a Confederate soldier coming straight at you. Get over there and attack him like you mean it. Because if you don't kill him first, he's going to kill you. Do you understand?"

"Yes, sir!"

Wilhelmina thrust with all her might, but she didn't have her feet under her. She lost her balance and tumbled forward. The bag, suspended from a wooden A-frame, swung toward her and hit her in the face. Her eyes teared and her vision blurred as Maynard Harrison led a chorus of raucous laughter.

"If he's the best of what Philadelphia has to offer," Maynard said, "I don't want to see the worst."

"Jesus, Mary, and Joseph," the drill sergeant said. "Don't sit there sniveling, boy. Move your scrawny ass out of the way so the real men can take their turn."

Erwin Weekley picked up Wilhelmina's cap and rifle and offered her a hand up. "It's okay, son. You gave it your best effort."

Wilhelmina put her cap back on and wiped sand from her mouth with her sleeve. "But my best wasn't good enough."

"It will be, son," Erwin said, giving her an encouraging pat on the back. "It will be."

For the first time in her life, Wilhelmina was on her own. Dependent upon strangers to keep her safe while others sought to do her harm.

And she had never been happier.

Clara wrapped her shawl tighter around her shoulders as she regarded the raised plant beds containing the onions, peas, turnips, and potatoes her family was counting on to get them through the rest of the winter. This time of year, spring always seemed like it was a lifetime away instead of only a few months. She was glad she had preserved as many fruits and vegetables as she could spare from the summer crops because the winter garden didn't look very promising. She pressed the tip of her spade against the ground and pushed down with her foot, but the tool barely made an impression in the frozen soil.

"Here. Let me try."

Enid Bragg was a good fifty pounds heavier than Clara. She took the spade and leaned her weight against it. Her family lived on the farm on the other side of the river. She and her daughter, Mary, came over every morning to offer Clara a helping hand, and she returned the favor for them after she fed Abram and Percy their midday meals.

Clara didn't mind the extra work—or the companionship. Until the men of Shiloh and the surrounding counties returned from the war, the Braggs were in the same dire straits as the Summerses.

Enid's husband, Joseph, had joined the Confederate Army the very day word came to town that war had been declared. Their son, Moses, had followed Joseph's example. According to the letters Joseph sent home every few months, he had fought in skirmishes all over Tennessee and even parts of Alabama without being wounded even once.

Moses, meanwhile, had been forced to return home last month after being struck in the head by a ball from a Union soldier's gun. He had survived the wound, but he had lost his sight as a result of the assault. He didn't leave the house much these days, preferring to stay behind closed doors rather than subject himself to pitying looks from well-meaning neighbors.

Some people might wonder how Moses could sense something he couldn't see, but Clara didn't have to speculate. You didn't have to use your eyes to see what was true. Some things you just knew.

She wished she had news of Papa's and Solomon's whereabouts, but Papa couldn't read or write anything except his name, and Solomon couldn't do much better, so neither sent letters home. Clara tried to tell herself that no news was good news, but she couldn't help fearing Papa or Solomon had fallen on some godforsaken battlefield far from home and were doomed to lie for the rest of eternity in an unmarked grave instead of a carefully tended plot looked after and visited often by family and friends.

She closed her eyes and whispered a prayer she was certain God received on a daily basis and had probably grown weary of hearing. "Please keep them safe."

She gasped and opened her eyes when she heard the sound of cracking ice. Thanks to Enid's concentrated effort, the tip of the spade slowly broke through the earth.

"You did it, Ma."

Mary clapped her hands in delight, the sound muffled by the old pair of her father's socks she was wearing as gloves. One of Moses's floppy hats he used to wear when he was tending the fields was clamped low on her head to help keep her warm, but her ears and cheeks glowed bright red from the bitter cold.

"Hold your merriment," Enid said after she pried a few vegetables from the unforgiving earth. "These potatoes are as frozen as the ground I pulled them from. Just like ours." She tossed the potatoes aside. They sounded like rocks when they hit the ground. "Do you have enough food set aside to get by, Clara?"

"As long as Abram keeps bringing in fresh meat, we won't have to use what's in the smokehouse. If he can bring down a deer one day, we'd have enough meat to last until the spring thaw. If he doesn't, we can make do on what we have plus the squirrels, raccoons, and opossums he keeps managing to find. How are you faring?"

Enid shrugged. "I don't rightly know. We've got the fruit and vegetables I canned last summer, but fresh meat is hard to come by. Moses can't hunt no more, I've never been much of a shot, and Mary is too tenderhearted to kill any living thing, whether it's a dumb animal or an even dumber human."

Life had been so bad for so long, Clara had almost forgotten how good it felt to laugh.

"If Abram and Percy bag some game today, I'll be sure to send over half of whatever they find."

Clara had never known any of the Braggs to accept charity, so she was surprised Enid didn't refuse her offer.

"Much obliged," Enid said, obviously humbled by circumstances that were sure to grow even worse in the weeks to come. "Mary and I had better head home. Moses gets as nervous as a long-tailed cat in a roomful of rocking chairs if he's left on his own too long." She lowered her eyes as well as her voice. "He still has nightmares about the things he saw while he was fighting. He won't tell me about them, but he wakes up screaming sometimes. When he gets in that state, the look on his face and the sound of his voice are enough to make your blood run cold. I want to help him, but I don't know what to do."

Clara touched Enid's arm to let her know she didn't have to fight the battle alone.

"I'll be over as soon as I get some food on the table for the boys. They should be home directly. Abram might not own a pocket watch, but his stomach always leads him home when it's time to eat."

"Why don't you come over to our house for supper tonight?" Mary asked. "We have some opossum stew left over from last night. Even if Abram doesn't find another one to add to the pot, there should be enough to go around."

"Are you tired of keeping company with me and your brother," Enid asked, "or would you rather keep time with Abram instead?"

Mary tried to protest her innocence, but Enid wouldn't hear of it.

"Stop trying to pretend you're not sweet on the boy. You're as lovestruck over him as he is over you." Enid tossed a wink in Clara's direction. "I used to think you and Moses would be the ones to bring our clans together through marriage, but I guess the young'uns will have to be the ones to do it."

Clara stomped her feet to keep them warm. Melting snow covered the tops of her shoes, and she could practically feel the ice through the thin soles on the bottom.

"Moses has always been like a brother to me."

"And he says you're like a sister to him. If you ask me, it's all talk. If Jedediah Ogletree wasn't hot on your heels, Moses would have asked your papa for your hand in marriage long ago. But none of that matters now with Moses being an invalid and all."

Clara hated to think of the sweet boy she had grown up with forced to grow old alone. Even though he would have his family near, he had always longed for a wife to call his own and children to bear his name. She hoped he hadn't given up on his dreams simply because he could no longer watch them come true.

"Any woman he marries would be lucky to have him."

Enid patted Clara's hand. "I appreciate you saying so. Able-bodied men are in short supply these days, so maybe the women in town will be able to look past what he can't do and see what he can." She paused and heaved a sigh. Her breath plumed in the frigid air like smoke from a chimney. "Even if none of them are able to stop comparing the man he is to the one he used to be, he won't lack for anything. Mary and I will continue to look after him. Family takes care of family. Even when they aren't related by blood."

"Yes, they do." Clara didn't have to try real hard to catch Enid's meaning. Enid and her kin were as close to Clara as family and always would be. "I'll see you at supper."

"Do me one favor first. Tell the boys not to ask Moses to tell them stories about the war. He doesn't like to talk about it. It upsets him something fierce."

"I understand," Clara said, though she doubted Abram and Percy would.

Her little brothers loved nothing more than hearing about the latest skirmishes. She didn't know what they would do for entertainment when the war finally ended, but she certainly couldn't wait to find out.

There had to be more to life than killing. All she needed to do was hold on until she discovered what it was.

Chapter Four

The steady back-and-forth movement of the train was almost soothing enough to rock Wilhelmina to sleep, but the pain in her hands kept her awake. She flexed her fingers as she regarded the blisters in her palms.

After her first few embarrassing attempts at using the bayonet attached to the end of her rifle, she had subjected herself to extra drills after chow. While her fellow soldiers slept soundly on their cots or sat around smoking hand-rolled cigarettes and lying about their experiences with women, she had attempted to master all the skills that came so easily to them but were a struggle for her. The muscles in her shoulders and arms ached from the extra effort, and her newly formed calluses assured that, even if she allowed her hair to grow back, she would never be mistaken for a society woman again.

"Rub some vinegar on those blisters, son," Erwin said as he puffed on his corncob pipe. "It'll ease the pain and make sure the wounds don't get infected. You won't smell so good, but you'll definitely feel better."

"Thank you, sir. I'll be sure to check in with the medical tent once we get to camp."

Wilhelmina looked around the darkened train car. Some light streamed in through a tiny window that provided her only vantage point to the passing countryside. What little illumination that remained was provided by the lit ends of nearly burned-out cigarettes or the brief bursts of matches used to light fresh ones.

The train was slowly rattling its way from Pennsylvania to Kentucky, where Wilhelmina and the other soldiers with her would join the rest of their infantry. The 77th had been bunked down in Munfordsville since December and were set to march to Bowling Green as soon as reinforcements arrived.

Wilhelmina had taken long journeys before, but never on foot. She hoped she would be able to keep up with the rest of her regiment during the more than fifty-mile march as she bore the added weight of her haversack, rifle, ammunition, and assorted supplies.

It had been three weeks since she had run away from home and disguised her sex in order to enlist. The constant drills and exercises she had undertaken since then had made her stronger in every way, but she knew she still had a long way to go if she hoped to pull her own weight on the battlefield. Training was one thing. Fighting was another.

She looked out the window as her rifle rested between her bent knees. Had the night sky always been this beautiful or the stars so plentiful? She had never noticed them when she was in Philadelphia. Now she couldn't look away.

"Get all the daydreaming out of your system now, boy," Maynard said. "Once we get where we're going, we've got Rebs to kill."

Wilhelmina chewed on a piece of hardtack to ease the hunger pains gnawing at her insides. She and the rest of the men hadn't eaten in nearly half a day, and there was no telling when they would be able to sit down to their next meal.

"You don't like me much, do you, Mr. Harrison?" she asked as she struggled to swallow the dry cracker.

"No, I don't."

She had tried not to draw attention to herself and made an effort to remain cordial with everyone she came across so no one would hold any grudges against her. The other men seemed to have accepted her into their ranks, but Maynard had always kept his distance. She had caught him staring at her from time to time with an odd look on his face. The first time it happened, she had feared he had seen through her disguise. When daybreak came and she hadn't found herself on a train bound for home, she had thought something else might be the issue, but she hadn't been able to figure out what it could be.

"Please tell me what I did to get on your bad side."

"You're the weakest link in this unit, Fredericks. The proverbial albatross around our necks. When we get to the front, make sure you stay as far away from me as you can. I don't want to wind up getting killed because you can't defend yourself. Or anyone else, for that matter."

"I'm sorry you feel that way."

"I'm not the only one, believe me."

When some of the other men looked away rather than meeting her eye, Wilhelmina realized what Maynard had said was true. They didn't trust her to keep them safe from harm.

"Face it, Fredericks. You're the worst man in this regiment. Don't be surprised if no one wants to partner with you once we start seeing action. We've all got families we want to get back to. We don't need you standing in our way."

Wilhelmina tried to think of something to say in her defense, but words failed her. The uncomfortable silence stretched on for several minutes before Erwin's deep voice breached the peace.

"Forgive me if I'm wrong," Erwin said, "but the last time I looked, the enemy was wearing gray not blue."

Maynard batted the air with his hand. "With your fondness for books and poetry, you're as bad as the boy. The two of you deserve each other."

Erwin clenched the stem of his pipe between his teeth and inhaled deeply. "I could think of worse company." He moved closer to Wilhelmina and pulled a tintype from the recesses of his haversack. "My family. My wife, Sarah, and our daughters, Beatrice and Pauline."

Wilhelmina angled the photograph toward the moonlight. She squinted to see the faces of a petite woman with blond hair and the two children who were the spitting image of her.

"How old are your daughters?" she asked, returning the photo.

"Eight and six," Erwin said proudly, "though they often seem much older. Some of the words and phrases that spill from their lips make them sound like women rather than children. When I'm finally able to return home, I wouldn't be surprised if they didn't have families of their own." He kissed the photograph and returned it to his haversack. "Do you have someone waiting for you to return? A young lady, perhaps?"

Wilhelmina hesitated only briefly before she reached for the tintype tucked inside her uniform. "That's Libby."

Erwin took a long draw on his pipe as he regarded the photo. "Quite a comely woman. As Lord Byron would say, she walks in beauty like the night."

"Thank you, sir. I think so, too," Wilhelmina said as she returned the tintype to its hiding place. Next to her heart, as Rose had directed.

"Do you intend to make her your bride one day?"

"I'd like to."

"But?"

Wilhelmina didn't know how much information she should share. Should she tell a version of the truth, or come up with a plausible lie?

"I would like to make her mine, but she's betrothed to another."

"I see." Maynard took another puff on his pipe. "Does she love him?"

"She says she does."

"Yet that doesn't stop you from writing to her every day."

Wilhelmina felt her cheeks redden and was grateful for the gathering darkness. She knew she wasn't the only one who constantly sent missives home, but her letter-writing campaign might be the only one that could be considered a lost cause.

"I've known Libby since we were young. I always imagined we would spend the rest of our lives together."

"God willing, you still can."

"Yes, sir," she said, wondering if He was still able or willing to answer her prayers, "God willing."

❖

Abram spooned some baked beans and roasted sweet potatoes into his mouth and followed them up with a big bite of fried chicken. He hadn't been able to scrounge up any game lately so Enid had sacrificed one of her hens to make tonight's meal.

"What do you miss most about the war, Moses?" Abram asked as he slathered butter on his cornbread.

Clara tried to kick Abram's leg under the table, but he dodged the attempted blow. This was their third trip to the Braggs' for Sunday supper in as many weeks. Abram had been able to hold his curiosity at bay during the first couple of trips, but his thirst for information had gotten the best of him tonight. Clara had given him and Percy a talking-to before they left the house. Same as she did every week. Both boys knew they weren't supposed to mention the war to Moses, but they had barely sat down to eat before Abram did what she had expressly told him not to.

Moses stuck the fingers of his left hand in his plate to gauge where his food was before he attempted to gather some with his spoon. Both Enid and Mary had offered to feed him, but he had insisted on trying to fend for himself. Clara admired his desire to remain as independent as possible, though she hoped he wasn't too proud to ask for help when he truly needed it.

"I don't miss any of it, to be honest."

Moses's sightless eyes wandered the room as if looking for a place to land. His gaunt face, pale skin, and lank hair made him look like a ghost. It was almost as if he had died in battle and someone had forgotten to tell him.

"I don't miss the hours of marching, the sound of gunfire, or the smell of death. I don't miss wounded men calling for help or dying ones begging for water to slake their unquenchable thirst."

His hands shook as they hovered above his plate. He looked like someone suffering from the palsy. Before he was shot, he had never been sick a day in his life. Now he seemed to have as many ailments as an old man and he was only twenty-one years old.

"I don't miss the flies, the maggots, or any of the innumerable insects that spread disease. In a way, I'm happy for what happened to me because I would much rather be here than there."

Abram's eyes widened and his mouth fell open in disbelief. Clara had never heard someone speak so honestly about the war. She hoped Moses's words had managed to end Abram's fascination with both the conflict and its combatants.

"You still think our side's going to win, don't you?" Percy asked.

His expression was as innocent as his question. Clara wished he could remain that naïve forever, but she knew his innocence to the ways of the world wouldn't last for much longer. If Percy kept peppering Moses with questions about the war, his guilelessness might not last past supper.

"I used to," Moses said, chewing on a drumstick. "Now I'm not so certain."

"What do you mean?" Enid asked. "Preacher Parsons said just last week that God's on our side."

"Preacher Parsons may know more about heaven and hell than the average man, but he don't know a thing about war," Moses said. "He's never fought a day in his life, which means he's seeing with his heart instead of his head. The plain truth is the Federals have more money, more provisions, and more men than we do. They can take us at any time. I'm surprised they haven't already."

"That's because we have Jefferson Davis and Stonewall Jackson on our side," Abram said. To him and thousands of boys like him, the Southern generals were more than heroes. They were practically gods. "Those two can take anything the Yankees try to dish out."

Moses's smile held more sorrow than mirth. "Unfortunately, Davis and Jackson aren't the ones doing the taking. The men in the trenches are. Men who are devoted to their cause but are as blind to the results of their outcome as the man you see before you now."

"But—"

"Enough talk of madness and mayhem," Clara said. "Let's move on to more pleasant subjects before we ruin what's left of our dinner."

"Agreed," Enid said. "Mary, fetch Abram another piece of your fine cornbread since he seems to be enjoying it so much."

"Yes, ma'am."

Mary got up from the table and headed over to the stove, where a plate of cornbread had been left to warm.

"Mary's an awful good cook, isn't she, Abram?" Enid asked with a teasing smile. "She'd make some man a fine wife one day."

Abram's face turned redder than the flames flickering in the fireplace as Mary held the plate of cornbread out to him.

"Yes, ma'am, I suspect she would." He took two pieces of cornbread and mumbled a bashful, "Thank you, Mary."

"You're welcome, Abram." Mary covered her mouth with her hands to hide her delighted smile as she set the plate on the table and returned to her seat.

"Ain't young love grand?" Enid said as she sucked the marrow out of a chicken bone. "I remember when Joseph and I started sparking. He was even more shamefaced than Abram is now. He could barely look me in the eye the first year we were courting, and I can count on the fingers of one hand how many words he said to me during that time." Her laugh was fond as she recalled the memory. "I guess not much has changed. He still—"

"Someone's coming," Moses said quietly.

"How many?" Enid asked, looking alarmed.

Moses listened for a minute or two.

"One, but he's coming fast."

"How can you tell?" Clara strained her ears but couldn't hear anything.

"Since I lost my sight, the rest of my senses have improved to make up for its absence."

"Now he can hear a butterfly flapping its wings five miles away."

Enid grabbed the rifle hanging above the mantle. She checked to make sure the rifle was loaded, then pressed the stock against her hip. She rested one hand on the barrel of the rifle and the other against the trigger. Both shook worse than Moses's had when he was talking about the war.

"Here, Mrs. Bragg," Abram said, reaching for the rifle, "you'd better let me have that."

Enid gave Clara a skeptical look as she held fast to the rifle. Clara nodded her assurance that Abram was up to the task for which he had volunteered.

"Let him have the gun."

After Enid finally handed him the rifle, Abram raised it to shoulder level and pointed it at the door.

"Have you ever drawn down on a man before?" Moses asked, sitting so still he barely took up space.

"No." Abram closed one eye as he took aim. "But it can't be much different from the time that black bear wandered out of the mountains and thought he could use me for food. I showed him a thing or two that day. I'll be glad to teach whoever winds up on the other side of that door the same lesson."

Abram had crossed paths with the bear while out hunting one day last spring. The animal hadn't been fully grown and was half-starved after hibernating all winter, but Abram had stood his ground and put it down after it had charged toward him. The family had dined on the meat for weeks and, at Abram's insistence, Clara had turned the hide into a rug. The thing smelled worse than all get-out, but it was the most prized possession Abram owned.

"Killing an animal is a lot different than killing a man," Moses said. "We'll see if you have what it takes when it's time for you to pull the trigger."

Abram swallowed hard, and Clara thought she saw a bead of sweat form on his forehead when the pounding of a horse's hooves announced their visitor's presence for all to hear, but his aim never wavered.

"Who do you think it is?" Enid whispered. "A Yankee scout on patrol or one of our boys?"

Moses cocked his head and listened intently.

"A scout doesn't ride this hard unless he's rushing back to his regiment to tell his commanding officer what he found while he was out. This man is moving toward us, not away from us."

Enid drew Mary to her side and held her tight to her bosom.

"I heard tell of a marauding group of Yankees who raped and murdered scores of women when they marched through Virginia," she said, smoothing Mary's hair. "If one comes through that door, Abram, make sure you hit him where it hurts."

"Yes, ma'am, I surely will."

Clara rested her hands on Moses's bony shoulders to let him know he wasn't alone. He covered one of her hands with his. His skin felt cold despite the warmth of the fire blazing in the hearth.

"I should be protecting you, not the other way around."

"We all have a part to play in this war, even if we might not understand our roles at the time."

"Everybody, quiet down," Moses said when the hoofbeats stopped. "He's coming up the steps."

Mary buried her face in Enid's chest, and Abram tightened his grip on the rifle. His knuckles were as white as his face.

Clara flinched when someone pounded on the door hard enough to shake the rafters.

"Who goes there?" Abram asked, his voice high-pitched with fear.

"It's me. Jedediah Ogletree. I've come to warn you of the Yankee invasion."

"Invasion?"

Enid released Mary, crossed the room, and snatched the door open. Abram sagged against the table with relief when he saw Jedediah standing alone on the other side.

"The Yankees are coming to Shiloh?" Enid asked.

Jedediah doffed his hat as he came inside and closed the door behind him.

"Not yet, but they're on the way. A trainload of them reached Kentucky a fortnight ago and they've been on the move ever since. Our scouts say nearly fifty thousand of them are bedded down in Nashville now with gunboats and artillery at the ready."

"Nashville?" Moses said. "That's about a hundred and fifty miles from here. If the Federals keep up a steady pace, they should be here in a little over a week."

"Fifty thousand men?" Enid asked. "Are you sure, Jed?"

"Sure as shooting. And Ulysses S. Grant himself is said to be leading them."

"What should we do? Pack up and run? I've got family in the mountains. We could stay with them until it's safe to come home."

"Don't worry yourself, Mrs. Bragg." Jedediah drew himself up tall. "Grant drinks so much he's apt to march his men in circles rather than a straight line. You'll be safe here in Shiloh as long as the men of my company and I are around to protect you."

The local branch of the Hardin County Reserves was a defense troop primarily composed of men either unqualified or unwilling to go to war. Some had their hearts in the right place. Others like Jedediah seemed satisfied preening around on their horses while grateful women swooned over their apparent bravery.

Would Jedediah and his men be able to fight off an armed invasion from a trained unit of soldiers, or would they drop their guns and raise their hands in surrender before the first shot was fired? Clara was inclined to think the latter was true.

"You're looking well, Moses," Jedediah said.

Moses flashed a rueful smile.

"I'll have to take your word for it, I'm afraid."

Jedediah turned to Mary rather than take time to apologize for his unfortunate choice of words.

"You're looking awful pretty tonight, Mary. If young Mr. Abram doesn't mind my saying so, of course."

"Why would I mind?" Abram asked irritably. Clara couldn't tell if he was more upset by Jedediah's attention to Mary or the giggles that flowed from Mary in response.

"Clara, you are a beacon as always." Clara didn't respond to his flattery so Jedediah turned back to Enid. "I didn't mean to interrupt your supper, Mrs. Bragg. I just came to deliver the news and offer to escort Clara and her family home."

"How did you know to find us here?" Clara asked.

"Where else would you be? There are only a few places a respectable woman would be at this time of night if not in her own home. When I didn't see you at the church, I figured you would be here." He offered his arm. "Would you allow me the pleasure of escorting you home?"

"No offense, Mr. Ogletree, but Percy and I can look after our sister," Abram said.

Jedediah grinned.

"I'm not trying to take your place, boys. I'm simply offering a helping hand."

"The same kind of helping hand your papa offered mine when he tried to steal his land out from under him?"

Jedediah's smile faltered.

"You're tall for your age, but you're still just a boy, Abram. Do yourself a favor and don't make pronouncements like the one you just uttered until you're old enough to defend them."

Jedediah pushed his coat aside so Abram could see the pistol holstered around his waist. Just like he did when the bear bore down on him, Abram stood his ground.

"I ain't scared of you, Mr. Ogletree. You and your papa might be rich, but you're still just men." He jabbed a bony finger into Jedediah's broad chest. "And you ain't man enough for my sister so you best stay away from her, you hear?"

Jedediah ruffled Abram's hair to show him he still thought of him as a boy instead of the man he was trying to be.

"Why don't we let your sister have final say? She has a mind of her own. We might as well give her a chance to speak it. What do you say, Clara? Would you like me to see you home?"

He offered his arm, but Clara didn't take it. She didn't cotton to the way he treated Abram or the way he talked down to her.

"Thank you for the offer, but we can see ourselves home. Come on, boys. Let's go before it gets too dark for us to find our way."

"As you wish." Jedediah bowed and made his way to the door. "I'll come back this way tomorrow to check on you. Your farms are pretty close together, but your nearest neighbors are miles away. A bunch of women with no men around to protect you. We wouldn't want anything to happen to you while you're out here all alone."

"We aren't alone," Clara said. "Enid and Mary have Moses to look out for them, and the boys and I can take care of ourselves."

"A blind man and two boys without so much as a hint of peach fuzz on their chins aren't any protection at all. Like it or not, you need me, Clara. My men and I are responsible for everyone in this town. That includes you and everyone else here. It's my job to keep you safe from harm. That means protecting you from the Yankees as well as yourselves. Loyalties are divided in this war. Opinions differ from house to house."

Jedediah paused as if something had just occurred to him.

"You do know this is Rebel territory, don't you?" he asked.

"What are you trying to say?"

"Part of my job is to root out Yankee sympathizers. Oftentimes the people you least suspect of giving aid to the enemy are the most guilty. Do you keep pushing me away because you're afraid of what I might find if I got too close? If I searched your barn, I wouldn't find any yellow-bellied Yankee deserters hiding under the pine straw, would I?"

"Are you accusing them of being traitors, Jed?" Enid asked. "Clara and her kin are as loyal to the Confederacy as the rest of us. Her father and brother are off fighting the Yanks right now. I've known Clara since she was born. There's no way she would ever turn on her own."

Jedediah rested the heel of his hand on the butt of his pistol.

"That's good to hear. I like loyalty in a woman. Especially in one I plan to make my wife one day." He tipped his hat. "I'll see you in the morning, Clara."

"That boy's as big a bully as his father was when we were growing up," Enid said after Jedediah strode down the steps, mounted his horse, and rode away. "I wish someone would put him in his place one day."

Like the end of the war, Clara feared that glorious day might never come.

CHAPTER FIVE

Wilhelmina moved closer to the flames as Erwin roasted a rabbit on a spit over a roaring fire. The mood in camp was relatively upbeat tonight. Everyone had finally recovered from the long march from Bowling Green, Kentucky, to Nashville, Tennessee, and they were making themselves busy getting to know their new colleagues. The regiment's numbers had swelled after the 77th Pennsylvania Infantry joined forces with the 5th Brigade, 2nd Division of the Army of the Ohio. Their current camp along the banks of the Tennessee River teemed with so many men it was practically a city in itself.

Wilhelmina was still getting used to all the new faces. She had come to recognize a few but still didn't know most of them by name. Rivalries had formed between the different companies that composed the overall regiment. Their commanding officers had assured them they didn't have to like each other in order to move as one unit, but Wilhelmina hoped someone's grudge against a fellow Union soldier didn't result in unnecessary bloodshed.

Violin music drifted from the open mouth of one tent. A group of men played a raucous game of poker outside another. Wilhelmina watched as money changed hands, most of it winding up in Maynard Harrison's possession. Pay for Union privates was only thirteen dollars per month, though officers received much more. Based on the pile of bills in front of him, Maynard had enough money to pay a colonel's salary.

Most men slept three and four to a tent. Wilhelmina shared her quarters with Erwin and twelve-year-old drummer boy Billy Freeman. Erwin snored louder than a freight train and Billy didn't stop tapping on his drum even in his sleep, but Wilhelmina would rather put up with their noise than some of the other men's bluster.

"Did you hear the news?" Erwin asked as he sawed a piece of meat off the rabbit with his pocketknife. "We're moving out tomorrow."

Wilhelmina took two pieces of meat, one for Billy and one for herself. The meals she and the rest of her fellow soldiers prepared from the small game they trapped and the fruits and vegetables they foraged from the fields and orchards they marched through weren't as fancy as the ones Rose used to dish up back in Philadelphia, but they would do in a pinch.

"Where are we headed this time?"

"Savannah."

"Georgia?" Wilhelmina asked incredulously. "Surely they don't expect us to walk that far."

"No, son," Erwin said with a chuckle. "Savannah, Tennessee. It's a small town just north of the border between Tennessee and Mississippi. We should be able to make the journey in a week to ten days rather than the months it would take for the trip you're proposing."

Wilhelmina smiled at Erwin's gentle ribbing. It was different when Maynard teased her. When Maynard made fun of her, he seemed to do it out of spite. When Erwin did it, it was obviously out of affection.

"I think Mississippi is General Grant's ultimate destination," Erwin said. "The Mobile and Ohio Railroad is located in Corinth, Mississippi. It serves as a vital supply line for the Confederate forces in Tennessee and Virginia. If we make it to Corinth unscathed, we can strike a blow straight to the heart of the Confederacy. Are you finally ready to fire that gun of yours at a moving target rather than a stationary one?"

Their path from Pennsylvania to Tennessee had been uneventful thus far. Weeks of marching, days of drills, and hours of idleness, but no skirmishes with the enemy. Wilhelmina wasn't surprised by the lack of action. There wasn't much fighting during the winter months. In some campsites, soldiers were too busy building huts and log cabins to pick up their rifles. Wilhelmina sensed that was about to change. And soon.

She reached for her rifle, which her commanding officer insisted should never be too far away.

"The two most important pieces of steel in this war," he had said the first time he addressed the supplemental troops, "are the one in your hands and the one between your legs."

Wilhelmina was one piece short by her count, but she never let the other out of her sight.

"I'm ready, sir."

Erwin dug a half-rotten potato out of the coals and sliced it open. "You don't have to call me sir, son. I'm a private just like you."

"I can't help it, sir. My father taught me to treat my elders with respect."

"I've never heard you call Maynard sir. He's your elder, too, isn't he?"

"He's also an arrogant bastard. My father never said anything about having to respect them."

Billy snickered at the expletive, and Erwin laughed so loud even the poker players stopped telling lies about the scores of women they had allegedly bedded in order to take a long look at him.

"He sounds like a wise man, your father," Erwin said.

Wilhelmina sliced two more pieces of meat and gave Billy the bigger hunk. They usually ate at least twice a day, but the boy never seemed to get full.

"He can be about some things."

"And the rest?"

Wilhelmina chewed thoughtfully as Billy licked his greasy fingers.

"Let's just say he and I agree to disagree."

Her father had always claimed not to understand her, but he had never attempted to rectify the situation. She had given up on trying to curry his favor years ago, though she still ached to earn his respect.

"Don't let your differences drive too deep a wedge between you. In my humble opinion, the most important things in life are loyalty and honor, but there's nothing more important than family."

Wilhelmina wondered how her family was reacting to her absence. She hadn't been foolish enough to tell them she planned to enlist. Only Libby and Rose were privy to that information. The letter she had left behind said she was leaving to help the war effort, but she hadn't provided any specifics. Her father had most likely assumed she had run away to become a nurse in one of the overflowing makeshift infirmaries that were popping up all over the country. Churches, schools, barns, and even houses had been turned into hospitals to treat the wounded, sick, and dying men that had walked, crawled, or been carried from the battlefields. There were plenty of people lined up to protect and care for those men. The ones who needed her help the most were the comrades they had left behind.

She wished she had news from Libby. Before she left home, she had sworn to write to Libby every day. She had kept her promise, penning long letters by the dim light of her lantern after Erwin and Billy had fallen asleep. But she had yet to receive any return correspondence. Had Libby received her missives and failed to reply to them, or was the mail delivery system so slow that Libby's letters had not had an opportunity to reach her before the regiment abandoned one position for another? Perhaps tomorrow's arrival of the supply train would result in much-welcomed mail in addition to much-needed food and equipment.

"I shall return momentarily, son. I'm afraid I need to heed the call of nature." Erwin grimaced as he rubbed his stomach. "Perhaps taking a chance on that potato wasn't such a good idea after all." He grimaced again. "If you hear trumpeting, I doubt it will be the bugler playing 'Reveille.'"

Wilhelmina suppressed a smile, not wanting to make light of his discomfort.

"I hope you feel better soon, sir."

Erwin grabbed his rifle and headed off to a thick patch of woods along the edge of camp. For her sake, Wilhelmina hoped the area he had chosen was downwind. He had been gone only a few minutes when she heard a commotion coming from the spot she had seen him walking toward. She heard a gunshot, followed by a shout of, "Halt! Who goes there?"

"The Rebs are here!" another voice yelled. "The Rebs are here!"

The cry echoed around camp.

As the men around her picked up their weapons and began to run toward the noise, Wilhelmina did the same. Her regiment ran through drills several times a day, sometimes for hours at a time. The actions they performed were so familiar they had become automatic. Until now.

She tried to remember her training as she joined the horde of men streaming toward a common cause, but her thoughts were a jumble. She felt on the verge of panic. She couldn't even remember the proper way to load her rifle, the simplest and first task she had learned after she enlisted.

What was she supposed to do first, place the percussion cap or load the cartridge? Hopefully, instinct would kick in. As she ran past flickering campfires toward an unseen enemy, she had no idea what she would do when she met them face-to-face.

She skidded to a stop when she saw Erwin holding his pants up with one hand while he led two bedraggled men out of the woods at gunpoint. There was an unwritten rule that enemy combatants didn't shoot each other while they were relieving themselves, but Wilhelmina didn't know if the same rule applied to taking prisoners.

The men in Erwin's custody were Confederate soldiers, though their uniforms—if you could still call them that—were so filthy the gray cloth looked black. Their greasy hair was crawling with lice. One was an older man with a heavy salt-and-pepper beard. The one beside him was several years younger. Beneath the dirt caked on their faces, they looked enough alike to be father and son. They walked with their hands up, their wide eyes trained on the half-eaten food resting on the soldiers' abandoned plates.

"Please," the younger man said, "we don't mean no harm. We just want something to eat. My papa's sick, and he could use a decent meal."

"We'll let Colonel Stumbaugh decide that," Maynard said. "Fasten your pants, Weekley. Nobody wants to see your flabby pecker flapping in the breeze. I'll see to these Rebs while you make yourself decent."

A few men laughed nervously, but most kept their eyes on the prisoners as Maynard herded them toward Colonel Stumbaugh's tent.

"Move, you two!"

Maynard shoved both men forward. The older one stumbled and went down. He tried to get up, but he fell face-first on the ground. His body shook as a coughing attack seized him. His stringy hair framed his face as he sprayed blood on the snow.

"Are you okay, Papa?" the younger man asked.

The older man nodded and tried to speak, but his eyes rolled back in his head and his body went limp.

"Talk to me, Papa. Can you hear me?"

The younger man frantically shook the older one by his scrawny shoulders and redoubled his efforts when he didn't receive a response.

Erwin fell to his knees and wiped the blood off the older man's chin after he shoved the younger one out of his way.

"Somebody get the doc over here. I think this man has pneumonia."

"Let him die," Maynard said heartlessly. "It'll be one less Reb for us to kill."

Erwin rested the stricken man's head in his lap.

"That isn't a very Christian attitude."

"The Union isn't paying me to be a Christian," Maynard said. "It's paying me to be a soldier."

He dragged the younger man away.

"I'm taking this one to Colonel Stumbaugh. You can do what you want with that one."

The other men looked back and forth between Maynard and Erwin as if trying to decide which one to side with.

"I'll help you take him to Doc Gibson's tent, Mr. Weekley," Wilhelmina said, making her choice. "You take his arms. I'll grab his legs."

"Thank you, son," Erwin said gratefully.

After they tucked their rifles under their arms, they carried the Confederate soldier to the medical tent and deposited him on a wooden table. Bottles of various liquids and jars of smelly ointments lined another table. Next to them lay a neat row of tools. Saws, hammers, pliers, knives, and chisels. All the equipment Dr. Theodore Gibson needed to separate men from their wounded or infected limbs.

"What do you think?" Wilhelmina asked. "Is he going to make it?"

Dr. Gibson looked into the soldier's eyes and listened to his chest.

"I don't rightly know," he said, scratching his head. "His lungs are full of fluid and his heart is racing fit to beat the band. I can bleed him to see if that helps, but he's coughing up so much blood I don't know how much he has left to spare. I think I'll mix a mustard plaster and spread it on his chest. The heat will warm him up a little and hopefully break up some of the congestion in his lungs. Aside from that, I'm afraid there really isn't much I can do for him. I was a dentist before this war began, not a physician."

He ran a hand through his unkempt hair.

"If he survives, what do you plan to do with him? We aren't equipped to house prisoners, and until the supply train arrives with fresh provisions, we'll barely have enough food to feed ourselves, let alone two extra men. You can't let him go and you can't kill him. That would be tantamount to murder, and I want no part of that."

"Just do what you can, Doc," Erwin said. "Let Wil and me worry about the rest."

❖

Clara looked away from the bowl of boiled eggs she was peeling in the kitchen to glance at the clock over the mantle. Abram and Percy had been gone since breakfast, and it was now an hour past lunch. It never took them this long to return from their morning hunts. Had something happened to them, or had they simply lost track of time?

Under normal circumstances, she wouldn't have been worried if Abram and Percy were a few minutes late for a meal. But nothing had felt normal since Jedediah had stood in the middle of Enid Bragg's dining room and announced that fifty thousand Yankees were camped out in Nashville and planning to head this way.

Fifty thousand. The number was almost higher than Clara could count. How could Jedediah and the couple dozen men under his command expect to make a stand against a group that large? If they tried to put up a fight, they would be swept under like the Egyptians in the Red Sea.

Boots thumped on the porch and Clara heard the front door swing open.

"It's about time you boys showed up," she said without turning around. "Your food's on the stove. Wash your hands before you eat."

"I've never known you to be quite so inviting, Clara. I should show up unannounced more often."

Clara whirled around to find Jedediah standing almost on top of her with a ravenous look in his eyes.

"What are you doing here?"

"My job, of course."

He stuck his fingers in a jar of honey and slowly licked them clean.

"It's my sworn duty to protect you, and I'm here to carry out my mission since your brothers are nowhere to be found." He took a step toward her. "I think that deserves some kind of reward, don't you?"

Clara didn't take her eyes off him as she ran her hand along the countertop, looking for something—anything—she could use to fend him off.

"What do you want from me?"

Jedediah let his eyes drift from her face to her breasts.

"I'm a man. You're a woman. No one is around. No one would ever know if we spent a little time getting to know each other better."

"I'm not that kind of woman, Jedediah."

"I wouldn't think any less of you if you were, and it won't matter if I'm the one who takes your virtue since I intend to make you my wife anyway. Consider it a preview of our wedding night. Give me a little taste, Clara. I want to know if you're as sweet as that honey."

He twirled a lock of her hair between his fingers and moved to kiss her. As soon as he leaned forward, she brought her left hand up and pressed the tip of a butcher knife under his chin. She could tell he wanted to pull away, but fear held him fast.

"You don't want to make an enemy out of me," he said as a thin trail of blood began to stream down the blade of the knife.

"And you'll never make a wife out of me, so do us both a favor and stop asking."

She pulled the knife away from his chin, but didn't let down her guard. She brandished the knife like a sword, daring him to come after her again.

Jedediah slowly reached into his pocket and pulled out a handkerchief, which he pressed against his chin to staunch the blood from his wound.

"I always knew you were a wildcat. Perhaps I should make you my whore instead of my wife."

She thrust the knife at him.

"Get out of my house before I slit your throat instead of giving you a little nick."

Jedediah flinched but didn't back away. He glanced disdainfully at the blood staining his handkerchief, then turned his angry gaze on her.

"When I see something I want, I don't stop until it's mine. That goes for you and your father's land. I aim to stake my claim to both before all is said and done."

Clara knew he held all the cards. If he came at her and she used the knife to keep him off her, the sheriff would get drawn into the conflict and it would be her word against Jedediah's. Odds were she couldn't beat Jedediah in a court of law or in the court of public opinion. His family had everything and hers had little more than the clothes on their backs. Who would believe someone like her over someone like him?

It would have been so easy for her to crumble in the face of Jedediah's wrath and let him have his way, but she forced herself not to lose her nerve. She forced herself to believe she was worth more than his low opinion of her.

"I told you to get out. Don't make me say it again."

He slowly backed toward the door as she tightened her grip on the knife.

"I'm getting, but I'll be back. And I might not be such a gentleman next time."

Abram and Percy ran up the steps and into the house. Even though they had returned from their hunt empty-handed, Clara had never been so happy to see them.

"Afternoon, boys," Jedediah said. "Your sister has prepared a fine-smelling meal for you. You'd best get it while it's hot. I would join you, but there are urgent matters requiring my attention."

"What did he want?" Abram asked as he watched Jedediah untie his horse and climb into the well-oiled saddle.

Clara closed the door and slid a thick piece of wood into place to make sure it stayed that way.

"Something he will never have."

CHAPTER SIX

Wilhelmina stood guard outside the medical tent while Dr. Gibson looked after the prisoner. The stricken man hadn't opened his eyes since he had passed out on the edge of the woods three days ago. Some of Wilhelmina's fellow soldiers said he was faking his condition, but his fever was almost impossibly high and kept getting higher every day. Dr. Gibson seemed amazed he was still alive but didn't dare offer a prediction as to how long he might remain that way.

"Any change in his condition?" Erwin asked after he showed up to take Wilhelmina's place.

Just in time, too. Her bladder was so full she was afraid it might burst, but she hadn't been willing to leave her post in order to find a safe place in which to relieve herself.

"No, he's still unconscious. Has the other one said anything?"

"Nothing we can use."

Maynard had marched the younger man to Colonel Stumbaugh's tent the night he and his companion had arrived in camp. The colonel and his men had been interrogating him ever since, but he had refused to break.

"He keeps telling the same old story," Erwin said. "He and his father got separated from their unit and stumbled across our unit while they were foraging for food and herbs they could use for medicine to treat his father's cough. He says he doesn't know where the rest of his regiment is, but I think he knows exactly where they are and doesn't want to give away their position."

"What would you do if you were in his shoes? Would you try to save yourself or protect someone else?"

"I would do the same thing he's doing. I would make sure my father was safe and do whatever I could to protect my men."

"I guess the Yankees and the Rebels aren't so different after all."

"No, son, I guess we aren't in some respects. Go get some sleep. You're going to need plenty of rest tonight. The regiment is marching out first thing in the morning."

"What about the prisoners? What will happen to them?"

"Colonel Stumbaugh plans to send them to the Louisville Military Prison in Kentucky for the duration of the war. The ambulance wagon will take them to the train station, where they'll be escorted to prison under armed guard. There was talk they might be executed without virtue of a trial, but the colonel's a good man. I knew he would find a reasonable solution if he was given a chance to consider the situation from all sides. All we have to do is make sure they both survive to make the journey."

Wilhelmina peeked inside the tent. The prisoner lay on a cot, his face and uniform drenched with sweat despite the bitter cold.

"I don't even know their names, Mr. Weekley. Do you?"

"The younger one says his name is Solomon Summers. His father's name is Lee. They're from Shiloh, Tennessee, and they've been fighting with the Fourth Tennessee Infantry Regiment for about six months now. That's the only information he's been willing to divulge. Has Lee said anything?"

"He talks all the time, but he's out of his head with fever. He's been having whole conversations with a woman named Saoirse, but there's no one in there but him and Doc Gibson most of the time. He keeps saying he'll see her when he gets to the other side."

Erwin nodded.

"The ghost of his dead wife, most likely. Sometimes loved ones who have already passed on appear at someone's deathbed to usher them from this world to the next."

"It's a good thing she's here," Dr. Gibson said, bending low to make his way under the tent flap. "The conditions are so bad in most prison camps, he'd be better off dead. Overcrowding, unsanitary conditions, and food not fit for man nor beast." He glanced behind him. "His uniform is rife with disease and needs to be burned, but I don't have anything to replace it with except civilian clothes. He'll be given a prison uniform when he arrives in Louisville—if he survives that long."

Wilhelmina felt an almost overwhelming sense of melancholy. If Lee and Solomon's story affected her so deeply, how could she consider them her enemy?

"Colonel Stumbaugh has asked for volunteers to escort the prisoners to Louisville," Erwin said. "I took the liberty of appointing ourselves to the position. Do you feel up to it?"

Wilhelmina felt honored to be trusted with such an important task.

"What will we be expected to do after we complete our mission? Are we to remain in Kentucky, or will we be expected to rejoin our regiment?"

"Three of us will ride the ambulance wagon to the train station, take the train to Louisville, and return to Shiloh after we turn over the prisoners. After we reach the train station, a supply wagon will be waiting to take us to our next campsite."

The trip sounded fraught with responsibility, which also made it ripe for disaster.

"Do you know who the third man is?"

Erwin shrugged.

"I don't think anyone has stepped forward yet. But it doesn't matter who the final guard turns out to be. I feel an obligation to these men. I captured them. I want to be assured that they are safe."

Wilhelmina rested her rifle against her shoulder.

"I'm willing to do whatever I can to help."

"Thank you, son. I knew I could count on you."

After she bade Erwin good night, Wilhelmina slipped into the woods and made sure no one else was around before she unbuttoned her pants and squatted to urinate. Fatigue wrapped itself around her like a blanket. Her eyelids were so heavy she could barely stay awake. She leaned on her rifle in order to remain upright. After she was done relieving herself, she stood and buttoned her pants, her fingers clumsy from exhaustion. She forced herself to hurry. She felt vulnerable at all times, but never more so than when she exposed herself like she just had.

She had been pretending to be a man for nearly two months. No one had seen through her ruse at this point, but how long could her good fortune hold out? And what would happen if her secret was discovered? She would surely be dishonorably discharged from service and her reputation would be ripped to shreds, but would she be spared her life? The army killed deserters. Were imposters given the same harsh treatment?

When she walked out of the woods, Maynard was standing on the edge of the clearing with a lit cigarette held loosely between his thumb and index finger. How long had he been there? Had he seen something he shouldn't?

"Evening," she said, too afraid to meet his eye lest he see right through to her soul.

Maynard took a long drag on his cigarette before he flicked it away.

"Erwin's guarding the prisoner you're both so fond of and the other one's in chains. Where are you off to in such a hurry?"

"Mr. Weekley and I have to escort the prisoners to Louisville tomorrow. I want to make sure to get plenty of rest before we begin the journey."

She tried to leave, but Maynard grabbed her arm.

"What's your story, boy?"

Wilhelmina broke free from his grip before he could feel the feminine softness beneath her newly formed muscles.

"I'm afraid I don't know what you're getting at."

"Sure you do. Everybody has a secret. What's yours?" He stepped forward, squinting to examine her face. "What are you running from, Fredericks?"

Wilhelmina felt her heart begin to race. Had Maynard been asking questions about her? Had her father been making inquiries that had raised suspicions about her identity? Did Maynard suspect she wasn't who she claimed to be?

"I'm not running from anything. I'm running toward something."

"What might that be?" Maynard asked through narrowed eyes.

"My destiny."

❖

Clara mixed flour, salt, sugar, butter, lard, and cold water with her fingers, then flattened the resulting ball of dough with a rolling pin. The boys had more of a sweet tooth than she did. They could eat sugary treats all day long if she let them, but she only got a hankering for something sweet when it was close to her time of the month. An apple pie made from one of the jars of preserves lining the shelves in the basement was just what she needed to prepare for the coming of her monthly curse.

Moses sat in a rocking chair near the pot-bellied stove. Jedediah's claims of fifty thousand Yankees readying to march on Shiloh had Enid so shaken up she didn't want anyone she cared about to be left alone. She hadn't resorted to having someone stand guard whenever anyone took a trip to the privy, but it was probably only a matter of time before the idea struck her. Lately, she had insisted on having Moses accompany her and Mary when they ventured to the Summerses' farm in case the Yankees raided their homestead while they were gone and burned the house down with Moses trapped inside unable to find his way out.

Clara appreciated Enid's concern but thought her fears were unfounded. An army fifty thousand strong wouldn't be able to sneak up on anyone. Dragging cannons, horses, rifles, and whatever else they needed to wage war, the men would announce their presence well before they arrived, giving everyone plenty of time to clear out if they wanted to. She was grateful for the company, however. Especially considering what had nearly happened the last time Jedediah Ogletree had come upon her while she was unaccompanied.

Moses draped his walking stick across his lap. Percy had spent almost two full days carving it for him out of a branch from the pine tree on the corner of the house. Instead of support, Moses used the walking stick like a second set of eyes. He poked it out in front of him as he walked so he could locate any obstacles that might be in his way. He still needed to take someone's arm from time to time, especially in areas with uneven footing, but he was able to make his way on his own more often than not. Clara had noticed a change in him the past few days. Gone was the sullen acceptance of his fate. In its place was something that looked an awful lot like hope. She wanted it to stay.

"What's troubling you, Clara?" Moses asked.

She looked up, startled. Had a miracle happened? Could he see the worry on her face? When she regarded him, his eyes were as cloudy as ever.

"What makes you think something's the matter?" she asked, returning to her chore.

"You're pounding that dough so hard I'd be surprised if it doesn't come out bruised. Is it Jedediah? Ma hasn't had a good night's rest since he came to the house last week."

"Neither have I." Though her discomfort had begun after his visit to her home, not the Braggs's place. "Aren't you scared of what he—I mean what the Yankees might do?"

Moses flashed a sad smile. The only kind he had been able to produce since he returned home.

"Half the stories you hear about the war are just that. Stories. Tall tales people tell because they want to be scared or scare someone else. If they weren't there to see it for themselves, how can you be sure what they're saying is true?"

"But the things you saw when you were in battle—"

"Were things done in battle. The Yankees aren't going after civilians any more than the Confederates are. They're just trying to find food to eat and a warm, dry place to sleep at night. If they come marching through here, we'll be fine as long as we give them what they want and stay out of their way."

"Wouldn't giving them food and shelter be considered aiding the enemy?"

Moses cocked his head as if he was listening to what Clara didn't say as opposed to what she did.

"So what Jedediah said did spook you."

"Not so much as what he did."

She covered her mouth with her hands, but the words had already slipped out and it was too late to take them back.

Moses's voice was quiet but forceful.

"What exactly did he do?"

Clara cast a glance out the window to make sure no one was in earshot. Enid and Mary were busy tending to a goat with a sore hoof. Abram and Percy were supposed to be mucking the horse's stall in the barn, but she could see Abram staring at Mary all moony-eyed as he leaned on his shovel.

"He tried to have his way with me a few days ago."

Moses gripped his walking stick so tightly Clara feared it might splinter.

"Please tell me he didn't succeed."

"No, I fought him off. I nicked him with a butcher knife and told him I'd cut his throat if he tried anything like that again."

This time, Moses's smile seemed to contain some of its former mirth.

"I believe you would, too."

"I'm glad you believe me, but I don't think he did."

"Have you told the sheriff what happened?"

"Why would I? Jedediah didn't leave a mark on me, and he's the one who came away wounded. If I said anything, I might be the one who ended up in jail instead of him."

"What can I do to help?"

"What can you do? His father owns most of the land in Hardin County and half the people in it. Your family and mine are the only holdouts."

"All the more reason for us to stick together."

Clara pressed the bottom pie crust into a pan and poured in the preserves. Then she laid the other pie crust on top, trimmed the edges with a paring knife, and poked several holes in the dough so steam could escape while the pie baked.

"Enid says you're sweet on me," she said after she set the pie in the oven. "Is that true?"

The steady rhythm of Moses's rocking faltered for a moment.

"It was a long time ago, but no more."

Clara poured herself a cup of coffee as she took a much-needed rest. She had been bustling about for hours, and this was the first chance she'd had to sit still for more than five minutes at a spell. "What happened to change your mind?"

"I knew the feelings you had for me weren't the same as the ones I had for you, so I told myself it wouldn't make sense to go chasing after lost causes."

Clara was glad Moses was able to resolve the issue without any awkwardness transpiring between them. She loved him in her own way. Just not the way he wanted.

"I wish you could teach Jedediah to follow your example."

"It wouldn't do any good. He's a more prideful man than I am. Turning him down the way you did most likely wounded his spirit, not just his flesh. Now he's probably looking to find a way to restore his pride and get back at you in the process."

Clara shivered despite the combined warmth of the fire in the stove and the cup of hot coffee in her hands.

"That's what I'm afraid of. I don't want something to happen to my family because of me. Jedediah wouldn't dare to attempt to take such liberties if Papa and Solomon were home, but I've got to accept the possibility that they might never come back."

She set the cup of coffee down and spread her palms on the table, finding strength in the worn wood surface.

"Maybe Mama was right. She always said a woman didn't need a man to survive. If that's the case, I don't need a man to look after my family. I can do it myself."

CHAPTER SEVEN

H ere," Maynard said as he tossed Wilhelmina two short lengths of rope.

"What do you want me to do with these?"

"Tie up the prisoners. And make sure you cinch them up good and tight. We don't want either of them getting any ideas about busting loose once we leave camp. The last thing we need is two escaped Rebs on our hands."

While Erwin trained his rifle on Solomon, Wilhelmina leaned into the ambulance wagon and tied one of the lengths of rope around Lee's wrists. Lee was still out of his head with fever and was probably too weak to hurt a fly, but Wilhelmina couldn't disobey Maynard's order. He had been promoted from private to sergeant after "his" capture of the prisoners and had been showing off his new stripes ever since like a society lady flashing a shiny new bauble.

When she approached Solomon with the second length of rope, he fixed her with a baleful glare.

"Turn around."

She pitched her voice even lower than she normally did to show she wasn't afraid of him, even though the hateful look in his eyes struck fear in her heart.

Solomon spit at her feet but did as she asked. He slowly turned around and placed his hands behind his back so she could bind his wrists.

"Whoa, now," Maynard said from his perch next to the wagon driver, "what do you think you're doing, Fredericks? Tie his hands in front of him not behind him. Unless you want to volunteer to pull his pecker out and hold it for him every time he has to piss."

"What's this predilection you seem to have with peckers, Sarge?" Erwin asked good-naturedly. "First mine, now this boy's. I'm of a mind to think you're a mite obsessed."

Solomon snickered at the joke. Truth be told, Wilhelmina found it pretty funny, too, though she didn't dare laugh because Maynard obviously didn't seem to find the humor in it. His face turned purple with rage and his voice shook as he said, "Every one of you better wipe those smiles off your faces right now or I'll show you what for."

"Calm down, Maynard," Erwin said, trying to placate him. "I didn't mean any harm. I was just trying to bring a little light to the darkness in which we currently find ourselves."

"This 'darkness,' as you put it, ain't no laughing matter. Neither is my reputation. I won't have it sullied by the likes of you or that Rebel trash you found in the woods."

"To paraphrase the great William Shakespeare," Erwin whispered, "I think the fellow doth protest too much."

"Quit your mumbling, Weekley, and get your ass in this wagon," Maynard said. "You, too, Fredericks. It's time for us to perform our assigned duty and take these sorry excuses for soldiers to prison. I'll deal with your insolence when we get back from Kentucky."

"He ain't right in the head," Solomon said after Wilhelmina helped him into the wagon and sat him next to the stretcher where his father lay prone. He jerked his chin at Maynard's back. "I've seen people like him before. Mean for no reason is what he is. And you bastards are dumb enough to follow him."

Maynard whirled around.

"Keep talking, Reb, and I'll show you exactly how mean I can be."

He pulled a filthy handkerchief from his pocket, blew his nose in it with great fanfare, and tossed the soiled cloth in the back of the wagon.

"Gag him with that, Weekley, so I won't have to listen to that annoying Tennessee drawl of his all the way to Louisville."

Erwin looked at the handkerchief but didn't move to pick it up.

"Are you disobeying a direct order, soldier? If you are, I'm sure I can find you a spot in the same cell as your newfound friends here."

"I'm sorry, son," Erwin said under his breath as he slipped the handkerchief into Solomon's mouth and tied it around the back of his head. "I'm just doing what I'm told."

Solomon mumbled something that sounded like "Ain't we all?"

The ride to the train station was bumpy, the wagon's wheels bouncing over the deep ruts the heavy artillery carts had left in the narrow dirt road. Wilhelmina placed her hand on Lee's chest to keep him from rolling off his stretcher. She could feel his lungs rattle each time he breathed. He sounded more like a hissing cat than a man. She laid a blanket over him to keep him warm.

"You've got a fine bedside manner, Fredericks," Maynard said. "You ought to quit trying to be a soldier and try your hand at nursing instead."

"This man may be my enemy, but he still deserves respect."

"The only thing he deserves is to be put out of his misery. The way he's sounding, it won't be long now."

Solomon couldn't speak clearly with the gag in his mouth, but the expression in his eyes as he looked at his father was more eloquent than any words he could have uttered. Lee wouldn't survive in prison. They all knew it. He was too weak to fend off any predatory inmates he came across, and the virulent diseases endemic to such places would wreak havoc on his diminished immune system. He and Solomon were supposed to remain in the Louisville Military Prison until the end of the war, which could occur in a matter of months if Union forces pressed their advantage and kept pushing farther south, but the indefinite term seemed more like a death sentence.

"Ain't right," Solomon mumbled around the gag. "It just ain't right. A man should die in his own house with his loved ones gathered around him to say fare-thee-well, not locked up in some godforsaken prison camp far from home."

Wilhelmina pondered her own fate. What would happen to her if she were wounded or killed? Would anyone she loved claim her body and visit her crypt to keep her memory alive, or would she be tossed into an unmarked grave and quickly forgotten?

"Whoa." The driver pulled on the reins and urged the horses to stop as the wagon neared the train station.

Maynard stood on the platform with Solomon after Wilhelmina and Erwin helped him climb down from the wagon. Wilhelmina and Erwin struggled to lift Lee's stretcher and carry him onboard the waiting train. Even though he was only skin and bones, his dead weight seemed much heavier. As Wilhelmina's arms trembled with fatigue, she was eager to free herself of her terrible burden.

The train was similar to the one Wilhelmina and her fellow recruits had ridden from Pittsburgh. Most of the cars were filled with nothing but empty space to leave as much room as possible for supplies. The few passenger cars were outfitted with wooden benches instead of the plush seats and luxurious accommodations common to the first class cabins Wilhelmina had inhabited in the past.

She and Erwin placed Lee's stretcher on one of the benches and took a seat on either side of him. Wilhelmina sat on the bench in front and Erwin on the one behind. Wilhelmina spread her legs, taking up as much room as she could. Men, she had observed, never seemed to have enough space. They sat, stood, and walked like they were on the lookout for more.

Maynard escorted Solomon near the front of the car and positioned himself so he could keep an eye on his prisoner at all times.

The ambulance driver took off his hat and waved it in the air as the train whistle blew and the cars began to move.

"Good luck, boys. Don't run into any booby traps along the way."

Most of the countryside had been sabotaged by the Confederates. Rail lines had been heated and twisted out of shape and the wooden cross ties burned to slow or halt the Union army's flow of supplies from the North. Telegraph poles had also been chopped down, their vital lines of communication cut. Some farmers had even poisoned their wells and ponds so advancing troops couldn't have fresh water. None of it made sense. How could citizens of the same country turn on each other so completely?

As the train slowly chugged out of the station, a few local boys ran after it to throw rotten eggs at the windows.

"Go home, Yankees. We don't want you here," they catcalled as the odor of sulfur permeated the car.

Maynard lowered the window closest to him, stuck his rifle into the gap, and fired a shot in the air. The egg tossers scattered like leaves on the wind. "That'll show them."

"No, don't!"

Wilhelmina's attempted warning came too late. Solomon was on Maynard before he could turn around. He shoved Maynard face-first into the window. Maynard's head hit the thick glass with a fearsome thud. Wilhelmina tried to rise to her feet, but she felt strong hands around her neck dragging her down.

"Don't make me do it, boy," Lee whispered hoarsely in her ear as the train began to pick up speed. "Please don't make me."

Wilhelmina clawed at her neck as the rope around Lee's wrists bit into her flesh, cutting off her air. She heard the sounds of a struggle as Solomon and Maynard wrestled for control of the pearl-handled pistol Maynard always wore tucked into his belt.

"I'm done for, Solomon," Lee said. "Don't worry about me. Save yourself."

Wilhelmina's head swam, and her vision started to go gray around the edges. She tried everything she could but was unable to break Lee's grip. She felt herself begin to weaken as her arms and legs grew impossibly heavy. Then, just before she thought she might lose consciousness, the weight pressing against her back was lifted.

Erwin cracked Lee in the back of his head with the butt of his rifle. Lee fell limply to the floor, blood streaming from a gash in his scalp.

"Can you manage, son?" Erwin asked, pulling Wilhelmina to her feet.

Wilhelmina tried to say, "Yes," but she couldn't stop coughing long enough to get the words out. The skin around her neck felt like it had been rubbed raw. The inside of her throat felt much the same way. Each breath burned as she tried to force air into her lungs.

"Stay here."

Erwin deposited her on the bench and headed to the front of the car.

"Drop the gun, son."

Solomon wrapped one arm around Maynard's neck and positioned Maynard's body in front of him like a shield.

"Don't come any closer," he said, pressing the pistol to Maynard's head as he edged toward the door, "or I'll blow his head clean off."

"Think about what you're doing," Erwin said. "If you kill him, the Union will hang you. If you try to escape, they'll hang you for that, too. If you survive the fall after you jump off this train and try to return to your unit, the Confederacy will shoot you for desertion."

"Sounds like I'm dead either way, don't it? I might as well take as many Yankees with me as I can."

Solomon shoved Maynard to one side and threw himself out the door. Even over the roaring of the engine and the clattering of the train's wheels against the steel tracks, Wilhelmina heard the thud when Solomon's body hit the ground. She screwed up her courage and peered out the window, fully prepared to see Solomon's broken body lying in the meadow they were passing at breakneck speed. She was amazed to see Solomon on his feet, dragging his left leg awkwardly behind him as he half-ran, half-shuffled toward the woods.

"Shoot him, Weekley," Maynard said, gesturing toward Solomon's rapidly disappearing form. When Erwin remained rooted in place, Maynard grabbed Erwin's rifle and took aim. "Fine. I'll do it myself."

Just before Maynard pulled the trigger, Erwin struck the barrel of the rifle with the heel of his hand, causing the shot to fly well off target.

"What in tarnation do you think you're doing?" Maynard asked. "I had a bead on him."

"My conscience wouldn't allow you to shoot an unarmed man in the back."

"Unarmed?" Maynard sputtered. "But he's got my—"

Erwin bent and retrieved the pearl-handled pistol Solomon had tossed on the floor before he leaped from the train.

Maynard snatched the pistol from Erwin and tucked it into his belt.

"I ought to recommend you be brought up on charges of insubordination. I wouldn't hesitate to do so if we didn't need every man we have, even ones as pitiful as you."

He poked his finger in Erwin's chest.

"But make no mistake. When we get back to camp, you are taking the blame for this, Weekley, not me. Step aside."

He touched the lump on his forehead to make sure it wasn't bleeding, then marched down the aisle and stood over Lee.

"I knew you were fooling the whole time, old man. So stop your pretending and get on your feet. I told you to get up."

He nudged Lee with the toe of his boot, but Lee didn't move. That was when Wilhelmina realized the awful rattling in Lee's lungs had stopped. She pressed her fingers against the side of his neck, but felt nothing but cooling flesh.

"This man's dead," she said, sitting back on her haunches.

"And the other one is as good as." Maynard scraped a hand over his whiskers. "This might not turn out to be such a bad day after all."

As she stared at the first dead body she had ever seen, Wilhelmina couldn't imagine how a day could feel much worse. But with a major battle looming, she knew she was probably about to find out.

❖

Clara churned butter on the porch while Abram and Percy played checkers beside her. There was still a great deal of work to be done around the house and on the farm, but she didn't see anything wrong with letting them have a little fun for a while.

"King me," Percy said proudly after he moved one of his pieces into the proper position on the board.

"How did you do that?"

Percy hooked his thumbs in the straps of his overalls. "You might be the second-best shot in the county, but I'm still better than you at checkers. Now king me."

"Cheater."

"Sore loser."

Clara laughed as she listened to her brothers squabble. It had been so long since they had been able to act like children, she was glad to see they hadn't forgotten how. Her laughter died in her throat when she saw a soldier coming out of the woods. Trying not to scream, she shoved the churn aside and waved Abram and Percy toward her.

"Come on, boys, get in the house."

"What for?" Percy asked. "We haven't finished our game yet."

Clara watched the man move closer. His dark wool uniform hung off him, and he walked with a limp made more pronounced by the tree branches tied to his left leg as a makeshift splint. He wasn't carrying a gun, but that didn't mean he wasn't armed. Or dangerous.

"Don't argue with me, Percy. Just get in the house."

Abram stood and followed her line of sight.

"That's not a Yankee, Clara. He's wearing a gray uniform, not a blue one. That makes him one of ours. And I think—" He squinted and took a step forward. "It *is* him. Solomon. Hey, Solomon!"

He ran down the steps and made a beeline for the figure lurching toward them. Percy took off after him.

"Boys, get back here."

Clara reached for them but was able to grasp only air.

The soldier staggered and nearly fell when Abram slammed into him and crushed him in a bear hug. Percy wasn't too far behind, wrapping his arms around the soldier's uninjured leg and holding on for dear life. Clara wanted to believe her eyes weren't playing tricks on her, but she didn't dare get her hopes up. Could it really be Solomon, alive and home from the war? But if he was here, why wasn't Papa with him?

"What's the matter, sister? Don't you recognize me?"

Tears flooded Clara's eyes when she heard Solomon's voice. Heard his familiar laugh.

"I can't believe it's you."

After he laboriously climbed the porch steps, she touched his arm to convince herself he was real.

"What are you doing home? What happened to your leg? Where's Papa? And when was the last time you had a bath? You smell worse than the hog pen in the middle of summer."

"I missed you, too, sister." He went inside the house and sat down hard in the closest chair. "I'll tell you everything in a minute," he said, rubbing his splinted leg, "but I gotta have something to eat first. I haven't had a bite of food in three days and my stomach is practically touching my backbone."

"I'm glad you're home, brother."

Clara patted his shoulder before she headed to the stove to fix him a plate of ham, biscuits, and redeye gravy.

"Abram, run tell Mrs. Bragg your brother's home."

"Don't you move, Abram," Solomon said sharply. "I don't want nobody to know I'm here."

"Why not?" Abram asked.

Clara shushed him and set the plate of food in front of Solomon, who attacked it like he hadn't eaten in weeks instead of days. After he swallowed the last bite, he held out the empty plate to ask for more.

"What's wrong, Solomon? Where's Papa?"

Solomon drank greedily from a cup of water. Clara refilled it as Solomon wiped his mouth with the back of his hand and slowly began to tell a tale she wasn't certain she wanted to hear.

"He caught the pneumonia about a month ago and kept getting sicker and sicker every day. We left camp one night to try to find some herbs to brew into a tea, but we got captured by a bunch of Yankees up in Nashville. Their doctor did his best to help him, but Papa kept getting sicker. The Yanks ordered us to be sent to a prison camp. They put us on a train to Louisville and would have locked us up sure enough, but Papa gathered what little strength he had left to help me get away. He choked one of the guards half to death and probably would have killed him if the other guard hadn't cracked him on the head with his gun. I bunged up my leg jumping off the train after Papa fell. It's probably broke, but I ain't got time to fret about it. I've been on the run for nearly a week now."

Clara wiped her streaming eyes with the hem of her apron.

"You left Papa behind with a bunch of strangers?"

"He told me to go so that's what I did."

Solomon gripped her hand, and the years that had been added to his features during the months he had been gone fell away. He wasn't a nameless, faceless soldier anymore. He was her brother once more.

"He knew he wasn't going to make it, sister. I doubt those soldiers got the chance to take him to the prison. He probably died right there on that train car. He gave his last breath to save me."

Clara held out hope.

"But you left him with those men so you don't know for sure if he's dead or alive. That means there's a chance he might come walking out of the woods one day like you did just now."

Solomon shook his head.

"No, Clara. His body could be buried anywhere from Tennessee to Kentucky, but his soul's with Mama now. I know it in my heart. Quit your sniffling, you two," he said as Abram and Percy began to cry. "You're getting too big to be bawling like babies."

Abram and Percy tried to put on brave faces, but their masks refused to stay in place. Solomon wrapped his arms around their waists.

"Papa died a hero. Don't ever forget that, hear?"

Abram and Percy nodded dutifully. Percy was the first to find his voice.

"Are you home to stay, Solomon?"

"It would be too dangerous for all of you if I stayed here. I've got both sides after me. The Yankees want to hang me for being an escaped prisoner and the Rebs want to shoot me for being a deserter. I ain't neither one of those things. I'm just a soldier doing his job."

"What are you planning to do?" Clara asked.

"What I signed up to do: kill as many Yankees as I can. I spotted a whole host of them setting up camp around the church."

Clara's heart lurched.

"They're already here?"

She clutched the ring she always wore on a cord around her neck. The ring was her mama's and had passed to her after Mama died. Touching it offered her comfort in times of trouble, and she had never needed comfort more than she did now.

"Does Preacher Parsons know? Why didn't the Reserves sound the alarm?"

"The preacher probably thinks the Yanks will disappear if he prays hard enough. And the men in the Reserves ain't been trained. They probably turned tail and ran as soon as they saw that wave of blue as vast as the ocean heading toward them. I ain't scared, though. I know these woods better than anyone around these parts. I'm going to find a place to hole up until the war's over and if any blue coats cross my path, I'll pick them off one at a time. Hand me the rifle and a box of cartridges. That ought to hold me for a while. I'll come back if I need more."

Clara took the rifle down from its place above the mantle and set it and a box of ammunition next to Solomon's right hand.

Abram eyed the rifle, obviously unwilling to see it change hands.

"How am I going to hunt with no gun? We've got to have meat, don't we?"

"We've got half a hog hanging in the smokehouse," Clara said. "If we ration it right, that should be enough to tide us over. I'll take the wagon to town tomorrow and go see Mr. Stallings at the general store. He may have some rifles in stock. If he don't, he can order one." She ruffled Abram's hair to rub away the sting of loss. "It's past time you had a gun of your own anyway."

Abram's chest swelled with pride. Except for the bear rug, he had never owned anything except Papa's and Solomon's hand-me-downs. The new rifle would be the first thing he ever had that was his and his alone. Clara hoped they had enough credit left at the store to be able to buy it for him. If they didn't, what would they do then? The Braggs needed their rifle to protect themselves. They couldn't go lending it out like it was a library book. But she couldn't worry about that now.

"Percy, go and fetch your brother some clean clothes," she said. "Abram, drag the washtub off the porch and take it into the bedroom. After you fill it up, I'll add a bucket of hot water to it so Solomon can scald off the six months' worth of dirt he's carrying around."

"But I ain't had a chance to ask him how many Yankees he's killed yet," Abram said.

"Not as many as I'm going to," Solomon said. "Now mind your sister and do what she said." After the boys left to perform their assigned tasks, he turned back to Clara. "How are you holding up?"

"Fair to middling. Some days are better than others. But any troubles I may have are nothing compared to yours."

She longed to tell him everything that had happened while he was gone—especially how Jedediah wouldn't give her a minute's peace—but he already had enough worry on his plate. He didn't need an extra helping. He had never shown more than a passing interest in her life in the past. They didn't have time to change that now.

"I hate to leave you alone like this when the three of you have been on your own for so long," Solomon said, "but I don't see no other way around it. With Papa dead, the land passes to me. It would go to you if I got killed, but you're a woman so you ain't got a head for business and you don't have a husband to make the decisions for you. Abram's too young to hold the deed so that leaves him out. With the ownership in doubt, anyone could swoop in and snatch this place right from under you. Those damned Ogletrees would be first in line. Papa worked too hard to build this place up. I won't let anyone have it who ain't family. I'll keep my eye on all of you as best I can, but I can't stay here with you."

"I don't want you risking your life trying to protect ours. Don't worry about us. Just do what you have to do to keep yourself safe. The boys and I have managed this long. We'll find a way to manage a little longer."

"From the looks of things, you don't need me around here nohow." He seemed surprised to see the farm hadn't fallen apart without him and Papa around to tell her what to do.

"Don't start thinking we don't miss you around here because we do. We could always use an extra hand," Clara said as she put some water on to boil. "Enid and Mary help out as best they can, and we try to do the same for them since they're in the same situation we are with Mr. Joseph away and Moses unable to see."

Solomon tossed his greasy hair out of his eyes as he sopped the gravy off his plate with the remains of his third biscuit.

"I'll take a broke leg over losing my sight any day."

"Moses doesn't seem to mind it too much. Not like he did in the beginning."

Solomon looked at her out of the corner of his eye.

"How do you know so much about it? Has he been courting you while I was gone? Plenty of able-bodied men have shown an interest in you over the years, and you didn't pay them no mind. Why did you finally set your cap for one who doesn't have all his parts in working order?"

Clara took offense both to what Solomon said and the manner in which he said it. He'd always had something of a mean streak, but he never used to direct his ire at his family and friends.

"Moses is a good man. He would make someone a fine husband someday despite his infirmity."

"Would you want to marry him?"

"No, but not for the reasons you're saying. I'm not interested in him in that way. I never was even before he got hurt. He keeps me company while I do my chores, but that's all there is to it. Besides, I think one of the Franklin girls has her eye on him. She drops by the Braggs' place every Sunday afternoon to bring a cake or a pie, or just to sit with him for a while. Enid's waiting for one of them to make their intentions clear, but both of them are proving too shy to say anything. Just like Abram and Mary."

"Abram's sparking with little Mary Bragg? That little devil. I didn't know he had it in him."

"He doesn't have anything in him yet. Neither one does. You can't even mention one's name to the other without having them turn red in the face."

"Do you want me to tell him about the birds and the bees before I go?"

"He's spent his whole life on a farm. He knows where babies come from. And he's much too young to even think about making or providing for one of his own."

"It's getting kinda late for you, though, isn't it? You're going to be twenty soon. Isn't it time for you to think about settling down?"

"Not if it means settling for less. I'm not going to marry someone I don't love just to please someone else."

Clara forced herself to stop staring at the water on the stovetop. A watched pot never boiled and this one was surely proving the adage.

"It don't seem right not to tell Moses and the rest of the Braggs the news about Papa," she said, returning to the table. "Papa and Mr. Joseph have always been fast friends."

"Mrs. Enid knows how to keep a secret. It probably wouldn't hurt none to let her know what's happened, but we don't want word to get around to too many people. You never know who might be a Union sympathizer."

"You sound like Jedediah Ogletree."

"I'd rather rip my tongue out of my mouth than be compared to that overstuffed peacock. Has he been keeping you company, too?"

"No, he rides by when he's on patrol for the Reserves, but I've made it clear he isn't welcome in our house."

"Good. I don't care if you never get married as long as you don't get mixed up with the likes of him."

That was the best news Clara had heard in months.

"The washtub's full," Abram said after his third trip from the well to the house. A trail of splashed water marked the path.

Solomon peeled off his uniform and socks and sat shivering in his drooping long johns. He handed the soiled clothes to Abram.

"Take these out in the yard and burn them. The coat's filled with so many lice, it'll probably sound like you're cooking popcorn once it hits the flames."

Abram held up the filthy rags.

"Don't you want to keep your uniform as a souvenir? I could wash it up real good and save it for when you come home to stay."

"I've got all the souvenir I need right here," Solomon said, rubbing his left leg. "I'm sure to remember the war every day for the rest of my life, especially when rain's coming."

He tried to push himself to his feet but fell back in the chair. Clara took him by the arm and helped him up. She couldn't get over how much weight he had lost. He had never been a big man, but now his cheeks were hollow, his chest was as scrawny as a boy's, and his arms and legs were as thin as twigs.

"You need fattening up," she said as he limped his way to the bedroom.

"When the war's over, I'll find a wife to help me put some meat on my bones, but I ain't got time for that foolishness now. I've got Yankees to kill. Three in particular. One goes by the name of Maynard. I don't know his Christian name, but I know his face. He was the one who was so hateful to Papa and me when we were at the Yankee campsite. If I see that sorry son of a bitch again, I'm going to put a bullet right in the middle of his forehead. Then I'm going to smile as I watch him die. After that, I'm gonna find his friends. None of this would have happened if the one named Weekley had let Papa and me go when we ran up on him taking a piss in the dark. We wasn't armed or nothing. That Weekley fella could have looked the other way if he wanted to, but he didn't."

"Why didn't you and Papa have your guns?" Abram asked. "You weren't running, were you?"

"Watch your mouth, boy." Solomon cuffed him on the back of his head. "I told you me and Papa was out hunting herbs. You don't need guns for that."

"You do if you know there's Yankees around," Percy said.

"I'm not going to argue the point with either one of you because you wasn't there," Solomon said sharply. "Now where was I? Oh, yeah. The last one I'm gonna get is named Fredericks. From the looks of him, he couldn't be a day over sixteen. But if he's old enough to shoot a gun, he's old enough to get shot at."

Clara had never heard Solomon speak so coldly about seeking revenge. He'd had conflicts in the past, usually over some girl he and another fella both had their eye on, but he had always resolved those issues with his fists instead of reaching for a gun.

"I'm going to miss Papa, too," she said, pouring hot water into the tub, "but killing those men won't bring him back."

"You're a woman, Clara. That means you have limitations. I wouldn't expect you to understand something this complicated. Just know I have to do it for the sake of our family's honor as well as mine. You understand, don't you, boys?"

Abram nodded fervently as he handed Solomon a washcloth and a bar of lye soap.

"Kill them twice, Solomon. Once for Papa and once for me."

He looked at Solomon with eyes filled with adoration. Abram had learned most of the things he knew about life and the world from his older brother, but Clara wished this was one lesson he had never been taught.

CHAPTER EIGHT

Wilhelmina's arms, shoulders, and back screamed with pain, and bile rose in her throat. She didn't know which was worse, the stench of the open latrine or the laborious task of adding ten more feet to the trench. She adjusted the handkerchief she had tied over her nose and mouth, but the smell still seeped through. She could even taste it on her tongue. She clenched her stomach muscles to keep from vomiting.

As punishment for their part in the failed prisoner transfer, Maynard had been stripped of his sergeant's stripes, and Wilhelmina and Erwin had been assigned to thirty days of latrine duty. A host of men had been ordered to dig the latrine at the campsite in Savannah, Tennessee, but only Wilhelmina and Erwin had been compelled to complete it. Once her assignment was over, she would be more than happy if she never saw a shovel again.

Most men headed to the woods when they felt the need to relieve themselves. Doing so offered more privacy and the smell wasn't nearly as overpowering while they did their business. The latrines were mainly used by those too sick, too desperate, or too lazy to find a secluded spot. Wilhelmina gagged at both the sight and the odor of the waste those men's bodies had expelled as they tried to rid themselves of the various virulent diseases spreading through the ranks like wildfire. Influenza. Smallpox. Malaria. Measles.

"The next time you want someone to volunteer to help you do something," she said, tossing another shovelful of dirt aside, "ask someone else."

Erwin chuckled behind his mask.

"Point taken, son. Point taken."

The officer tasked with monitoring their progress had positioned himself safely upwind. He pinched his nostrils shut as he approached them.

"Okay, you two. That's enough for today." He looked at the expanded latrine with disdain. "General Grant should have you digging trenches we can use for defense, not for taking a crap in, but he'd rather have us run you through drills and teach you how to march nice and pretty than prepare you for a fight. Put those shovels back in the supply wagon and get cleaned up. Dress parade is in an hour."

"Yes, sir."

Wilhelmina automatically snapped off a salute, forgetting until the smell hit her even harder that her clothes and hands were dotted with excrement. Her boots were more brown than black. If the water weren't so cold and she didn't risk exposure in more ways than one, she would strip naked and immerse herself in the river to scrub herself clean. She settled for washing her face and hands, then scraping the soles of her boots against the bark of a tree.

When she and Erwin got back to their tent, Billy was practicing his cadences as usual. Drummers were responsible for communicating officers' commands both on the battlefield and in camp. Attack, retreat, eat, sleep. Every possible action was dictated by the tap, tap, tap of a drummer's sticks against the instrument strapped to his shoulders.

"This came for you while you were gone." Billy continued to practice one-handed as he picked up a wrinkled envelope and handed it to Wilhelmina. "It smells pretty. Is it from your mama or your girl?"

Wilhelmina held the envelope under her nose and inhaled deeply. The faint smell of Libby's favorite perfume soaking the paper made her forget the malodorous latrine. Seeing her new name written in Libby's handwriting made her forget everything else.

Erwin's eyes twinkled as he lit his pipe.

"The smile on his face is all the answer you need, Billy."

Wilhelmina ducked out of the tent, intending to find a place she could read Libby's letter in private. A tough task considering there were men everywhere she looked. The population of the camp currently exceeded that of some of the towns they had passed through.

To her left, a group of soldiers were playing poker with a set of cards featuring images of naked women. To her right, another group was singing a lovelorn ballad about a maid with golden hair. The longing in the men's voices and the plaintive sound of the harmonica music accompanying them plucked at Wilhelmina's heartstrings.

Deciding she was better off where she was, she sat on her bedroll with her back to Erwin and Billy. Spreading her shoulders to hide the words, she opened the envelope with shaking hands and began to read.

Dearest Wil,

I pray this letter finds you well. Thank you for keeping me informed of your whereabouts and the state of your health, though I must admit some passages of your letters are difficult to read.

I sorrow for the trying times you are enduring—until I remind myself no one forced you to enter the life you are currently living. Despite the danger, deprivations, and hardships, you chose this path of your own free will. I feel compelled to ask yet again. Is it worth it?

Is your sense of duty so great you are willing to risk life and limb for the "privilege" of marching for hours on end, sleeping under a thin blanket on the frozen ground, surrounding yourself with thousands of strange men, and putting yourself in the line of enemy fire? Is your belief in your cause so complete you are willing to die in order to see it achieved? For the life of me, I cannot understand it.

I did not attempt to dissuade you from your stated course the night you told me of your plans because I doubted the veracity of your words. It is now painfully clear how utterly I misjudged everything that took place that night, including your declarations of love. There are certain subjects I cannot and will not broach, especially on paper, but I am begging you to throw down your weapons and return home. It is not too late for you to find salvation.

Your family misses you terribly. Your mother has been sick with worry since the discovery of your letter and its vagaries about your intentions to join the war effort. Your father has exhausted all efforts to find you. He has sent letters to dozens of officials inquiring if you are currently in their employ. After receiving nothing but negative responses, he now fears you might be dead. I want to assuage his concerns, but how can I do so without betraying your trust?

Stephen and I will be married in three weeks' time. Although it is my deepest desire that you will be here to witness the occasion, I am asking you not to attend the ceremony if this letter finds its way into your hands prior to the appointed date. If I looked upon your form on that happiest of days, I fear I would not see the face of the woman I know and love but the visage of a soldier I do not.

You have changed, Wil, and not for the better. There is a hardness about you now that did not exist when you were home where you belong. I know I often teased that you would make a better husband than you would a wife, but now the image is nearly complete.

With each line of your letters I read, I recognize less and less of the Wil I once knew. Even though your words affirm you are still alive, I have already begun to mourn the passing of my boon companion.

I am mightily sorry for my delayed response to your letters, but it has taken me this long to find the courage to say what I feel I must. You have placed me in an untenable position, Wil, and I can no longer be party to your lie. I can also no longer be part of your life.

Though I give my word I will not reveal your secret, I beseech you not to write me again unless it is to say you have regained your senses and are returning to the life you once led. That you are ready to resume being the woman you are instead of the man you are pretending to be.

I cannot say it any plainer. Stop this nonsense, reveal yourself, and come home!

Yours truly,
Libby

Libby's words left Wilhelmina feeling devastated, but she blinked away her tears because men weren't supposed to cry.

Libby, the woman she had longed for for years, was now lost to her in every way. She pressed her hand against her stomach to keep from sobbing. The dreams she'd had about making a future with Libby—of having Libby see her and accept her for who she really was—were just that. Dreams.

She bolted to the fire, intending to drop the letter into the flames, but her fingers wouldn't loosen their grip. Her charade would come to an abrupt end if the letter fell into the wrong hands. In a way, her life would end as well. How could she go back to what she was when she had seen what she could be?

She always kept Libby's picture next to her heart. She put the letter in the same hiding place.

"Bad news, son?" Erwin asked after she returned to the tent.

"In a way."

Erwin nodded soberly.

"A letter of dismissal then."

"How can it be a dismissal letter, Mr. Weekley?" Billy asked innocently. "I thought you said the letter was from Wil's girl, not his employer."

Erwin patted Billy's knee.

"Hush now, son. I'll explain it to you later."

Erwin draped his arm across Wilhelmina's shoulders like a father consoling his child. Wilhelmina's own father had never shown her this kind of tenderness, yet Erwin had not hesitated to attempt to offer her comfort. He had been more of a father to her over the past few months than her actual father had in nineteen years.

"Romantic entanglements are difficult in the best of times, but never more so than in times of war," Erwin said. "Though it might not seem like it at the moment, rest assured another young lady will come along one day. One always does. By the time you reach my age, you're likely to have had several affairs of the heart. If you're lucky, they will each have more pleasant outcomes than this one."

Wilhelmina wished she could tell him she was forbidden to have the kind of love she sought, but how could she without giving herself away?

A sharp whistle alerted Billy it was time for him to gather the troops. Soldiers across the campsite gathered their rifles as he performed the cadence for the call to dress parade.

"Thank you for the advice, sir," Wilhelmina said as she fell in line with the rest of the men from her regiment. "I'll do my best to take it to heart, but right now I've got a war to fight."

❖

The farm's output allowed Clara and her family to be relatively self-sufficient. The crops they planted provided food for them as well as their livestock. Ground corn from the corn crop fed the chickens, and the horse and mules munched on oats and hay from the pasture. The only time they needed to go to town was to mail a letter at the post office or visit the general store to stock up on staples like flour and sugar. Or, like today, to purchase a new rifle and a box of ammunition.

Abram was so excited about the upcoming purchase—and the chance to catch a glimpse of the Yankee troops camped upriver—he couldn't sit still as he rode in the back of the wagon.

"Give those mules the whip, Percy. You drive slower than Mrs. Bragg, and everybody knows her mule team's as slow as molasses."

Clara had allowed Percy to take the reins today to give him something to be proud about instead of pouting over the fact that Abram was getting something new and he wasn't.

"Don't pay Abram no mind," she said. "You're doing just fine. You don't have to hold the reins so tight, though. Pharaoh and Nicodemus have made this trip often enough to know the way."

Percy loosened his grip, but not by much.

"I'm afraid they might get spooked. I heard noises in the woods last night, and I thought it might be Yankees."

Clara glanced toward the thick woods, searching for signs of movement. She had heard strange sounds last night, too, but she had hoped it was just her imagination playing tricks on her, not Yankee infantrymen on a reconnaissance mission. She jumped every time she heard a twig break nowadays, but she tried not to let her nervousness show. She didn't want to put the boys any more on edge than they already were.

"It was probably a bear waking up from hibernation and looking for something to eat."

"Sounded more like a man than a bear." Percy's face brightened. "Maybe it was Solomon. He said he would look after us, didn't he? Maybe it was him sneaking out of his hiding place to show a few of those Yankees what for."

Clara squeezed his arm to make sure he was paying attention to what she was about to say.

"If anyone mentions Solomon, you haven't seen him since he and Papa left for the war, you hear? His being home is supposed to be our secret, so you can't make comments like that where someone outside the family can hear you. You can keep a secret, can't you?"

Abram snickered.

"About as well as he can walk on water."

"I can, too, keep a secret, and I'm a heap better swimmer than you are, Abram." Percy stuck his tongue out at Abram, then turned back to Clara. "I won't say a word to nobody about Solomon. I promise."

"Good. The same goes for you, too, Abram. Enid Bragg is the only one aside from the three of us who knows Papa's dead and Solomon's hiding out in the woods. Let's make sure we keep it that way. If we don't, it could mean serious trouble for all of us, Solomon especially."

"I won't say nothing," Abram said, "but if we can't tell nobody that Solomon took the rifle to shoot Yankees with, what are you gonna say to Mr. Stallings to explain why we need another one? You know he loves poking his nose in other folks' business."

Clara leaned back in her seat, trying to gather her thoughts.

"I haven't planned that far ahead yet, but I'm sure I'll come up with something when the time comes."

"Just make sure you think of something good," Abram said. "Mr. Stallings is worse than a hog when it comes to rooting up dirt."

Clara clutched her empty satchel to her chest, hoping she hadn't set out on a fool's errand. Would Mr. Stallings let her buy what she needed when Papa already owed him money?

Papa didn't like buying things on credit because he didn't like being beholden to anyone. Whenever he owed someone, he always fretted about it until the debt was repaid. He had left owing Mr. Stallings for the new boots he and Solomon wore when they set out on foot to join the Rebel army, but he had vowed to pay for the purchases as soon as he returned. Mr. Stallings had agreed to the transaction, probably thinking as Papa did that the war wouldn't last more than a few months. Now Papa was buried in the cold ground somewhere far from home and Solomon's ethereal presence was haunting the family like a ghost.

Clara wished she was allowed to grieve Papa's memory, but she couldn't wear the customary black mourning clothes or show a sad face to the world because no one could know Papa was dead. She was supposed to act like everything was fine when the world felt like it was falling apart all around her.

Percy pulled on the reins to signal the mules to stop. Abram jumped down and tied the wagon to the hitching post in front of the general store, then ran up the steps as fast as his legs would carry him.

"Where are you going in such a hurry, Abram Summers?" Mrs. Stallings asked after Abram almost plowed into her as she tried to make her way into the store. "If you've got money burning a hole in your pocket, make sure you spend some of it on me. I haven't had a new hat in Lord knows when."

"Yes, ma'am. I'm sorry, ma'am." Abram slipped past her and darted into the store, Percy hot on his heels.

"They're certainly energetic, I'll give them that," Mrs. Stallings said. "Abram reminds me of Solomon when he was that age. Percy, too. I can see the Summers blood in both of them. But you, my dear, are the spitting image of your mama. God rest her soul."

Clara felt a twinge of renewed sadness at the reminder that she had lost both her parents in a matter of only a few years.

"Thank you, Mrs. Stallings. I'd better get inside before the boys stuff their pockets full of candy we can't afford."

"A little treat won't hurt them every now and then." Mrs. Stallings followed her inside. "Mr. Stallings and I haven't seen you in town for months."

"Has it been that long?" Clara counted backward in her head. She had bought ten pounds of flour and ten pounds of sugar last August but hadn't been back since. "Yes, I guess it has."

"I hear the Yanks are set up pretty close to your place. About five miles or so? They haven't been worrying you none, have they?"

"They've been worrying me plenty, but I haven't seen any of them wandering onto our land. Not yet anyway. That's kind of what brings me here today."

"In that case, don't be shy. Come on up here and tell Mr. Stallings what you want."

Mrs. Stallings grabbed her by the arm and pulled her to the front of the store. Mr. Stallings was standing behind the counter with his glasses perched on the end of his nose like a schoolmarm.

"What can I do for you today, Clara?" he asked.

"It's time for Abram to own his first rifle, and I brought him in so he could pick one out."

Mr. Stallings fished a key out of his pocket and unlocked the gun case behind the register.

"Do you have your eye on one in particular, Abram?"

Abram pointed to one of the rifles.

"That one there. The forty-caliber Graham. It looks just like Old Betsy, the rifle Davy Crockett used to kill a hundred twenty-five bears and become King of the Wild Frontier."

Mr. Stallings looked at Clara over the tops of his half-moon glasses.

"I assume you have money to pay for it."

Clara twisted her worn satchel, wishing it was filled with money instead of air.

"No, sir, I don't. I was hoping to buy the rifle and ammunition on credit. Along with ten pounds of flour, ten pounds of sugar, and maybe a trinket or two for Percy so he won't have to go home empty-handed."

Percy's eyes lit up. Then he ran to the toys piled on a display table and began sorting through them to see which one he wanted most.

His expression as sour as the lemons he favored in his tea, Mr. Stallings locked the gun case and slipped the key back into his pocket.

"Cash only, Clara. Your credit's no good here."

"But—"

Clara shushed Abram before he could begin to whine.

"Since when, Mr. Stallings? Papa's always been square with you, hasn't he?"

When Mr. Stallings spoke again, he had managed to whittle the edges off his sharp tone.

"It ain't your papa I'm worried about."

"Who, then?"

Mr. Stallings ran a feather duster over some of the items on display as if he would rather do anything else than meet Clara's eye.

"Mr. Stallings?" she said.

Mr. Stallings sighed and dropped his hands to his sides.

"Jedediah Ogletree came in here last week and said I wasn't to sell you nothing on credit. He didn't give me a chance to ask why."

Mrs. Stallings furrowed her brow, none too pleased at having been kept in the dark.

"Buck Stallings, you didn't mention a word of that conversation to me. If you had, I—"

Mr. Stallings's face reddened from anger, embarrassment, or both as he went back to whisking away dust that wasn't there.

"It ain't your place to know everything, Maudie. Jedediah came to me and asked if we could talk man-to-man."

"From the sound of it, you were a couple men short."

Percy stared disconsolately at the toy in his hand.

"What's Jedediah trying to do, starve us out because you won't marry him? You didn't cut him too bad. Unless you look real hard, you can barely—"

"Hush up about that, Percy," Clara said. "Isn't there anything you can do, Mr. Stallings? Until the spring crops come in during harvest time, the boys and I won't have two plug nickels to rub together."

Mr. Stallings eyed the other customers milling around the store as if he was afraid they might be more interested in his conversation than the items they were pretending to be browsing.

"I'm sorry, Clara, but cash only. That's the way it has to be."

Abram turned to look at her, his eyes filled with defeat.

"Jedediah's beaten us once and for all, hasn't he?"

It broke Clara's heart to see him like that.

"Not yet, Abram. Not yet."

She had to do something to take that pitiful look off his face. She decided to make the ultimate sacrifice so he could feel proud instead of beaten down. She reached inside the collar of her dress and revealed her most prized possession.

"This was my mama's ring, Mr. Stallings. Papa saved up a slap year to buy it for her. I don't know how much it's worth, but it's the most valuable thing I own." She untied the cord and placed the ring on the counter. "Is this enough to buy the things I asked for?"

Mr. Stallings eyed the ring.

"It's more than enough. It will pay for everything you want and erase your papa's debt to boot, but I can't take it."

"Pshaw." Mrs. Stallings snatched the ring off the counter and pressed it into her husband's hand. "You can take it and you will." She closed his fingers around the ring. "And when their crops come in this spring, you're going to sell it back to them. You know why? Because you're a better man than Jedediah Ogletree has frightened you into being. Now get a move on, Buck. Don't keep your customers waiting."

Mr. Stallings stashed the ring in the pocket of his vest, set the rifle on the counter, and began to gather the rest of the items Clara had requested.

"If the South sent its women to fight the war instead of its men," he grumbled under his breath, "the North wouldn't stand a chance."

CHAPTER NINE

Wilhelmina's regiment was camped at Pittsburg Landing on the west bank of the Tennessee River. The name reminded her of home. Of the life she had left behind. Of the life she might be about to lose. Scouts said a large group of Confederate soldiers—perhaps as many as forty thousand—were marching toward Shiloh, Tennessee, a town only twelve miles from where she was located and only five miles from where General Grant and his men had set up near Shiloh Church. Surely a confrontation was imminent.

She pondered what the future might hold for her. Or how long the future might last. As she watched the waters of the Tennessee River rush downstream, she allowed memories of the recent past to wash over her.

She remembered disguising herself as a man two months ago in order to hear Frederick Douglass speak. She remembered being so galvanized by what she heard that night that she had decided to wear the disguise full-time so she could take up arms. She remembered sneaking out of the house and traveling from Philadelphia to Pittsburgh in order to enlist. She remembered meeting the men of her regiment for the first time. She remembered being so afraid they would be able to see her for who she was instead of who she was pretending to be, then being pleasantly surprised when they had readily accepted her as one of their own. Except for Maynard. He had never accepted her and probably never would, but his issues with her, whatever they were, didn't seem to have anything to do with her sex. If they did, he would have turned her in long ago.

She laughed at her own ineptitude as she remembered trying and failing at drills, then trying again and again until she got the exercises right. She remembered marching for hours, sometimes days at a time. She remembered feeling like she couldn't possibly take another step, then finding the strength to take another and another and another until she finally reached her destination. She remembered learning to shoot, to fight, to be a man. And most of all, she remembered wanting to dissolve into girlish tears after she read Libby's long-awaited letter. The letter that could be her undoing. The letter that had broken her heart.

She pressed a hand to her chest to reassure herself that the letter was still in her possession. That it hadn't tumbled out during a game of horseshoes or a round of drills. She felt the scratch of wool, the firmness of folded paper, and beneath both, the softness of the muslin binding her breasts.

She couldn't understand Libby's change of heart. Libby had seemed so understanding when she had told her about her plan. Now Libby had withdrawn not only her support but her affection as well. Despite everything they had shared over the years, Libby had excluded her from the most important day of her life: her wedding day. Libby hadn't invited her to the ceremony because she had known Wilhelmina wouldn't be able to attend. She hadn't invited her because she didn't want her there. Because she was too afraid to see what she had become. Too afraid to see who she was.

I fear I would not see the face of the woman I know and love, Libby had written, *but the visage of a soldier I do not.*

Wilhelmina longed to show Libby that the woman and the soldier were one and the same, but what good would it do? Libby was Stephen's wife now. Her heart and soul belonged to him and would never be hers. The friendship they had long shared had come to a bitter and rather ironic conclusion. Ended not by a lie, but the truth.

Wilhelmina took off her forage cap and plunged her head in the river to hide the tears that were threatening to fall.

"If you're trying to drown your sorrows," Maynard said after she came up for air, "you'll need to try harder than that."

Wilhelmina shook the excess water from her hair and replaced her cap.

"What do you want?"

She didn't bother trying to hide her irritation. Maynard had given her and Erwin a wide berth since the incident on the train, but she had heard talk around the campfire that he blamed them for his demotion and was waiting for the right time to exact his revenge. If he was spoiling for a fight, she meant to give him one. Even though he outweighed her by a good thirty pounds, she would try her damnedest to get a few good licks in before he managed to get the upper hand.

She balled her hands into fists, hoping the bruises he was about to put on her body would take her mind off the ones that had already been inflicted on her heart.

Maynard backed up with his hands raised.

"Easy now. Save some of that spunk for the Rebs. Don't waste it on me."

Wilhelmina heard something in his voice—saw something in his face—that his bluster and harsh words had thus far been able to hide.

"That's why you were willing to shoot Solomon in the back," she said, thinking out loud. "Because you couldn't do it while you were looking him in the eye."

Maynard's eyes widened.

"What are you trying to say? Don't start quoting Shakespeare like Weekley does when he's trying to make a point. Speak it plain."

"You pick on those you think are weaker than you, but you shrink when someone challenges you. You're a coward. I can't say it any plainer than that."

"Watch your mouth, boy. I'm not the one crying over a woman when there are plenty of others in the world to choose from. I'm not the one who couldn't even scratch the enemy with his bayonet, let alone poke a hole in him. I'm not the one who's yellow, Fredericks. You are."

"Keep talking." Wilhelmina unclenched her fists. "When the fighting starts, we'll see who the real man is."

❖

Clara had always heard that April showers brought May flowers, but she feared the two days of heavy rain that had just mercifully come to an end might have washed away all the seeds she, Abram, Percy, and the Braggs had worked so hard to plant.

"Your fields look about as bad as ours," Enid said as she, Clara, and Mary walked the rows. "At least you've got a few seedlings, pitiful though they might be. On our place, we still don't have anything but dirt."

"Don't you mean mud, Mama?" Mary asked as she struggled to reclaim her shoe from the muck. The hem of her dress was as brown as the mud through which it trailed.

"It could be worse." Clara lifted her face to the sun, basking in its unseasonable warmth. "It could still be raining."

"That it could," Enid said. "One thing the rain did accomplish was to melt the last of the snow. Joseph and the kids love playing in the snow every winter—making snowmen and getting into snowball fights—but I've never cottoned to it. It's right pretty when it first starts to fall. There's something downright soothing about that smooth blanket of white, but it leaves a godawful mess behind once it's gone." She fingered the leaves of a collard that had survived the harsh winter only to nearly drown during the torrential rains. "But like every tribulation, this too shall pass."

"Where's Moses this fine Saturday morning?" Clara asked.

"Like you don't know. He and Nancy Franklin are drinking sweet tea on my front porch, each waiting for the other to say something more substantial than 'Good afternoon,' 'Good morning,' 'Good night,' or 'Fine weather we're having.' They're taking so long to get together, my first grandchild won't be the only one gumming its food."

"Moses was good company. I'm glad he's happy, but I miss having him around. We've talked more since he's been back than we have in our whole lives."

"Sitting with you helped him find his way back to himself. And that walking stick Percy made for him has turned him into a new man. I've got my son back, and I've got you and Percy to thank for it."

Clara had a hard time accepting the praise. She didn't feel like she had done anything special. She had seen a friend in need and had taken the time to listen to what he had to say. She had done what she wished someone would do for her. Moses had tried, but there were still so many things she had left unsaid. Things she couldn't say to anyone. Not even herself.

"Has Jedediah stopped sniffing around trying to keep company with you?" Enid asked.

"I haven't seen him since the Yankees showed up. It sounds strange, but maybe it's a good thing they're camped so close. Having them near has kept the bad apples away, that's for sure."

"But doesn't it give you a fright knowing you might run up on a horde of them while you're taking a trip to the privy in the middle of the night?"

"Not with the Summers boys on duty."

Clara looked over at Abram and Percy, who were patrolling the riverbank like a couple of sentries. Abram had his rifle resting on his shoulder. Percy used a fallen branch from a pine tree instead.

"Between them and Solomon, I feel pretty well-protected."

"I'm so sorry about your papa, honey," Enid said. "I don't know how I'm going to break the news to Joseph when he gets home. He and your papa were as close as two peas in a pod when they were growing up. But at least Lee is with your mama now."

Clara briefly allowed herself to feel the sorrow she was usually forced to hide. She couldn't afford to wallow in sadness for long, however. She had to stay strong. For her brothers' sakes as well as her own.

"Papa's war may be over, but ours is just beginning. Percy and Abram said they saw a Union gunboat sailing down the river yesterday. They came running in the house to fetch me and tried to point it out to me, but once I got to the water, all I saw was a speck in the distance that could have been anything. Sometimes, I think I hear whispering in the woods, followed by a flash of blue or gray, but I can't be sure. Sound carries on the river. The men I think I'm hearing could be five miles away or five feet. Everything's so mixed up these days, it's hard to tell."

"The time's drawing nigh for battle," Enid said with a weary sigh. "It's getting closer every day. I can feel it. Caleb Brewster at the post office has a cousin who lives in Corinth, Mississippi. That's just twenty miles southwest of here. Caleb's cousin said fifty-five thousand Rebs were camped out in Corinth until General Johnston gave them the order to move out. They left two days ago headed this way."

Clara heard the sound of rifle fire in the distance.

"Sweet Jesus," she said as the volleys continued one after the other, "they're already here."

CHAPTER TEN

Wilhelmina heard Billy beating the cadence for the call to arms and reflexively reached for her rifle. Then she opened her eyes and saw that the sun had barely risen above the tree line. She threw one of her boots in Billy's direction to get him to knock off the racket.

"Wake up. You're drumming in your sleep again."

She placed her cap over her face, closed her eyes, and tried to get another hour of sleep before reveille. When she heard the cries of, "The Rebs are here! They're attacking the camp," sleep became the least of her priorities.

She tossed her covers aside, fastened the top button on her uniform coat, and tried to locate her boots. One was easy to find. The one she had thrown at Billy was harder to track down.

"Steady, son. Steady." Erwin placed the stem of his unlit pipe between his teeth and clamped down hard to keep his nerve. "Remember your training and you'll be fine."

"Yes, sir."

Wilhelmina filled her pockets with as many cartridges as they could hold and looped the strap of her leather cartridge box over her shoulder. Then she followed Erwin out of the tent. The camp, once orderly and neatly arranged, was a mass of confusion. Men, some fully dressed and others wearing nothing but their underwear, ran willy-nilly.

"Stay in your divisions!" an officer on horseback yelled. "Form your lines!"

Wilhelmina searched out the members of her regiment as gunfire sounded all around her. Heeding the cadence to move forward, she gripped her rifle and moved toward the front line.

"It's Sunday morning," someone said. "Leave it to the Rebs to attack on the Sabbath."

Wilhelmina crouched low and performed one of the many drills she had practiced time and time again.

"What's going on?" she asked after she ran into one of the men from General William Sherman's forces.

"The Rebs had set up camp less than three miles from us and no one knew they were there until a few hours ago," the man said. "Colonel Peabody sent men from the Twenty-fifth Missouri and the Twelfth Michigan on a reconnaissance mission at three in the morning. They ran into Rebs in the woods and came under fire. They fought them off, but ran into the Third Mississippi Battalion a few hours later. Now the Rebs are everywhere. We might be in serious trouble if they knew what they were doing, but they're nowhere near as experienced as we are. Keep your head and you'll be—"

He didn't get a chance to finish his sentence. A blast from an artillery shell blew off half his face before he could. The dappled roan he had been riding screamed in fright, then reared and pawed the air with his front feet. The man's body slowly fell from the saddle, but one of his feet got tangled in the stirrups. The spooked horse ran off, dragging the man's body behind him.

Wilhelmina wiped a spray of something warm and wet from her cheek and continued to move forward as the regiment fragmented around her. Some men, Maynard included, ignored the catcalls of their peers, threw down their arms, and beat a hasty retreat. They headed west toward Owl Creek, obviously more willing to take on the creatures in the swamps than the Confederate forces bearing down on them.

"Save your ammunition," an officer on horseback commanded. "Don't fire until I give the order."

Wilhelmina looked up and saw that it was General Sherman leading the charge, his close-cropped hair wild as he waved a sword in the air.

"Fire," General Sherman said as his troops' right flank began to crumble. "Fire!"

Wilhelmina tucked Maynard's discarded pistol into her belt, raised her rifle, and aimed at anyone wearing a gray uniform. She pulled the trigger, and a man closing in on Erwin went down clutching his neck.

She reloaded her rifle and fired again, the taste of gunpowder from her cartridge packet caustic on her tongue. Another man fell. Then another. And another.

Return fire flew past her ear. She heard the thuds when the bullets slammed into the trunks of nearby trees. Still she continued to move forward because retreat offered only shame, a fate worse than the almost certain death that awaited her.

General Sherman's horse was shot out from under him and he called for another. As he waited for his fresh mount, Wilhelmina ran toward a slightly sunken road where several Union soldiers had taken up a defensive position. A small cotton field bordered the road. The green leaves on the scrawny young plants were splattered with blood.

"No, son."

Erwin grabbed her by her collar as Confederate soldiers began assaulting the Union troops lining the road.

"If you set up there, you're sure to be captured or killed. The bullets are flying so fast it sounds like a hornet's nest up there. Let's fall back behind the church and wait for the fight to come to us."

They retreated several miles to Shiloh Church, where General Grant and his men had established their base of operations. Recovering from a recent injury incurred after his horse fell on him, General Grant plotted strategy as he hobbled around on crutches.

As the hours slowly crept past, Wilhelmina watched the Confederate troops creep closer and closer. The Rebs' units were disorganized, and the inexperienced troops seemed to be at a loss as to what to do, but the ferocity of their attack was enough to overcome their strategic shortcomings.

By noon, the men entrenched along the sunken road were surrounded, Confederate troops had overrun several Union positions, and Wilhelmina grew certain she was about to die. She had used all the ammunition in her pockets, and her cartridge box was half-empty.

"I've got twenty cartridges and the six bullets in Maynard's gun," she said as she and Erwin lay on their bellies underneath the log meetinghouse known as Shiloh Church. "What about you?"

Erwin peered into his cartridge box and took a quick inventory of his remaining ammunition.

"I've got sixteen cartridges. If I run out, I'll be forced to fight hand-to-hand. I like my chances one-on-one, but I doubt the odds will be that generous today."

Wilhelmina felt the taste of something cold and metallic in her mouth. The coppery taste of blood. The silvery taste of fear.

"Where are General Buell's men?" she asked. "The Army of the Ohio left Nashville days ago. They should be here by now."

"It seems ironic doesn't it?"

Erwin shot at an approaching Confederate soldier's legs. The man fell to the ground and writhed in agony. Another soldier dragged him out of the line of fire, leaving a trail of bright red blood on the bent grass.

"What does?"

Erwin turned on his side so he could reload his rifle.

"Shiloh means 'place of peace' in Hebrew. It seems ironic you and I will meet a violent end in a place of peace."

Conserving her ammunition, Wilhelmina fired her rifle only when a target was within range. She didn't shoot to kill, only to incapacitate. She didn't want to take men's lives. She simply wanted to spare her own.

During the pauses between shots, she listened to the sounds of the pitched battles taking place all around her. The sounds of gunfire, officers yelling commands, drummers tapping cadences, horses neighing in fear, and men screaming in pain.

She wanted to cover her eyes, but she couldn't look away. She wanted to cover her ears, but she couldn't block out the noise. So she did the only thing she could do: she decided to be honest.

"I need to tell you something, Mr. Weekley. Something about me. My real name isn't William. It's actually—"

"Not now, son."

Erwin stretched his arms in front of him and ducked his head as he scrambled out from under the church. When he stood, his uniform was covered with dirt, and cobwebs dangled from the brim of his cap.

"The men defending the sunken road seem to be keeping most of the Rebs occupied, which gives us a chance to help shore up the line around Pittsburg Landing until reinforcements arrive. Follow me if you're so inclined."

Wilhelmina gathered her courage and crawled out from under the church. She and Erwin met up with a host of stragglers crowding the bluff over the landing, then boarded a ferry to cross the river and join the left side of the line. After they reached the shore, they positioned themselves along River Road.

"If Lew Wallace's men ever show up," one of Colonel David Stuart's men shouted over the roar of cannon fire, "they should come marching down that road. We have to keep it open so they'll have a chance to join the fight. If we don't, we're going to die out here. Sooner rather than later."

Backed by a ring of more than fifty cannons and naval guns from the *USS Tyler* and the *USS Lexington*, the two Union gunboats anchored in the river, Wilhelmina, Erwin, and the intermingled troops tried to repel the Confederate charge.

Two Rebel brigades tried to break through the line of blue but were turned back. As the sun began to set on twelve hours of fighting, Wilhelmina prepared for another wave of attacks. The sunken road, by most accounts, had already endured at least eight of them. To her relief, she heard a bugler in the Southern ranks blowing the call for retreat.

"Why did they stop?" she asked as she and Erwin slowly made their way back to what was left of their camp. Some Union campsites had been taken over by the Rebs. Theirs had not changed hands, but the number of men in it had been considerably reduced due to death, injury, or desertion. "They would have had us if they'd kept coming."

Erwin's legs seemed to give way as he sank wearily onto his bedroll.

"They're just as exhausted as we are, if not more. There's only so much fighting a man can do before the need for food, water, and rest takes precedence over victory."

He lay back and placed his arm over his eyes.

"Get some rest and find yourself something to eat, son. The Rebs will still be there in the morning. As they proved today, they damned sure know where to find us."

"The shooting probably scared away any game that might be in the area. There's a small farm a few miles from here. I saw it when we were running back and forth between here and Shiloh Church."

"What are you going to do, knock on the door and ask them if they'll let you borrow some things from their smokehouse? I doubt the folks around here are feeling too hospitable toward men dressed in blue these days."

"Do you have any other ideas?" Wilhelmina asked with a shrug. "If so, I'm open to suggestions."

"I wish I had some, but my mind is too clouded by gun smoke to think clearly. Do you want me to come with you? I think I could manage it if you need the company."

Despite his assertions to the contrary, he looked so tired Wilhelmina thought he would drop from exhaustion if he were asked to take another step.

"No, stay here and wait to see if Billy shows up. If he comes back and finds us both gone, he'll probably think we're dead."

"If he isn't dead himself."

Even though drummer boys weren't fighters themselves, they were often caught up in battle. They shadowed officers and used drumbeats to deliver the orders to the soldiers who couldn't hear the spoken commands over the noise of war. When they weren't needed to sound the calls, they performed the even more difficult job of stretcher bearer, walking around the battlefield looking for wounded men in need of medical care.

"I'll check the medical tent to see if Doc Gibson's seen him." Erwin pushed himself to his feet. "Be careful out there. And bring back something good. My mouth is watering for a nice piece of ham." He clapped Wilhelmina on the shoulder. "I'm proud of you, son. You did a fine job out there today. Far better than those who abandoned their posts."

Wilhelmina remembered the fear she had seen on Maynard's face as he'd run from the approaching Confederates. She wondered if he had managed to escape to the woods he had been so desperate to reach or if he had been captured by the Rebels and taken prisoner. Either way, she doubted she would ever see him again. In this life or the next.

She grabbed her rifle and ducked out of the tent.

"Son?"

Erwin's voice prompted her to turn back.

"Yes, sir?"

"What were you trying to tell me earlier? When we were taking cover under the church, you said something about your name, but I can't recall now what it was. What did you want me to know?"

Wilhelmina wanted to tell him the truth about herself, but she didn't want to risk losing the two things she had tried so hard to earn: his trust and his respect.

"Nothing, sir. It seemed important at the time, but it doesn't matter now."

"Okay, then. Don't forget about that ham. My stomach and I are depending on you."

"You can count on me, sir. I won't let you down."

❖

"Is it over?" Percy asked tremulously after the sounds of gunfire slowed, then stopped altogether.

Earlier, the fierce fighting had been so close Clara had heard bullets hit the house. The shot that had punched a hole in her bedroom window had sent her scrambling for cover. She had turned a table on its side and held Abram and Percy close as they took shelter behind it.

She strained to hear. Though the rifles had fallen silent, the ground shook as the Union gunboats continued shelling Confederate positions.

"Yes, it's over." Clara turned the table upright and lit a candle to banish the darkness that had fallen during the battle. "For today, at least."

"I'm hungry," Abram said.

Clara's stomach growled at the reminder they hadn't eaten since breakfast. The shooting had started around six and hadn't let up until now.

"Bring some sausages from the smokehouse. I'll make biscuits and gravy for supper."

Abram lit a lantern and held it in front of him as he headed for the front door.

"Make it quick," Clara said before he removed the wooden barricade holding the door shut. "There might be Yankees roaming around out there somewhere. Take your rifle just in case."

Abram tucked his rifle under his arm and darted out the door. Clara tossed wood into the stove and sprinkled kerosene on the logs so they would burn faster.

"What's taking Abram so long?" Percy asked as he played with the cup-and-ball toy Clara had used Mama's ring to purchase for him from the general store. "He should be back by now, shouldn't he?"

Clara looked at the clock. Ten minutes had passed since Abram had left to fetch the sausages. Even if he had stopped to relieve his bladder first, he'd had plenty of time to complete his task.

"He's probably out there pretending to be Davy Crockett."

"I'll fetch him."

"No, you stay." Clara wiped her hands on a dish towel after she placed the biscuits in a cast iron skillet. "I don't want both of you running around in the dark."

She lit another candle and used her hand to protect the flickering flame from the wind as she headed down the steps. The smokehouse was located on the far side of the barn, situated so the fumes from the burning hickory and cherry wood Papa used to cure the meat wouldn't blow into the house.

Clara peered into the growing darkness. Light from Abram's lantern spilled from under the smokehouse door.

"I thought you were hungry, slowpoke," she said. "What's the matter? Can't find what you're looking for?"

She blew out her candle and pulled the door open.

"Stay back, Clara." Abram stood with his rifle trained on a Union soldier holding an armful of meat. "I caught this Yankee trying to steal from us."

Clara didn't know whether to move forward or retreat to the safety of the house.

"Careful, Abram. He might be dangerous."

"I don't mean any harm, ma'am," the soldier said. "I was hungry and looking for something to eat."

"So you saw our smokehouse and decided to help yourself?" Abram asked.

"I'm not looking to hurt anyone. See? I'm not even armed."

For Clara, the man's reassuring words offered cold comfort. Though he didn't appear to be carrying a weapon, she couldn't tell if his intentions were pure. Something about him—something in his eyes—didn't sit right with her.

"I don't trust him, Abram."

"I'm sorry you feel that way, ma'am," the man said. "What are you going to do? Order the boy to shoot me? He can barely hold that rifle, let alone fire it. Be sensible, boy. Give me that rifle before you hurt yourself."

The soldier reached for the rifle, but hesitated when Abram put his finger on the trigger.

"Stay back or I will shoot you," Abram said.

"If you were going to shoot me, you would have done it already." The soldier's expression changed from innocent to something almost sinister. "You should have let me go when you had the chance."

"What are you going to do?" Abram asked. "I'm the one with the gun."

"Not anymore."

Moving quicker than Clara would have given him credit for, the man dropped the meat and backhanded the rifle away from Abram. The rifle discharged with a roar that sounded even louder in the small, confined space. The bullet tore a hole in the back of the smokehouse, and the rifle clattered to the ground.

"He's reaching for the rifle." Clara pushed Abram forward. "Get it before he does."

Abram reached for the rifle, but the soldier snatched it up before Abram's fingers could close around it.

The soldier picked up the dropped meat, slapped Abram across the face, and brandished the rifle like a baseball bat.

"Back up, boy, or I'll split your head wide open."

His voice shook as if he were the one in peril instead of the one making the threat.

Clara moved Abram behind her. A trickle of blood ran from his split lip.

"You've got what you want, mister," Clara said. Abram clutched her dress as they slowly backed out of the smokehouse. "Now go about your business and leave us alone."

The soldier gnawed on a piece of ham. He looked more like a wild animal than a man. A cornered animal, which made him even more dangerous.

"Who's in the house?" he asked, pieces of meat and gristle clinging to the stubble on his chin. "Are you alone out here, or is it just the two of you?"

Clara thought of Percy—alone, defenseless, and waiting for them to return.

"No one. There's no one else."

"Where's your man? Is he out trying to round up dinner, or is he off hunting Yankees?"

"If my brother were here, he'd put a bullet in you, for sure," Abram said.

"But your brother isn't here, is he?" the soldier asked.

He looked around and nodded appreciatively.

"This seems like a good place to hole up for the night. When both sides start trying to kill each other again, I can make my way north, where life is a lot more civilized than it is down here."

He turned the rifle around and jerked the barrel toward the house.

"Get in there and cook me some dinner. Tonight, we're going to be one big, happy family."

Clara turned and walked toward the house. The soldier made her nervous. She feared for what he might do to her or the boys. The rifle was empty now, but there was plenty of ammunition in the house. If he got his hands on it, neither she, Abram, nor Percy might survive the night.

"Please, mister," she said, "just take the meat and go."

"Not until you give me a meal, a change of clothes, and some bullets for this gun. A little Southern hospitality would be good, too. Now stop jawing and keep moving."

"I'm sorry I couldn't pull the trigger," Abram said, wiping the blood from his face. "Moses was right. It's a lot different killing an animal than it is killing a man."

"Hold your head up," Clara said. "You accounted well for yourself. No matter what happens, there's no shame in your actions tonight."

"But what if he—"

Abram broke off mid-sentence. Clara whirled around when she heard heavy footsteps coming up fast behind him. The soldier turned around, too, but not fast enough.

"There's another one!"

Abram pointed at the second Union soldier.

This soldier was smaller than the first. Younger, too. Lit by the pale light of the lantern, his cheeks looked as smooth as a baby's. He couldn't have been more than fifteen or sixteen, but his eyes made him seem much older.

"Wait, Wil," the first soldier said as the younger one raised his rifle. "There's more than enough here for both of us."

The younger soldier—the one the other one had called Wil— didn't say anything. He just took the butt of his rifle and slammed it into the older man's jaw. The first soldier dropped to his knees, then slowly fell forward.

"Are you all right, ma'am?" Wil asked.

His voice was deep. Unexpectedly so for someone his size. He was tall for his age, but slight of build.

"Did he hurt you or the boy?"

"He knocked my brother around some," Clara said, "but he didn't leave any permanent damage, if that's what you're asking."

Wil glanced at the angry red mark on Abram's cheek and the fresh wound on his lip, then bent and pulled the rifle from underneath the first soldier's unconscious body.

"Is this yours?"

"Y-Yes, sir," Abram stammered.

"Here. You might need it."

Wil held out the rifle. Abram hesitated before taking it and holding it tight to his chest.

"Why are you doing this for us, mister?" he asked, echoing Clara's thoughts. "Why are you siding with us instead of one of your own?"

"When it comes to doing what's right, there's only one side to choose."

Clara admired Wil's gentle nature. Despite his tender years, he was quite handsome. He had rich brown eyes, a strong jaw, and full lips that looked ripe for kissing.

"What are you going to do with him?" she asked as the first soldier moaned and began to stir.

"He deserted during the battle this morning. I'm going to take him back to camp and deliver him to the officers in charge. They'll decide his fate."

"My brother says they shoot deserters," Abram said. "Is that true?"

"Yes, it is. Which means he probably won't be needing this."

Wil reached into his belt and pulled out a pearl-handled pistol.

"Take it," he said, handing the pistol to Clara. "With so many soldiers around, you'll need all the protection you can get."

Clara took the gun, unsure how to hold it or if she even wanted to.

"Do you know how to shoot it?" Wil asked.

"No."

"Don't fret none, mister," Abram said. "I'll show her how."

"You're a good brother," Wil said. "How old are you?"

"Thirteen, going on fourteen. How old are you?"

"Nineteen, going on twenty."

Abram looked from Wil to Clara and back again. "That means the two of you are the same age."

"Is that right?" Wil asked.

Clara's stomach turned a funny little flip when Wil looked at her. Was that the feeling her mama had said she was supposed to have the first time she looked into the eyes of the man she loved? She had never felt that feeling before. She wanted to feel it again.

She didn't have to wait long. When Wil asked, "You're not married, are you, ma'am?" she felt like an army of butterflies was marching around her insides.

Abram answered for her.

"No, she ain't married. She's had men chasing after her for years, but she ain't never showed no interest in none of them. Mrs. Bragg says she's determined to become an old maid."

Clara dug her elbow into Abram's ribs. Abram yelped with pain, but at least he stopped telling such embarrassing tales about her.

"Thank you, Wil. For everything."

"You're welcome."

Wil looked at the meat the first soldier had dropped on the ground, and his stomach growled so loud Clara could hear it from five feet away.

"Are you hungry?"

Wil's blush was his only reply.

"Take it. It's yours."

Wil reached into the pocket of his uniform pants and pulled out a wad of bills.

"Let me pay you. I don't have much, but—"

Clara touched his wrist, which was surprisingly delicate for a man's. His skin was smooth beneath her fingers and warm to her touch. Clara didn't want to let go.

"Keep your money. The stores in town only take Confederate bills, not U.S. ones. And after what you did, you don't owe us a thing. We're the ones who owe you."

Wil tipped his cap. His short brown hair was lush and full. More like a woman's than a man's.

"Thank you, ma'am."

The first soldier pushed himself to his knees and rubbed his jaw as if it ached.

"I have to get him back to camp," Wil said, snapping to attention, "but may I ask you a question before I go?"

"Of course."

Wil flashed a shy grin.

"What's your name?"

CHAPTER ELEVEN

Y ou've been grinning from ear-to-ear since you returned from that farm you found," Erwin said, picking his teeth with a matchstick.

He, Billy, and Wilhelmina had eaten like kings after she returned to camp. The food the cooks served up in the mess tent was enough to keep the men on their feet, but the small portions weren't enough to keep them satisfied. Especially when the supply trains were slow to arrive or only half-filled when they finally did show up. Groups of men often slipped out of camp at night in search of whiskey, cigarettes, fresh meat, or a little female companionship. Tonight, Wilhelmina had followed their example. Now very little of the bounty she had received from Clara and her brother remained. Just a few links of sausage and a couple of slices of ham she planned to fry up for breakfast before tomorrow's scheduled assault began.

"What did you find in that smokehouse besides a deserter and the best ham I've ever tasted?"

"Nothing, sir."

"Come on, son. It's just the three of us talking. You can be straight with us. You met a girl, didn't you?"

Billy rolled his eyes and quietly tapped out a cadence on his drum.

"Girls. Who needs them?"

"You'll change your tune in a year or two." Erwin rubbed his full belly as he leaned toward Wilhelmina. "I told you another young lady would come along, didn't I? Now go on, son. Tell me about your lady friend."

"When I got to the farm, I heard a commotion in the yard and saw Maynard holding a woman and a boy I thought was her son at gunpoint. The boy turned out to be her brother. One of them, anyway. The other one was hiding out in the house."

"What's the woman's name?"

"Clara."

The name was like honey in Wilhelmina's mouth. Warm, soft, and oh-so-sweet.

"Is she pretty?"

Wilhelmina smiled just thinking about Clara's warm, friendly face.

"She's the prettiest girl I've ever seen. She's got red hair, green eyes, and skin as fair as cream."

"She does sound comely. Are you going to see her again?"

Wilhelmina wanted nothing more, but she didn't know what, if anything, could come of it. Would Clara break her heart like Libby had, or would she even let her get close enough to try?

"I don't see how I can. I took an awful big chance tonight going out there on my own. I don't dare take the risk again unless I'm part of one of the patrols."

"Don't you think she's worth the risk?"

Wilhelmina remembered the smile that had stolen across Clara's face when she'd asked Clara her name. A smile that had made it seem like the answer was a secret to be held between only the two of them. For a moment, she had forgotten about the war. She had forgotten about everything. Everything except Clara.

"Yes, sir, I think she is, but I don't want any of the men in our regiment to mistake me for a deserter if they catch me sneaking out of camp on my own."

Outside, a firing squad was being assembled to execute Maynard and the other deserters that had been rounded up and forcibly returned to camp. Wilhelmina had helped dig the graves. The men's bodies would be buried on a separate plot of land from the men who had fallen in battle today so their presence wouldn't tarnish the other soldiers' memories.

Executions were normally performed at dawn, but the officers in charge had decided to adjust the timetable this time to boost the morale of the men who had performed their duties, and to serve as a deterrent for the ones who might be thinking of running when the next round of fighting began.

"No chance of that," Erwin said. "Not after the valiant way you performed today. When I heard the drummers beating the call to action, I nearly soiled myself. With so many of them drumming in unison, the sound was like a thunderbolt from on high. Most of the sounds that followed were like something that had escaped the gates of hell. I can still hear all those men pleading for water, for help, or their mothers. No wonder so many of the able-bodied ones decided to run."

"Why didn't you?"

"I want to be able to look my children in the eye when I see them again." He fished the tintype of his family from his haversack and kissed the images of his wife and daughters. "Why did you stay?" he asked, replacing the picture.

Wilhelmina wished her answer could be as high-minded as Erwin's. She settled for honesty instead of nobility.

"I stayed because I didn't have anything to run to."

"Ready," a hoarse voice called out in the distance. "Aim. Fire."

Wilhelmina flinched as the firing squad performed its duty. She heard the muffled thuds as the deserters' bodies hit the ground.

"I heard some of the men say they think General Grant was drunk during the battle, and that's why he performed so poorly," she said. "Do you think there's any truth to the matter?"

"I think men will say anything after they've lost a fight they expected to win," Erwin said solemnly. "We were unprepared, undermanned, and outfought. Plain and simple. How much whiskey General Grant did or didn't have last night didn't alter today's outcome."

He turned onto his side with a grunt of effort.

"Now let's get some sleep. Tomorrow's bound to be another long day, though I can't say I would blame you if I woke up and discovered you had decided not to face it with me."

Though Wilhelmina was still committed to the cause and was willing to do whatever she could to guarantee a Union victory, she wasn't eager to pick up her rifle again after today's crushing defeat.

The Rebs had clearly won today's battle. Their victory would have been even more decisive if they had pressed their advantage, but they had chosen to retreat, giving the Union troops time to reorganize and regroup. She hoped General Grant and his men were busy crafting a winning strategy to see them through tomorrow's conflict rather than drowning their sorrows.

She lay on her bedroll and listened to a thunderstorm rumble overhead. Rain pounded down, driving the men in camp inside their tents. Lightning lit up the sky, ensuring they would remain there for the duration.

Wilhelmina had never experienced such a miserable night, but she suspected there would be many more to come.

❖

"You like that Yankee, don't you?" Abram asked as he cleaned his rifle. "That Wil fella."

Clara didn't turn around as she washed the dishes from breakfast. If she did, she knew Abram would see the true answer on her face rather than the one she sought to provide with her words. "He saved both our hides. That's reason enough to like him, isn't it?"

"That's not reason enough to make eyes at him, though, is it?"

"I did no such thing."

"Oh, Wil, you're so big and strong," Abram said in a falsetto voice that made Percy double over with laughter. "Take all the meat you want. Let my brothers go hungry. I'm sure they won't mind."

Clara threw her dish towel at Abram after she turned to face him.

"Is that what you think? That I was favoring him over you?"

"No." Abram put down his cleaning cloth. "I don't know what would have happened to us if Wil hadn't shown up when he did last night, but what would Jedediah say if he knew we willingly gave some of our food to a Yankee? What would Solomon say, for that matter? You know he hates all of them for what they did to him and Papa."

"Jedediah's opinion doesn't matter to me one way or the other. He's not part of this family and never will be. As for Solomon..."

Clara paused to listen to the sounds of battle. The fighting had begun around half past five, but the gunshots seemed to be coming from farther away than the day before, meaning that the tide had apparently been reversed. Whoever had ended the day with the upper hand was now struggling to retain it. Did that mean good news or bad?

"Solomon wants to see us safe. Last night, Wil kept us that way. How could Solomon find fault with that?"

"Because the Yankees are the reason Papa's dead," Percy said.

"Did the Yankees give Papa pneumonia? Did the Yankees cause his lungs to fail?"

"No," Abram said, taking up the cause. "But they captured him and Solomon and tried to send both of them to prison. Solomon won't rest until the three men responsible are dead. They're our enemies, Clara. That means we're supposed to hate them, doesn't it?"

Clara dried her hands and sat across from Abram and Percy. "Last night, when he prevented that man from doing God knows what to us, did Wil feel like your enemy?"

"No," Abram said as if the admission came at a cost, "he felt like my friend."

To Clara, Wil had seemed like he could be much more. She told herself she shouldn't allow herself to be attracted to someone who wasn't much older than a boy, but she couldn't stop thinking about him. The chivalrous way he had acted. The shy way he had looked at her. The curious way he had said her name after she had told him what it was.

"Clara," he had said as if he had never heard anything more beautiful. "Pleased to meet you. I'm Wil."

"I know. I heard that man call out your name right before you socked him in the jaw."

"Of course."

Wil had shifted his weight from foot to foot as if he wanted to ask if he could call on her sometime. Clara had found herself receptive to the idea. She had imagined Wil presenting her with a bouquet of flowers, offering his arm as they walked along the river, kissing her as they stood under the moonlight.

She had never felt that way about any other man. How could she feel that way about one she had just met?

"I don't understand." Percy rested his chin on his hands. "How can we be at war with someone who was so good to us?"

"I don't know, Percy. I don't understand it either."

She felt like she was at war, too. Except the battle she was waging was with herself. How long was she supposed to put her family's needs ahead of her own desires? And how could she want to be with someone so badly when she didn't even know his last name?

"I hope your Yankee doesn't come back," Abram said.

"Why not?"

"Between Jedediah sniffing around and Solomon wanting to kill every Yankee he sees, I fear something bad will happen to Wil if he does show up here again."

Clara shared Abram's fear, but the thought that the first time she had laid eyes on Wil was also the last time wasn't one she was sure she was willing to accept.

"Hello, the house," a familiar voice called from outside.

"It's Jed," Abram said.

The door rattled as Jedediah tried to open it but couldn't get in. "Clara, are you in there?"

"Where else would we be?" Clara asked without opening the door. "There's a war going on outside in case you didn't know."

"That's why I'm here. Let me in."

"You're not welcome here, Jedediah. Mr. Stallings told me what you said about not giving us credit at the store."

"That was a misunderstanding. I was only looking out for our business owners' best interests. I didn't want the women in town running up a bunch of debts their men might not be able to pay when they return."

Clara's temper flared, and she snatched the door open so she could look Jedediah in the eye when she told him exactly how she felt about him.

"So what did you expect us to do, come to you for help? I would rather die first."

A corner of Jedediah's mouth twitched into a semblance of a smile.

"No need for anything quite so drastic. I would miss you too much." He looked past her and regarded the full cache of supplies in the kitchen. "Besides, you seem to have managed just fine on your own. I always knew you were a clever one."

"Is that what brings you by today? You came to sing my praises? If so, I would appreciate it if you would change your tune."

Jedediah began walking through the house.

"Lots of people around these parts have reported having trouble last night," he said, peeking into cupboards and under beds. "Several of them found a couple of Yankees and a few Rebs raiding their smokehouses and chicken coops. Enid Bragg even spotted one trying to chase down a pig in the middle of her hog pen. Men from both sides are deserting left and right. My boys and I are going house to house to make sure no one's harboring any deserters, whether intentionally or against their will."

Clara gritted her teeth as he riffled through her things.

"I doubt you'll find any Yankees hiding out in my underwear drawer."

"You can't be too careful. Especially considering the size of that hole."

He pointed to the bullet hole in her bedroom window. The glass hadn't shattered, but spidery cracks were spreading through the pane.

"You'd better get that fixed pretty soon. Before you know it, all manner of varmints will come crawling in trying to get at you."

Clara saw the threat in his eyes long before she heard it in his voice. This time, he didn't even try to use one of his insincere smiles to cover it up. When his searching hands brushed against something solid, she knew he had found the pistol Wil had given her for protection.

"What's this?"

"Don't you recognize a pistol when you see one?" Abram asked.

Abram's question—and Percy's accompanying laughter—prompted a glare from Jedediah.

"Where did you get it? Mr. Stallings doesn't sell pistols this fancy down at the general store."

"We didn't buy it from Mr. Stallings," Abram said angrily. "We got it from—"

Clara stepped in before Abram could reveal the secret of Wil's visit.

"We took it off a dead Yankee. There are plenty of them lying just up the road. The burial detail wasn't able to move all the bodies before the fighting started up again."

Abram and Percy had ventured out early that morning to see the grisly sight. They had reported that most of the bodies had been picked over, robbed of boots, jewelry, and other "souvenirs" soldiers and citizens alike had felt compelled to claim. She had told the boys not to sink to the same depths, but Jedediah didn't need to know that.

"Finders keepers. Isn't that how the saying goes?" Clara asked.

Jedediah's fingers were slack from shock, making it easy for her to reclaim her property. She didn't intend to let it out of her sight again.

Jedediah poked his head in the boys' bedroom but didn't go inside. In fact, he seemed anxious to leave. Had she finally managed to convince him that her family didn't need his for anything?

"Don't you want to check the outbuildings to see if we're hiding Yankee soldiers in the barn or corn crib?" she asked as he headed for the door. "What about the smokehouse? Have you looked in it?"

He glanced at the gun in her hand.

"Any man would be crazy to try to steal from you."

She tapped the barrel of the pistol against her leg.

"Make sure you pass the message along to your father."

"If you're of a mind, you can tell him yourself."

"What do you mean?"

Jedediah held his hat in his hands.

"We could use your help," he said with uncharacteristic humility. "One of the Confederate generals dropped by our farm a few days ago and decided our place would make a good field hospital. He didn't give us any say-so in the matter. Now we've got wounded and dying soldiers everywhere, not enough people to tend to them, and no idea when any of them will be well enough to leave. Would you and the Braggs mind lending a hand? Most of the men don't want the slaves touching them, and the women in town are too delicate to do what needs to be done. We need someone like you."

"To do what? Enid, Mary, and I might end up doing more harm than good. We ain't nurses, Jedediah."

"And most of the surgeons wielding scalpels ain't real doctors. That's not stopping them from fulfilling their duty to their country, is it? What's stopping you? You don't need to be educated to hold a dying man's hand or fetch water for the living."

Abram tugged at Clara's arm.

"We've got to do it. For Solomon and for Papa. They would want us to help, wouldn't they?"

"Yes, Abram, I suspect they would."

Papa had given the war his all before he died and Solomon was still fighting it in his own way. Now it was time for Clara, Abram, and Percy to do their parts, too.

"Hitch the wagon, boys. Let's take a ride."

CHAPTER TWELVE

On Sunday, the Confederate troops had dished out a surprise attack. The next day, aided by the arrivals of General Buell's and Major General Lew Wallace's men, Union forces responded by returning the favor.

Wallace's men brought the fight first, meeting little resistance as they crossed Tilghman Branch and continued to move forward. The Confederates were driven back, their units falling into disarray.

Wilhelmina listened to the updates filter into camp as she fried the last of the meat.

"Good morning," she said after Erwin poked his head out of their tent.

"Talk about a pleasant surprise," he said. "When I woke and saw your bedroll was empty, I didn't think I would find you in camp."

"Just making a little breakfast." She handed one plate of food to Billy and another to Erwin. "It's bound to be a long day, remember?"

"Yes, son, I remember." Erwin rested his hand on her shoulder. "And I'm glad you're still with us."

Wilhelmina was undecided on the matter, but she had a duty to perform. Duty came before everything else.

The sunken road next to a cotton field had been claimed by the Rebs during yesterday's battle, resulting in the capture of thousands of men and the deaths of many thousands more. Its road cover and open fields of fire made the position a valuable commodity. Both sides wanted to claim it. The Rebs had it and the Yanks wanted it back.

"No drum today, Billy?" she asked as they prepared to part ways.

"Doc Gibson asked me to be a stretcher bearer instead. When yesterday's fighting ended, there were so many wounded men lying on the battlefield, we couldn't get to them all. Some might have been saved if we'd gotten to them fast enough. Today, the doc wants men picked up and brought to him as soon as they fall. Good luck today, sirs."

"The same to you," Erwin said, "though you might need more of it than we will. At least Wil and I will have rifles in our hands. The only thing you're going to be carrying is a wounded man."

"Don't worry about me, sir. I'm too fast for the Rebels to catch me."

Billy grabbed his hat and ran toward the medical tent, his short legs churning as if he were running across a playground rather than toward a battlefield.

Wilhelmina quickly downed the rest of her coffee and reached for her rifle when the order came to move out. Her regiment ran into a group of Confederate skirmishers almost as soon as they left camp.

Straining to see through the haze of gun smoke, she fought her way toward the sunken road. Each time she thought her unit had gained the upper hand, the Confederate troops under Brigadier General John Breckinridge's command pushed them back.

"We've got to keep fighting," Erwin yelled from his position behind a fence post pockmarked with bullet holes. "Wallace and Sherman have Bragg and Polk on the run. If we can take this position and the Corinth Road, victory will be ours."

Wilhelmina poked her head up long enough to fire a shot and take a quick look at the opposition.

"They're getting desperate," she said as she ripped into a cartridge packet with her teeth. "I think we've got them outnumbered. Part of their line looks ready to fall."

"Then let's finish knocking it down."

Wilhelmina fired and reloaded. Fired and reloaded. Fired and reloaded. She increased her pace with each shot as she and the men around her slowly pushed the Rebs defending the sunken road to the brink of submission. She cheered when Brigadier General Breckinridge's men began to retreat, but she knew the overall battle still had not been won.

Breckinridge's men headed south toward Shiloh Church. A portion of Wilhelmina's unit, Erwin included, stayed behind to hold the sunken road. Wilhelmina fell in with the men pursuing the retreating Rebs.

She ran with her rifle held high. The attached bayonet sliced leaves and small branches from the trees, leaving a trail of debris behind her.

"Careful, Private," someone said. "You're going to poke someone's eye out with that thing."

"Just make sure you don't poke me in the ass while you're at it," the man in front of her said.

Wilhelmina enjoyed the men's sense of camaraderie and their ability to make jokes even during a time of strife. She felt a sense of loss when the man she was trailing had his left leg blown off by cannon fire and the one running behind her lost part of an arm.

She called out for stretcher-bearers, but the fighting was too intense and the woods too thick for them to get through to the wounded men. The soldiers' only hope of survival rested in her hands.

Abandoning her pursuit of the Confederate troops, she dropped to her knees, tossed her rifle aside, and tried to help her wounded comrades.

The ground was covered with gore and both men were screaming in agony. Wilhelmina's fingers grew slick with blood as she fashioned tourniquets out of the first man's pants leg and the second man's sleeve.

The second man clutched at her with his remaining hand.

"Help me," he pleaded.

"I've done everything I know to do. Now you've got to help yourself. I'll take you to the medical tent. Can you walk?"

"I think so." He groaned as he pushed himself to his feet, but he managed to stay upright somehow. "What are you going to do about him?"

She had intended to provide support while the second man used his rifle as a crutch, but he had passed out from loss of blood or the pain of his wound.

"Carry him, I guess."

Getting him into a sitting position was easy. Getting him onto her shoulders and off the ground was a great deal more difficult.

"You're stronger than you look, Private. I didn't think you had it in you."

"Neither did I," Wilhelmina said as she staggered under the first man's weight. "Neither did I."

They laboriously made their way through the woods and back to camp.

"You look like hell, Wil," Dr. Gibson said after they finally made it to the hospital tent.

"Speak for yourself."

Dr. Gibson was operating on a man who had been bayoneted in the stomach. The white apron covering his clothes was matted with blood and gore. A growing pile of amputated limbs, some still sporting their former owners' wedding bands, sat in a corner.

"Where do you want them?" Wilhelmina asked, indicating the men with her.

Dr. Gibson absently waved one of the surgical instruments he was holding.

"Wherever you can find room."

Wounded men lay on every available surface. Some had already been treated. Others were still waiting to be seen. The man who had lost an arm sat on the ground. Wilhelmina deposited the one who had lost a leg next to him.

"Doc Gibson will take care of you from here. I'm going back for my rifle. I can't fight without it."

"There are plenty of others lying around," Dr. Gibson said. "Most of these men won't be using them again. Take your pick."

"No offense, but I would rather have mine, sir. It's my good luck charm. It's helped me get through this war without getting so much as a scratch on me."

Dr. Gibson shook his head.

"Soldiers and their superstitions. I'll never understand either one."

"What's your name, Private?" the armless man asked.

"Wil Fredericks."

"You're a good man, Wil Fredericks." He stuck out his remaining hand. His grip was firm despite the trauma his body had endured. "Thanks for your help. When you get back out there, give those Rebs hell, you hear?"

"I'll do my best."

Clara looked up at the arched sign hanging over the entrance to Thomas Ogletree's farm. Treetop Farms, the sign read, the black letters carefully burned into the faded wood.

The spread was enormous. Acres and acres lined the winding road that led to the house. The fields were laden with plants. Some seedlings, others more fully grown. The dozen or so slaves Thomas owned tended to the fledgling crops under the watchful eye of Raymond Stuart, their overseer. Clara didn't know Raymond well, but she had heard tell he was one of the meanest men in Hardin County. Second only to the man who paid his salary.

Clara flinched when Raymond cracked his long black bullwhip in the air to coerce the slaves into working faster.

"There's no call for that," Abram said.

He, Moses, and Mary rode in the back of the wagon. Percy, Clara, and Enid were jammed up front.

"Sometimes I wish I could give men like that a taste of their own medicine," Enid said. "See how they like being on the receiving end for a change."

"Careful, Percy," Clara said, drawing his attention back to the road.

Percy steered the wagon around a small band of soldiers slowly and painfully making their way to the large two-story house at the top of the hill. Though the soldiers could walk on their own, each was wounded in some way. One in the neck, another in the stomach, and yet another in the leg.

Clara looked toward the house. How many more injured men were waiting inside?

"Stop the wagon."

After Percy did as Clara asked, Abram and Mary helped the injured men climb into the back of the wagon.

"Much obliged," one of the soldiers said as Percy drove them the rest of the way.

Clara turned to look at them. They weren't much older than boys. Boys Wil's age. Had Wil come across them in battle? Was he, by chance, the reason they were in such sorry shape?

She didn't want to think of Wil in that way. She knew he was a soldier and it was his job to kill any enemy combatant he came across, but she didn't like imagining him with a gun in his hands. She supposed she should be grateful Wil had a gun and knew how to use it, however. If he didn't, she, Percy, and Abram might not be alive right now.

She, Abram, and Mary helped the men down after Percy tied the wagon to a hitching post mounted near the front of the house.

"Where do you want them?" Enid asked the weary-looking surgeon smoking a cigarette as he sat on the porch steps.

"Anywhere you can find room."

Clara helped the man with the stomach wound climb the stairs. Injured men lined the porch, foyer, and front room. Some had already been tended to. Others were waiting to be seen.

The formal dining room that had hosted its fair share of dinner parties over the years now served as an operating theater. A surgeon held a bloody saw in one hand and a man's arm in the other. He tossed the amputated limb out the window, used a long needle to close the wound, and called for his next patient.

The injured soldier on the operating table was carried away, and another was deposited in his place. The soldier's foot was black and swollen. The discoloration had spread halfway up his calf. Clara watched as the surgeon took a few tentative pokes at the man's leg.

"Gangrene," he said with a shake of his head. "That leg's got to come off."

He placed the saw just below the soldier's knee. Clara turned away before the serrated blade bit into the skin.

"I don't want to be a soldier no more," Percy said, clapping his hands over his ears to block out the sounds of the wounded man's screams.

"Me, neither," Abram said.

"That's the best news I've heard all day," Clara said.

"Who's in charge?" Enid asked no one in particular. "Where's the lady of the house?"

"She left as soon as we started showing up yesterday," a soldier with his arm in a sling said. "She said she didn't want to see her house covered in blood like the Plagues of Egypt. She's been camped out at her sister's house ever since. Mr. Ogletree and his son went riding off after her a little while ago, but they didn't seem real confident they would be able to talk her into coming back."

"When Jedediah said he was running short on women," Enid said under her breath, "did he mention his mama was one of them?"

If Mrs. Ogletree decided not to return from Corinth, Jedediah would be even more desperate to find a wife. He and his father could run the farm, but who would take care of the household?

"Who knows?" Enid said. "I might be visiting you here one day."

Clara looked around at the expensive objects lining the shelves and walls. The spacious house was magnificent, but, unlike her humble abode, it didn't feel like a home.

"I wouldn't go counting my chickens before they were hatched if I was you," the wounded soldier said. "If our boys don't finish what we started yesterday, the Federals will claim this house and take every man in it as their prisoner."

"They can do that?" Clara asked incredulously.

"This is war, ma'am. When you're on the winning side, you can do whatever you want."

Clara couldn't imagine the Ogletrees without their land, money, or power. If the war didn't go their way, however, they might lose all three.

Clara had been partial to the Confederates because of Papa's and Solomon's participation, but now she found herself rooting for a Yankee victory.

❖

As Wilhelmina retraced her steps in search of her lost weapon, the sounds of battle had drastically diminished. Morale on the Union side was high. A passing scout said Confederate troops were concentrated at Shiloh Church and on Corinth Road, but they were beginning to withdraw with Lew Wallace and his men hot on their heels. The victory Erwin had predicted earlier that day seemed close to coming to pass.

Wilhelmina felt tired but exhilarated. She had set out to make a difference in this war, and she was actually achieving her goal. The Union's march through Tennessee had resulted in the bloodiest battle yet. Would Mississippi bring more of the same, or would the Rebs concede defeat? She was excited to see what the future might hold—and for a chance to see Clara again.

"Yes," she said to herself as she planned another foray to Clara's farm, "she's definitely worth the risk."

She entered the woods and started looking for her rifle. The task was more difficult than she had thought it would be. The landscape appeared to have changed since she'd seen it last. Probably because she was no longer running at breakneck speed with bullets and cannon balls flying past her head.

She walked in circles for a while before she reached a patch of land that seemed familiar. There on the ground were three discarded rifles. One belonged to her, the other two to the men she had stopped to aid. As she bent to pick up her gun, she heard footsteps crunching behind her.

"Hey, Fredericks."

She turned at the sound of her name. The voice hailing her had a Southern accent instead of a Northern one.

"Solomon?" she said when she saw who had called out to her. "What are you doing here?"

"Hunting. Same as you."

Wearing overalls and a floppy hat rather than a uniform and kepi, Solomon was dressed like a farmer instead of a soldier.

"You all alone out here, Fredericks? Where are your friends?"

"Which ones?" she asked, thinking he meant the rest of her regiment.

Now that he mentioned it, the woods did seem strangely deserted all of a sudden. Had the Rebs surrendered? Had the war ended without her knowing? It was so quiet, it seemed like she and Solomon were the last two people in the world.

"Maynard and Weekley," Solomon said. "Wasn't that their names?"

"Mr. Weekley's around somewhere. Maynard got shot last night for desertion."

"I'm not surprised to hear that about your buddy Maynard. Considering the way he treated me and Papa, I wish I'd been there to put a bullet in him myself. Where's Papa buried?"

"At the military prison in Louisville. We had a service for him and two other prisoners who died before we got there."

"You couldn't see fit to bury him in Tennessee where he belongs?" Solomon asked, taking a step forward.

"You can always move his body after the war ends. I'd be happy to show you where it is, if you like."

Solomon had a rifle draped across his arm, but Wilhelmina didn't sense any danger from him. A wad of tobacco was wedged in his cheek, making him look like a chipmunk gathering nuts for the winter.

"I hate to do this, Solomon, but it's my duty to take you in."

"What for?" Solomon asked after he spit a stream of tobacco juice on the ground.

"You were in my custody when you escaped. You're supposed to be in jail, not out here running free. Drop your rifle and come back to camp with me. I'll put in a good word for you, I promise."

"That's right nice of you, Fredericks, but I'm not done hunting yet."

Before Wilhelmina could react, Solomon raised his rifle and fired. She felt something hot and hard slam into her chest. The blow knocked her off her feet. The searing pain stole her breath. She stared at the sky as the world grew dark around her.

Before her view faded to black, she heard Solomon say, "Two down, one to go."

❖

Clara closed the door to the chicken coop after the rooster and hens settled onto their perches for the night. After she made sure the horse and mules had enough fresh water to last until morning, she slowly made her way back to the house. She was tired from ministering to the dozens of wounded men temporarily taking up residence at Treetop Farms, but that wasn't the reason she was moving at a snail's pace. She was waiting for Wil. She repeatedly glanced toward the woods, hoping he would appear.

Wil hadn't said he would come back tonight—or ever again, for that matter—but she couldn't stop thinking he might show up. That he would smile at her, say her name in that funny accent of his, and she would feel that strange sensation in her stomach again. The one that scared her a little but thrilled her, too.

Being with Wil made her feel alive inside. What would she do when he was gone?

A ball of light appeared in the woods, its movement erratic as it moved through the trees. Clara thought it might be a lightning bug flying around, but the glow was too bright. Someone with a lantern was headed her way fast. She wanted to run, but her feet remained rooted in place.

"Clara!"

She sighed, relieved to hear Percy's voice, but disappointed not to hear Wil's.

"You and Abram have been wandering around the battlefield again, haven't you? Didn't you get enough of a taste of the war this afternoon? Get in the house. It's dangerous for you to be wandering around out here at night. Where's Abram?" she asked after Percy came out of the woods alone.

"He sent me to fetch you while he stayed with the body. You got to come quick."

Percy took her hand and tried to pull her toward the woods.

"Body? What body?"

She took him by his shoulders and turned him to face her. Her heart nearly stopped beating when she saw the tears rolling down his cheeks.

"Catch your breath and tell me what you're trying to say. Where's Abram?"

"He's with Wil. He's been shot."

Clara felt her hands begin to shake, along with her resolve.

"Abram's been shot?"

Percy shook his head from side to side.

"No, Wil. Abram and I found him when we were tracking a deer. He's been shot right here."

Percy put his hand on his chest, marking a spot halfway between his collarbone and his heart.

"There's blood everywhere, and I don't know if he's breathing."

"Oh, my Lord."

Clara covered her mouth with her hands. She'd just found him. Had she lost him already?

"Take me to him, Percy. Take me to Wil."

They hitched Pharaoh and Nicodemus to the wagon, and Percy drove the mules hard while Clara held up the lantern so he could see where he was going. The road was littered with hats, shoes, guns, and all sorts of things Clara wished the lantern's light hadn't allowed her to see.

After he tied the reins to a sturdy tree so the mules wouldn't wander off with the wagon, Percy grabbed the lantern and led her through the woods. Branches clawed at Clara's hair and face as she ran. One scratched her deep enough to draw blood, but she didn't dare take the time to stop and inspect the damage. She had to get to Wil before it was too late. If it wasn't already.

"Put out that light," Abram said in a fierce whisper after Clara and Percy found him sitting with his back against a tree and Wil's head in his lap. "Someone might see it and decide to take a shot at you next."

Percy moved to blow out the lantern, but Clara grabbed his arm.

"Wait. Let me hold it for a second."

She moved the lantern close to Wil's face. His eyes were closed and his skin was deathly pale. Blood had soaked through his uniform and covered the ground. Body parts were strewn across the grass. A leg, an arm, and what looked like an ear.

"Is he dead?" Abram asked. "I'm scared to look."

Clara put her hand on Wil's chest, but he was wearing so many layers of clothes she couldn't tell if his heart was still beating. She held her hand under his nose and felt a gentle puff of air that might have been a trick played on her foolish heart by the breeze. Then she pressed her hand to the side of his neck and nearly laughed out loud when she was rewarded with the feel of a faint pulse beneath her fingers.

She blew out the lantern and wrapped one of Wil's arms around her shoulders.

"He's alive. Get his hat, Percy. Abram, help me get him up so we can put him in the wagon and take him back to the house. I need to dig that bullet out of his chest before the wound closes up around it."

Abram took Wil's other arm. Wil's head lolled between them as they dragged him through the woods. Percy lit the lantern again after they reached the road. They loaded Wil into the back of the wagon, and Clara covered him with a blanket so no one could see him unless they climbed inside to take a closer look.

"Drive, Percy."

She smoothed Wil's hair with her hand. His face was so peaceful he looked like he was sleeping. Just like her mama had when she was lying in her casket.

"Drive like you've never driven before."

Pharaoh and Nicodemus chose that moment to get into one of their moods. They refused to move when Percy slapped the reins against their hindquarters.

"Stubborn animals."

"Slap 'em harder, Percy," Abram said.

"That won't work. They have to be sweet-talked when they start acting this way. Fellers, if you behave, I'll give you an extra bucket of oats and all the apples you can eat when we get home."

The promise of food goaded the mules into action.

"What are we going to do if Jedediah comes by tonight and starts searching again?" Abram asked as Percy maneuvered the wagon past the many obstacles in the road. "How are we going to explain having a half-dead Yankee in our house?"

Clara tore her eyes away from the road when Wil slid his hand from under the blanket, closed his fingers around hers, and gave them a gentle squeeze. She returned the pressure.

"We'll cross that bridge when we come to it."

CHAPTER THIRTEEN

Wilhelmina tried to open her eyes, but her lids were much too heavy. She felt hands pulling at her. Holding her up. Dragging her up a set of stairs. Pain shot through her at every turn.

"Everything's going to be all right, Mr. Wil," she heard a young boy's voice say. "You're safe now."

She must have blacked out again because the next thing she knew, she was sprawled across the first bed she had lain on in months. A soft pillow rested under her head instead of a lumpy haversack. Clean sheets lay beneath her instead of a dirty bedroll or scratchy oilskin.

"I've got to get the bullet out," a woman said.

Her voice sounded vaguely familiar, but Wilhelmina couldn't recall her name.

"It's going to hurt something fierce, so I'm going to find you something to bite down on, okay?"

Wilhelmina didn't know where she was or how she had gotten there, but she knew she couldn't allow the woman to undress her. She couldn't risk discovery.

"No."

She tried to push herself off the bed, but she didn't have any strength.

"Stay there. Don't try to move."

A hand touched her shoulder and pushed her down.

"Boys, I need you to do for me what you did for the surgeons at the Ogletrees' place this afternoon. Fetch me a sharp knife, plenty of hot water, and all the clean rags you can find. Quick as you can. Go."

Wilhelmina heard booted footsteps thumping against a wood floor.

"Let me get this bloody thing off you so I can take a look at that wound."

Wilhelmina felt hands unbuttoning her uniform coat. She tried to halt their inexorable progress.

"No. Please don't."

Strong hands closed around her wrists. Strong, but with a soft touch. The hands of a woman used to hard work.

"Stop fighting, Wil. It's Clara. Remember me? You saved me and my brother, Abram, from that soldier who robbed our smokehouse and tried to hide out in our house. I'm trying to help you, not hurt you."

"Clara?"

The name penetrated Wilhelmina's foggy brain, adding to her fear instead of taking it away. She remembered Clara, but Clara knew her as Wil, not Wilhelmina. Would Clara smile at her the same way—look at her the same way—if she knew the body of a woman lay underneath the man's uniform she was slowly removing?

"You don't understand." Her tongue felt thick and useless. She could barely get the words out. "I'm not—"

She groaned as Clara turned her first on one side, then the other. Her body jerked as Clara pushed her shell jacket off her shoulders and pulled her arms free of the sleeves. Air, crisp and cool, kissed her stomach. She shivered as goose bumps formed on her skin.

"Drink this," Clara said. "It'll help ease the pain."

Wilhelmina felt Clara's hand slip under her head and gently lift it off the pillow. Clara pressed something cold and hard to her mouth.

"I found a jug of whiskey in Papa's room. He used to say it's as smooth as spring water, but it tastes like liquid fire to me."

Something that smelled almost like kerosene splashed into Wilhelmina's open mouth and slid down her throat. The sensation was cool at first. Then heat bloomed in her chest, throat, and stomach. She coughed and nearly choked when Clara forced her to drink more.

"That ought to do it."

Wilhelmina heard a soft thud when Clara set the jug of whiskey on the floor.

"Why are you wearing these bandages around your chest?"

Clara's fingers touched the strips of muslin binding her breasts.

"Are you healing from another wound? This dressing doesn't look like it's been changed in ages. I'll cut it off and make a fresh one, but I'd better see what's under there before I go after that bullet."

Wilhelmina felt cold steel slide across her chest. Heard the sound of fabric being sheared away. She tried to raise her hands, but the whiskey made her feel clumsy and uncoordinated.

"Clara, don't."

With an effort, she finally managed to open her eyes. Then her breasts fell free and her lungs filled with air as the constriction around her chest disappeared.

"My God." Clara gasped, paused, then hesitantly cupped Wilhelmina's sex in the palm of her hand. "You're a woman," she whispered as she jerked her hand away and moved back from the bed.

"I can explain."

Wilhelmina sought out Clara's face, eager to bask in her beauty but reluctant to view the scornful look she expected to receive in return.

Clara looked down at her, her expression a mixture of confusion and what appeared to be curiosity.

"You're a woman," Clara said again, moving closer.

There was no use denying it so Wilhelmina didn't bother trying.

"Yes, I am."

The air felt charged. Electric. Wilhelmina could practically feel it crackling around her when Clara sat next to her.

"Then why do I still want to kiss you?"

❖

Clara hurriedly covered Wil's exposed chest with his—*her*—uniform coat when Percy and Abram burst into the room. Abram was carrying a steaming soup pot nearly overflowing with water, and Percy's arms were filled with the remnants of a clean sheet that had been cut into strips.

"We brought the things you asked for."

Abram eyed the terrible wound on Wil's thin frame. The center of the bullet hole was bright red, the edges charred black.

"Set the water on the nightstand, put the rags on the bed, and place the knife on the fire so the blade can get good and hot, then close the door behind you when you leave," Clara said. "I'll let you know if I need anything else."

"Can't we stay and watch?" Percy asked.

"No, there's going to be blood. A lot of it. If you faint from the sight of it, I won't be able to stop what I'm doing and tend to you, too. Go on now. I'll call you when I'm done."

Abram took a long look at Wil.

"Is he going to die?"

"Not if I can help it."

"Did he say who shot him?"

"Does it matter?"

"I guess not." Abram looked like he wanted to say something else, but thought better of it. "Come on, Percy. I'll let you beat me at checkers until Clara says it's okay to come back."

"You don't have to let me beat you. I can do it on my own."

After Abram and Percy left the room, Clara wedged a chair under the doorknob so no one could enter unexpectedly, and drew the curtains so no one could see in. Then she rolled her sleeves up to her elbows and scrubbed her hands with soap and water.

"You know. You saw." Wil's words were slurred by the effects of the whiskey. "And you want to kiss me anyway?"

Clara turned her back on him. On *her*. Why was the distinction so hard to remember when the truth was as plain as day?

"I'm just a woman. I don't know what I want."

Clara had heard the argument many times, but she never dreamed she would ever hear herself using it rather than trying to refute it.

"No one else can tell you what's in your heart," Wil said. "What is your heart telling you?"

The words Clara's heart was whispering were too frightening, too new to consider.

"Enough, Wil. I don't know why I said what I did."

But deep down, hadn't some part of her suspected Wil wasn't who she seemed? His gentle eyes, soft hands, and thin wrists didn't belong on a man. They belonged on a woman. They belonged *to* a woman.

Yet, knowing what she knew now, why did she still get a funny feeling in her stomach whenever Wil looked at her?

"What's your name?" Clara asked. "Your real name."

"Wilhelmina, but I prefer Wil." Wil looked around, her eyes wild. "I went back to get my rifle. Where's my rifle?"

"Under the bed."

Clara touched Wil's shoulder to calm her. Her thrashing was causing fresh blood to seep from her wound. If the bullet started moving around, it could cause even more damage than it already had.

"You can get to it anytime you want, but you're not going to need it. You're safe here."

After Wil settled down, Clara dipped one of the rags into the pot of water and wiped away the blood on Wil's chest as gently as she could. Wil stiffened at her touch but didn't cry out.

"Where are you from?"

Clara's gaze was drawn like a magnet to Wil's body. Wil's shoulders and arms looked strong, sporting more muscle than Clara had ever seen on a woman. Was that why Wil had been able to keep up with the men in her unit? Or had the training she had endured forged her into the fine physical specimen she was now?

"I'm from Philadelphia."

"Pennsylvania? How did you get so far from home?"

"It's a long story."

"Then tell me when we're done."

Clara moved her gaze lower. Wil's breasts were small but perfectly formed. Her light brown nipples were like little pebbles. Clara wanted to twirl them between her fingers. Tease them with her tongue. She had never had such thoughts before, but now they wouldn't stop coming. It was as if her body had a mind of its own and she was powerless to do anything except submit to its will. She tore her gaze away from Wil's breasts, picked up a hairbrush, and placed the handle between Wil's teeth.

"This next part's going to hurt. Bite down on the brush to take your mind off the pain. Ready?"

Wil nodded, and Clara poked her index finger into the hole in Wil's chest. She felt muscle, sinew, and a hint of bone, but no bullet. The muscles in Wil's neck bulged as she tried not to scream.

Clara pushed her finger deeper into the hole. Wil groaned and bit down harder on the handle of the brush. Clara watched her finger disappear up to her first knuckle, then her second. Finally, when she was just starting to think she would never find what she was looking for, the tip of her finger brushed against the base of the bullet.

"There it is."

Wil groaned when Clara spread the hole open and slipped a pair of tweezers inside the wound. Clara slowly pulled the bullet out and dropped it into the washbasin. Wil sagged with relief when the steel cartridge clattered against the metal bowl, but her ordeal wasn't over yet.

"There's a hole in your uniform, so there's a small piece of cloth somewhere inside the wound," Clara said. "I have to take it out, too, or it'll fester inside you and poison your blood. If that happened, you wouldn't last more than a couple weeks."

Wil teared up, either at the memory of what she had just endured or at the thought of what she was about to go through.

"I'll be as gentle as I can," Clara said. "I promise."

She explored the wound again, going deeper than before. Wil groaned and gripped the sheets with both hands. Clara wanted to stop causing Wil pain, but she knew she had to go on. She had to find the tiny piece of wool or the resulting infection might do more damage than the initial injury. She nearly cried when she finally located the blood-soaked piece of cloth and pulled it free.

Wil's brow was wet with sweat, her hair matted to her head. She spit out the hairbrush and glanced at the knife resting in the flickering flames of the fireplace.

"Before you pick up that knife," Wil said hoarsely, "I think I'm going to need some more of that whiskey."

Clara uncapped the jug and helped Wil drink more of the moonshine. Wil didn't sputter and cough nearly as much this time. Her cheeks took on a distinct rosy glow as the whiskey worked its magic.

"I'm ready now."

Wil let her head fall back on the pillow. Then she clenched the handle of the hairbrush between her teeth and waited for Clara to complete the unpleasant task.

Clara wrapped her hand with one of the cotton strips Percy had cut and gripped the handle of the knife.

"I'll make it quick," she said as she approached the bed.

Holding Wil down with her free hand, she pressed the heated knife blade against the open wound. She heard Wil's flesh sizzle even before she smelled it burn. Wil bucked beneath her, her body trying to arch away from the pain.

"I'm almost done."

Clara held the blade in place a few seconds more, then pulled it away. Wil's body went limp, and the hairbrush slipped from her slack jaw.

"Wil?"

Clara shook her by the shoulder, but Wil had passed out from the pain, the whiskey, or both.

"Just as well. It makes the rest of my job easier."

Clara dropped the knife in the basin, tossed the soiled rags into the fire, and washed the blood off her hands. After she removed Wil's boots, pants, underwear, and socks, she used soap, warm water, and a hand towel to clean Wil's body as best she could. With the amount of dirt crusted on her skin, Wil looked like she hadn't bathed in months. She smelled like it, too.

When she was done, Clara bandaged Wil's wound and bound her breasts. Not as tightly as Wil had, though. She wanted to make sure Wil had plenty of room to breathe.

After she slipped one of Solomon's nightshirts over Wil's head and covered her with the sheet and bedspread, she stepped back from the bed and took a long look at her most unusual houseguest.

Wil was sleeping soundly and probably would be for hours. She didn't look like a boy now. She looked like the young woman she really was. Her face was striking. She wasn't what most people would call beautiful. She was something altogether different.

Clara wanted to touch her face. Trace her smooth brow and the strong line of her jaw. Touch a finger to her full lips, then replace it with her mouth.

Stop, she told herself. Just stop.

Instead of fantasizing about what she wanted to do to Wil—and have Wil do to her—she needed to wash the blood out of Wil's uniform and mend the bullet hole in her coat. If Wil planned to go back to the war once she healed up, she might as well look the part.

Clara tossed the coat and pants over her shoulder and gathered her things. When she opened the door, Abram and Percy were standing right outside. Had they heard? Did they know Wil's secret?

"How long have you two been lurking outside this door?"

"We only came when we heard the moaning." Percy peeked into the room. "It sounded like you were killing him. Is he going to make it?"

Clara made sure to use the expected pronoun, not the one she had taken to using in her head.

"Once he sleeps off that hangover, I think he'll be fine."

"Can we sit with him for a spell?" Abram asked.

"He drank nearly half a jug of Myron Chamblee's most potent moonshine. You can sit with him if you like, but I doubt he's going to be too talkative for a while."

"But he might be scared if he comes to all alone and doesn't know where he is. You don't think he'd mind if we kept him company, do you?"

Clara's heart warmed at the concern she saw on her brother's face. At the compassion she heard in his voice.

"No, I don't think he'd mind at all."

Abram and Percy grabbed two chairs and placed one on each side of the bed.

"You boys were awful brave tonight," she said as they began their silent vigil. "I'm proud of you. Fetch me from the kitchen if he wakes up."

"We will."

She watched them a moment longer, then slowly walked up the hall. She was so tired all of a sudden. Whether from exhaustion or relief, she didn't know. But she couldn't rest now. There was still too much work to do.

She washed the blood out of the small piece of cloth she had fished out of the bullet hole, then found a needle and thread and sewed the tiny swatch back into place. When she was done, she held up the coat to inspect her handiwork. The dark blue wool had soaked up so much blood the material looked almost black. She didn't know if she would be able to get it clean, but she had to try.

She patted the pockets to make sure Wil hadn't left anything inside them. She always wound up with a treasure trove each time she washed Abram's and Percy's dirty overalls. You never knew what you might find when you started cleaning up after men. She laughed when she remembered Wil wasn't a man at all, but a woman pretending to be one.

She couldn't wrap her head around it. Why was Wil dressing contrary to her sex? Why was she off fighting a war when she could have been safe at home with her family? And why had touching her, even under such unpleasant circumstances, felt so good?

When she reached into the inside pocket of Wil's coat, she found a wrinkled envelope and an even more wrinkled photograph. The woman in the picture was beautiful beyond measure. She had long, wavy hair, bright eyes, and a dazzling smile. The dress she was wearing looked to be made of pure silk, the gloves on her hands sewn of the finest lace.

There was something written on the front of the photograph. The ink was so badly faded, Clara could barely make out the words.

"To My Dearest Wil," she read, bringing the photograph closer to the candlelight. "With Love, Libby."

The envelope was addressed from Elizabeth Reynolds to Wil Fredericks. The pages inside were perfumed with a mixture of Wil's natural scent and the artificial kind that came from a fancy bottle.

Clara wanted to read the letter but stopped herself from unfolding it. She set the photograph and envelope aside. Once

Wil's coat dried, she would return them where she had found them. Because some secrets weren't hers to share.

She filled a washtub with water and let Wil's clothes soak for a while. After the material had gotten good and wet and the dried-on blood had started to loosen up, she lathered the clothes with lye soap and scrubbed them against a corrugated washboard. She was so lost in thought, she left most of the skin on her knuckles behind.

She ran the clothes through a hand-turned wringer to get most of the water out, then hung them in the kitchen to dry. She hated getting the floor wet, but she didn't want to risk having someone see Wil's uniform hanging on the clothesline.

If Wil's heart belonged to another, she thought as she regarded the picture and envelope she had found in Wil's pocket, so be it. What did it matter to her, anyway?

Who was she trying to fool? There was a woman lying in her bed and, God help her, she didn't want her to leave.

"But soldiers leave. That's what they do."

And woman or not, Wil was a soldier. Duty-bound to follow orders, not her heart.

She heard Wil cry out and hurried down the hall to check on her. When she got there, Wil was sleeping peacefully and Abram and Percy were still sitting by her side.

"He's all right," Abram said. "He was having a bad dream is all, but he's settled back down. Go back to what you were doing. Percy and I will look after him for you."

Clara cocked her head.

"I thought you hated Yankees."

"Wil's not like the other ones."

"How many other Yankees have you met?"

Abram's ears turned as red as his hair.

"Aw, you know what I mean. Wil's...nice. He was good to us last night when he didn't have to be. He could have sided with that other Yankee against us out of spite, but he didn't. Plus he's sweet on you, and I think you might be a little bit sweet on him, too."

"So what's eating you?"

Abram picked at the covers with a grubby fingernail.

"Just because he's backing the wrong side in the war, does that give Solomon reason enough to shoot him?"

Clara's blood ran cold at the thought that her own brother might have fired the bullet that had almost taken Wil's life.

"What makes you think Solomon did this?"

"Because Percy and I saw him do it."

"Is that true, Percy?"

"Yes."

She kneeled next to his chair.

"Then why did you tell me you found Wil while you and Abram were tracking a deer?"

Percy hung his head, disconsolate.

"Because I didn't want to get Solomon in trouble."

"What happened in those woods tonight, Abram? I want the truth this time."

Abram shifted in his seat.

"Percy and I went out hunting, sure enough, but we didn't see any deer or anything else because of all the shooting during the battle today. We were about to give up and come home when we heard voices a few feet from where we were. I recognized Solomon's voice right away, but it took me a while to catch on to Wil's. Percy started to say something to them, but I told him to hush up so we could listen."

"What were they talking about?"

"Solomon asked Wil if he was alone. Then he started asking him about his friends and where they were. Wil said one was shot for deserting, but the other one was still alive. The men they were talking about were the same ones Solomon said were on the train with him and Papa. The ones that tried to haul them off to jail."

"Why were they talking about those men?"

"Because I think Wil was one of them. When Solomon asked him where Papa was buried, Wil knew the answer."

Clara choked up at the confirmation of Papa's death. Even though Solomon had told her not to hold out hope, she hadn't been able to let it go. Until now. Had Wil played a hand in Papa's death, or had she only borne witness?

"Where is Papa?"

"Buried at the prison in Kentucky, but Wil said we could move him down here after the war ends. He even offered to show Solomon the grave so he could pay his respects."

"What happened after that?"

Abram frowned as he struggled to remember.

"Wil said something like he didn't want to do it, but he had to take Solomon into camp with him because he was still a prisoner of war."

"He offered to put in a good word for Solomon and everything," Percy said. "He was real fair, but—"

Abram cut in, obviously anxious to be the one to tell the story.

"But Solomon wouldn't let Wil take him in. He shot him in cold blood, Clara. Wil didn't have his gun pointed at him or anything."

"Did Solomon see you?" Clara asked.

"No. After he shot Wil, he said he had one more to get. Then he ran off and didn't look back."

"But once he finds out Wil's still alive," Percy said, "he may try to finish the job."

Clara looked at Wil lying helpless on the bed. If Wil couldn't defend herself, who would? The woman in the picture? She was hundreds of miles away and looked like the type who would probably burst into tears if someone looked at her cross-eyed. Wil didn't need someone who would run. She needed someone who would stand her ground.

Clara picked up the pearl-handled pistol.

"Abram, I think it's high time you taught me how to shoot this thing."

"Whose side are you going to take?" Abram asked. "Solomon's or Wil's? Papa said family's always supposed to stick together."

"I know he did, but family ain't always right."

CHAPTER FOURTEEN

Wilhelmina didn't know where she was when she woke up, but the pain soon reminded her. She had survived two days of fierce fighting on the battlefields of Shiloh, Tennessee, only to be shot after the contest had been won. She had been so surprised to hear Solomon call her name. She had been even more surprised when he had pointed his rifle at her and pulled the trigger. She had let her guard down just for a moment, and she had very nearly paid the ultimate price for her mistake.

She didn't know which hurt worse, the ache in her chest or the one in her head. Her chest throbbed in conjunction with the rhythm of her heartbeat. Her head, on the other hand, pounded nonstop.

She tried to push herself into a seated position. Searing pain shot through the left side of her chest, the muscles rebelling as soon as she tried to use them. Her head swam, and she didn't feel strong enough to lift a cup of tea, let alone her own body weight. She felt like she was reliving her first day of training. Only ten times worse. Because this time she didn't have Erwin to offer her the encouragement she needed to keep going. This time, she had to do it herself.

She hoped Erwin wasn't too worried about her being gone. And she hoped even more that he was still alive so she could make amends to him when she returned to camp. If any Confederates who still might be in the area didn't shoot her first.

She settled back on the pillows and looked around to get her bearings. The room she was in was austere. A nightstand sat next to the bed. A small dresser was across the room. A washbasin and chamber pot were tucked into a corner, a nearby folding screen stood waiting to be positioned for privacy.

Two wooden chairs flanked the bed. Her uniform, laundered and neatly folded, rested in one chair. The other chair was occupied by a young boy with red hair and freckles. The boy, who looked to be about eight or nine years old, was whittling on a piece of wood. Based on the pile of shavings at his feet, he had been at the chore for a while.

"You're awake," the boy said, putting his knife away as he rose from his seat and approached the bed. "You don't know me, Mr. Wil, but my name's Percy. I was hiding in the house the night you met Clara and Abram. They're my sister and brother. They're off helping the Braggs tend to their fields. Clara wanted to stay and watch over you, but she thought Mrs. Enid would get suspicious if she didn't show up at her place like she always does, so she asked me to look after you in her stead. If anyone asks, I'm supposed to be sick in bed with a cold, but I don't really have one. Abram's the one who usually gets the sniffles, not me. Clara will be back directly. If you want something to eat, she left you some food in the stove. If you want some water, I'll have to pump you some from the well. I can fetch the chamber pot if you have to go too bad to make it to the privy, but you'll have to take care of business on your own."

Wilhelmina laughed when Percy finally stopped talking long enough to take a breath, but she immediately wished she hadn't. The action caused renewed pain in her chest. She cautiously peeked inside the nightshirt someone had put on her. A dressing had been applied to her wound, and fresh bandages were wrapped around her breasts, making her chest look as flat as a man's. Clara. No one else could have possibly been responsible for the handiwork. Wilhelmina was touched Clara had decided to help maintain her ruse instead of seeking to destroy it.

Memories of the night before came back to her in a rush. She remembered coming to on Clara's bed. She remembered Clara undressing her. Revealing her layer by layer until she discovered her secret, then touching her most private part to confirm that what she was seeing was true.

Wilhelmina had felt an indescribable thrill when Clara had touched her. It was like being struck by lightning. Hot and cold at the same time. The recollection made the hair on the back of her neck stand on end. She ached to feel Clara's touch again, but reality intruded on her fantasy before it could form.

"What time is it?" she asked after she noticed the beams of bright light seeping through the drawn curtains. "I've got to get back to my unit before roll call. If I don't, I'll be written off as a deserter."

"Here's your uniform, Mr. Wil." Percy picked up the folded parcel of clothes and set it on the bed. "Clara washed it last night and ironed it this morning. The creases in the pants are so sharp you might cut yourself if you aren't careful. She got most of the blood out and fixed the hole in the coat for you, too. It's almost as good as new."

Wilhelmina felt the inside pocket of her coat. Libby's picture and letter were where she had left them. Both seemed to be none the worse for wear, which meant Clara must have removed them before she laundered the clothes and replaced them after she was done. Had Clara read the letter before she returned it to his hiding place? Had she been so shocked by what Libby had written that she hadn't been able to face her today?

"She's a good cook, too," Percy said, continuing to sing Clara's praises. "She'll make some man a real fine wife someday. And I'm not just saying that because she's my sister. I'm saying it because it's true. You're not married, are you, Mr. Wil?"

"No, I'm not."

Her prospects hadn't been very good before she left Philadelphia. They would surely prove even worse if she were to return.

"But you got a girl back home, don't you?" Percy asked.

Wilhelmina thought of Libby as she pulled on her socks, but she quickly banished the images of her from her mind.

"No, I don't."

"Why not?"

"Because no one will have me."

"Why do you say that? You're kinda skinny, but you ain't bad-looking."

"I'm glad you think so, Percy, but no one else seems to."

"Then that's their loss."

"That's one way of looking at it."

Ignoring the ache in her chest and the pounding in her head, she reached for her Army-issue underwear and tried to stand. The room began to spin before she made it halfway off the mattress. She sat on the bed and waited for the wave of nausea to pass.

"Hold on," she said after Percy grabbed her clothes and carried them across the room. "Where are you going with my uniform?"

"I'm putting it where you can't get to it." He set her uniform on the dresser and turned to face her, his expression earnest. "I know you want to, but you can't fight, Mr. Wil. You ain't got the strength. You shouldn't be trying to go nowhere except back to bed. Get some rest until Clara comes back. If I let you try to walk out of here looking this poorly, she'll have my hide for sure."

"If you don't let me leave, my commanding officer will have mine." She swayed when she finally managed to drag herself to her feet. "Now give me back my pants."

"Trust me." Percy took her arm and led her back to the bed. "You'd be better off on the Army's bad side than Clara's. Ask Jedediah Ogletree. He'll tell you."

"Who's Jedediah Ogletree?"

"A fella who keeps asking Clara to marry him." Percy held the covers up so she could slide her feet between them. "She keeps saying no, but he keeps right on asking. He's stubborn like that."

"Do you think she'll give in?"

Libby had turned Stephen down the first two times he'd proposed, but she had only been biding her time to make sure he was truly as interested in her as he said he was. Wilhelmina couldn't imagine someone as kind as Clara appeared to be toying with someone's emotions that way, but how well could she truly know someone else's heart? She had known Libby for years and had never dreamed Libby would completely reject her without even attempting to understand her point of view. Her way of life.

"She might say yes if you were doing the asking," Percy said, "but she'll never say yes to Jedediah. Even if his daddy is the richest man in the county."

"What makes me a viable alternative?"

"What now?" Percy scratched his head. "You talk so funny I don't understand half the things you say, Mr. Wil."

Wilhelmina could have said the same about him. He spoke slower than most of the people she knew, but that didn't mean she comprehended everything he said.

"What makes me a better choice than Jedediah Ogletree?" she asked, simplifying her question.

"Oh. Well, why didn't you say that in the first place? Jedediah's meaner than a two-headed snake, but that ain't the only reason Clara would choose you over him."

He leaned over and fluffed her pillow. The jostling made her feel sick again, but Percy's words made her feel even worse.

"Clara feels grateful to you for helping her out the way you did the other night. More than that, though, she feels beholden to you on account it was our brother that shot you."

Wilhelmina grabbed Percy's arm to put an end to his "ministrations" since they were making her feel worse instead of better.

"How do you know who shot me?" she asked when what she really wanted to know was if guilt and gratitude were the only reasons Clara had shown an interest in her.

Percy sat in his chair and resumed whittling on the dwindling piece of oak.

"Abram and I saw the whole thing. We heard you and Solomon talking, then we saw him shoot you. Well, Abram saw it. I hid my eyes right before Solomon pulled the trigger. Don't tell nobody, though. They'll think I'm a coward if you do. You don't think I'm a coward, do you, Mr. Wil?"

"No, Percy. You, Clara, and Abram are some of the most courageous people I've ever come across. I admire you."

Her upbringing had been vastly different from theirs. Money had never been an issue for her the way it seemed to be for them.

She had received the best education and all the finest things her father's riches could buy. She had never wanted for anything except love, which the Summers clan seemed to have in abundance. While Percy beamed with pride, Wilhelmina gently steered him back to the subject at hand.

"Solomon Summers is the man who shot me. He's your brother?"

Percy nodded.

"He's the oldest, Clara's second, Abram's third, and I'm the youngest. That makes me the baby, but I hate when people call me that."

Wilhelmina felt like she was trapped behind enemy lines, her foe was closing in fast, and she couldn't see what direction he was coming from. For the past two days, she had shot to wound rather than kill. From here on out, she might have to change her strategy.

"Where is Solomon now?"

"He's been hiding out in the woods since Papa helped him get away from you and those other fellers on the prison train." He looked up at her. "Is it true Papa's dead?"

"Yes, I'm afraid so."

Percy's narrow shoulders drooped so far one of the straps on his overalls slid down to his elbow.

"Was it you and those men that killed him, Mr. Wil, or was it the pneumonia? That's what Mama died of, but they called it something different back then. Constitution, or something like that. I don't remember her anymore. I was only four when she left us, and we ain't got no pictures of her to look at to remind me what she looked like. Everyone says Clara looks just like her, though, so I guess that's good enough."

"If your mother resembled Clara, she must have been a very beautiful woman."

"Thank you for saying that, but what about Papa? You're not responsible for killing him, are you, Mr. Wil?"

Wilhelmina didn't know how to answer his question. Erwin had hit Lee pretty hard to get him to release the grip he had on her neck, but had the blow been a fatal one? She doubted it, but she couldn't say for sure.

"Your father attacked me, and one of the men I was with did what he had to do to get him off me. He wasn't trying to hurt your father, and I honestly don't know if his actions caused his death. If I had to hazard a guess, I would have to say no one was at fault."

"It don't really matter nohow. Dead is dead. Did Papa give you those marks on your neck?"

Wilhelmina touched the rope burns on her skin that had faded from bright red to pale pink in the days since the fateful train ride.

"He did, but I don't think he was trying to hurt me. I think he was doing whatever he could to help Solomon get away."

"Are you going to kill Solomon, Mr. Wil?"

"I don't want to kill anyone."

He frowned as if he was missing something. Some vital connection he couldn't find a way to make.

"But killing is what war is all about, isn't it?"

She opened her mouth to respond, but nothing came out. What could she say to a question that didn't have an answer? As she pondered her reply, she felt like she had been outmaneuvered by a master chess player.

"You got me there, Percy."

Clara knocked on the door and waited for a response. She wasn't used to having to knock to get into her own house. She didn't like it. Not one bit.

"How is Wil?" she asked after Percy removed the bar from the door and let her inside.

"He had a dizzy spell this morning, but he's fine now."

"A dizzy spell?"

Clara's heart leaped to her throat when she heard Wil might be sick. Had infection set in despite her best efforts to clean the wound? She rushed down the hall and threw open her bedroom door, but Wil was asleep, her face peaceful as she dozed.

"What happened?"

"He woke up in a God danged hurry to get back to his unit before they noticed he was gone," Percy said hotly. "He told me to hand him his uniform, but he nearly fell over before he could even put his underthings on. I put him back to bed and talked to him for a while to make sure he wasn't out of his head. He's been sleeping ever since."

"What did you talk about?"

Percy refused to betray Wil's confidence

"Man stuff," he said with a shrug. "You wouldn't understand."

"Oh, I wouldn't, would I?"

Clara suppressed a smile at the idea of Percy unknowingly having a man-to-man talk with a woman.

"What are you doing home so soon?" Percy asked. "Is it time for lunch already?"

He pushed the pile of wood shavings under the bed with his shoe when he thought she wasn't looking. She had told him time and time again not to whittle in the house because of the mess it made, but she didn't have the heart to yell at him now.

"Not yet. After I told Enid and Mary you had a cold, Abram laid it on so thick he made it sound like you were at death's door. Enid insisted I come home to check on you and make a pot of chicken soup."

"It's too hot for soup, but I'll take a ham sandwich and a glass of buttermilk."

"I'll fix it for you in a little while. Let me check on Wil first. Has he eaten?"

"Not yet. I told him there was food in the kitchen, but when he started swooning, he scared me so bad I forgot to ask him if he was hungry."

"I'll ask him when he wakes up."

Clara held the back of her hand against Wil's forehead. Wil's skin was warm but not overly so.

"No fever. That's a good sign."

She peeked inside the nightshirt to see if any blood had leaked through the bandages, but thought better of it when Percy moved forward to take a closer look.

"Leave us be a minute, Percy. I need to see if his dressing needs changing."

"Why can't I stay while you undress him? He doesn't have anything I ain't seen before."

Clara doubted his assertion but didn't bother to correct him.

"Just do as I say."

"All right then."

He left the room, though not before taking one last longing look at Wil as he closed the door. He and Abram had never had a man like Wil in their lives. Then again, neither had she. Someone who treated them like equals, not nuisances.

Papa had loved them, but he had done it with a hard hand. Harder when he was drinking. Hardest when the calendar crept closer to the anniversary of Mama's death. Solomon had spent time with Abram and Percy before the war began, but he had seemed more interested in putting them in their places than teaching them the difference between right and wrong. Since the war started, he hadn't been around to do even that much.

As for Moses, he was just beginning to pick up the pieces of his shattered life. Clara couldn't ask him to put his courtship of Nancy Franklin on hold to help her teach the boys how to be men. Wil was doing it without even trying. She was doing it just by being herself. For that reason alone, Clara had to do everything she could to keep Wil safe.

"When you're well enough to leave us," she whispered to Wil's sleeping form, "the boys are going to miss you as much as I will."

"If that doesn't sound like incentive to stay, I don't know what would."

Clara gasped when Wil opened her eyes.

"How long have you been pretending to be asleep?"

"For about an hour, I guess. I kept hoping Percy would get bored and leave me alone for a while so I could use the chamber pot without having to explain to him why I need to squat to pee."

Wil was taller than the privacy screen. Percy would have grown suspicious as soon as he saw Wil duck down behind it.

"You're right. That would require some explaining." Clara covered her mouth with her hand to hide her smile, then turned to leave. "The pot's over there. I'll leave you to it."

"Wait." Wil's cheeks colored and she couldn't meet Clara's eye. "I'm ashamed to say I don't think I can manage on my own. Could you…help me?"

"Of course. You don't have to be ashamed to ask for my help. I've played nursemaid so many times over the years, there isn't much I haven't done or seen."

Keeping her left arm tucked against her side to prevent herself from using the injured muscles, Wil offered her right hand to Clara. "Have you ever seen anyone like me?"

Clara helped Wil to her feet. Even though she was wearing shoes and Wil was barefoot, Wil stood nearly half a foot taller than she did.

"No," she said, looking up at her, "you are definitely a first."

Wil leaned heavily on Clara's shoulder as they slowly walked across the room. Clara reminded herself to ask Percy to make a cane for Wil to use until she got strong enough to walk on her own. She hoped Wil wasn't too proud to accept the gift.

"Do I frighten you?" Wil asked.

Clara didn't fear Wil. It was the unknown that gave her pause. The way Wil made her feel scared her to death. She wanted to kiss her. She wanted to lay with her as she would with a man. It was normal to feel that way before she discovered Wil was really Wilhelmina. Now that she knew different, why hadn't the feeling gone away? In fact, the feeling seemed to be growing stronger rather than weaker.

When Enid had suggested she come home early to check on Percy, she had been all too happy to leave. She had been doing more harm than good, anyway, her thoughts focused on Wil rather than the corn rows she was supposed to be tilling.

"No, you don't frighten me, Wil. I just don't know what to make of you is all."

Wil lifted the hem of the nightshirt. Clara held her hand so she wouldn't keel over as she positioned herself over the chamber pot. She averted her eyes so she wouldn't get caught staring, but she couldn't help but hear Wil's sigh of relief as she emptied her bladder.

"Better?" she asked.

"Much."

Clara helped her stand.

"Is there anything you want to ask me?" Wil said.

"Yes, there is." There were a hundred questions running through Clara's mind, but they all came back to the same thing. "Why?"

Wil laughed. Even her laugh sounded like a man's. Did it always sound like that, or was she so used to pretending that she didn't know how to stop?

"Why what?"

"Why are you taking part in a war no one asked you to fight when there's someone waiting for you at home?"

Wil stepped in front of her.

"There's no one."

Wil trembled as she said the words. She must have been in pain because her face was gray and a fine sheen of sweat covered her skin.

"I wasn't trying to be nosy," Clara said, "but I saw her picture when I was washing the blood out of your uniform. Her name's Libby, isn't it?"

Wil looked at her strangely.

"You saw her picture, but did you read her letter?"

"No."

"Why not?"

"Because it wasn't addressed to me."

Despite her interest in the letter's contents, Clara hadn't been willing to trade satisfying her curiosity for betraying Wil's trust.

Wil regarded her for a long moment as if trying to determine if she was telling the truth or lying to avoid having to admit she had snooped through her possessions.

"Thank you for respecting my privacy, Clara, but I don't want to keep any secrets from you."

She sat on the bed and gestured for Clara to sit next to her. Clara did so but kept a respectful distance between them, which felt odd considering the intimate act she had just helped Wil carry out and the even more intimate acts she had performed when she had washed Wil's naked body.

"Libby and I grew up together," Wil said. "We met when she was three and I was two, so it's no exaggeration to say we've known each other all our lives. We shared everything together. First words. First teeth. First steps. First day of school. Even first crushes, though mine turned out to be on her rather than someone else. From the moment I knew what love was, I knew I was in love with her. I knew she didn't feel the same way, but I kept hoping her feelings would change. They didn't."

Even though she suspected the story didn't have a happy ending, Clara found herself wishing it did. For Wil's sake.

"Does Libby know how much you care for her? Have you told her how you feel?"

"The night I decided to disguise myself and enlist, I visited her dressed as a man and told her of my plans. She didn't try to talk me out of it because my mind was made up and she knew me well enough to realize there was nothing she could do or say to sway me from my chosen path. I didn't know if I would ever see her again, so I told her I loved her and I begged her to kiss me."

Clara couldn't believe Wil's audacity. Or the courage it must have taken for her to speak her mind when she knew the most likely outcome was rejection.

"What did she say?" she asked, eager to hear the answer. "What did she do?"

"She laughed at me. She thought I was teasing her so she didn't take me seriously. I let her think that way because I had no choice. I didn't want her to look at me like she didn't know me. Like she didn't want to know me." Wil's voice broke, but she kept going. "But now she's had time to think about what happened that night, and she realizes I meant what I said. She wrote to tell me she doesn't agree with what I'm doing or who I am. We've known each other for seventeen years, but she wants nothing more to do with me."

"Oh, Wil, I'm so sorry." Clara touched her arm to offer her some much-needed comfort. "I've never given my heart to someone, so I can only imagine how hard it was for you to read those words."

"You've never been in love before?"

"No."

Wil looked skeptical.

"What about Jedediah Ogletree? Percy says he's asked you to marry him more than once, but you've turned him down each time. He must care for you. Do you feel nothing for him in return?"

Why wasn't Clara surprised to hear the "man talk" Percy boasted of had involved women?

"Percy talks too much."

"Yes, he does."

Wil grinned, and the sadness left her eyes. Clara was glad to see it go. If only for a little while.

"But he makes a lot of sense, too. How old is he?"

"Nine going on ninety. Is that how you two spent your morning, gossiping about me and Jedediah?"

"No, we talked about Solomon, too." Wil's face turned serious again. A weight seemed to settle on her shoulders. "He told me Solomon is your brother."

Clara felt a weight settle on her, too. Except she carried hers in her soul.

"Like I said, Percy talks too much. I wanted to tell you about Solomon myself when you were strong enough to hear it."

"I'm strong enough now. Is that why you saved my life? So you could prevent your brother from committing murder?"

"No, that's not it at all."

Clara felt something changing. A wall forming between them that she didn't know how to tear down.

"I know it's hard to believe and probably even harder for you to accept, knowing what you know about me, but I am a Union soldier, Clara. You're a citizen of the Confederacy. For you, helping me is tantamount to committing treason. You could be hanged for it. You, Abram, and Percy, too."

"I know."

"Then why take the risk?"

Clara hadn't taken the time to consider the consequences when she had helped load Wil's limp body into the wagon last night. Would she have taken the same course if she had stopped to deliberate what might happen if they were discovered?

"I couldn't leave you to die, Wil. It wouldn't have been right."

"For who? Me or Solomon?"

"What I did doesn't have anything to do with Solomon."

"Are you sure? Because I didn't do this to myself." Wil pulled the collar of the nightshirt aside so Clara could see the bandages wrapped around her shoulder and chest. Then she ripped some of the bandages free so Clara could see the angry red wound and bruised skin underneath.

"Don't."

Clara tried to look away, but Wil put two fingers under her chin and gently turned her face in her direction.

"Do you feel the need to atone for your brother's actions?" Wil asked, her voice as kind as her eyes. "Is that the only reason you're taking care of me?"

"No, Wil."

"Then why did you take me in?"

Clara didn't know whether she should say what was on her mind or if she should keep it to herself. What good would it do for her to say what she was feeling when no one—not her friends, not her family, and perhaps not even Wil—would understand?

Even though Libby had not returned her feelings, Wil had always known what and who she wanted. Clara hadn't been as fortunate. She had always known she didn't want to be with Jedediah or Moses or any of the other men who had crossed her path over the years, but she hadn't known why. Had she been unable to find the right man because her heart was waiting for her to meet the right woman? She didn't know any other women who felt that way. No one except Wil.

Wil saw her struggling to come to terms with her emotions and took her hand in hers.

"Please talk to me, Clara. I need to know what you're thinking. What you're feeling. Why are you going out of your way to protect me? Why are you risking your own life in order to save mine?"

"Because you make me feel things I thought I never could," Clara said in a rush. "You make me feel—You make me *feel*."

Tears rolled down her cheeks, but she didn't bother to wipe them away.

"I didn't know how lost I was until I found you, Wil. You came out of the woods that night like an avenging angel and you saved me. Not just from Maynard. You saved me from having to go through life not knowing what it's like to want someone more than you want air. More than you want food. More than—"

Wil silenced her with a kiss. Her lips were the softest things Clara had ever felt. The sweetest things she had ever tasted. She slid her hands up the back of Wil's neck and buried them in her hair. Wil kissed her harder. Hard enough to leave a bruise. Clara would feel proud to bear the mark if one formed. Because each time she looked upon it, she would remember this moment. And she would know that it was Wil's kiss that had made it.

"Clara."

Whispering her name, Wil laid her on the bed and covered her body with her own. Clara felt her weight. Needed to feel her skin. She slipped her hands under the nightshirt and slid her fingers over Wil's stomach. Wil shuddered against her. The tip of Wil's tongue touched her lips, asking for and receiving entry.

As Wil's tongue filled her mouth, Clara felt her body rising off the bed. She felt her body, her heart, and her soul rising to meet Wil's.

"Clara."

Wil's lips were on the side of her neck now. Kissing her. Searing her skin.

"Wil." Clara took Wil's hand and placed it on her breast. "I need you to touch me."

She moaned when Wil gently kneaded her flesh. Moaned because she had never felt anything as wonderful as Wil's hands on her.

"Wil—"

"Clara, can I have my sandwich now?"

She pushed Wil away when she heard Percy calling for her. Heard his footsteps coming down the hall.

"Stay there, Percy. I'm coming." She tucked Wil back into bed. "I'll be right back."

"Hurry."

YOLANDA WALLACE

The urgency in Wil's eyes spurred Clara to move faster. She wanted to finish her task as quickly as she could so she could spend more time behind closed doors with Wil. Sitting with her. Talking to her. Kissing her. How much longer would they be able to share these stolen moments? A few days? A few weeks? Because surely a lifetime was too much to ask.

After she made Percy's lunch, she put Wil's food on a tray and carried it down the hall. When she opened the door, she discovered Wil had fallen asleep again. Wil wasn't pretending this time, if the soft snores coming from her were any indication. Clara set the tray on the nightstand, fixed the torn bandages as best she could, and kissed Wil on her forehead.

"What am I going to do with you?" she asked, even though she knew Wil couldn't answer. "It's too dangerous for you to stay here, and you'll be found out if you leave. If you show up at camp with a fresh bullet wound in your chest, you'll get sent straight to the infirmary, the doctors will find out who you are, and they'll send you home. If you stay, anyone could discover you're here and they won't wait long enough to find out who you are before they kill you. You would be lost to me either way."

She wrapped her arms around her middle to keep from falling apart. Though she hadn't realized it at the time, she had been looking for Wil all her life. Now that she had finally found her, how could she possibly let her go?

CHAPTER FIFTEEN

Wilhelmina woke up feeling hungry. Not just hungry. Starving. Thankfully, Clara had left a tray of food on the nightstand. Ham, eggs, and a big piece of cornbread drenched in butter. Wilhelmina didn't bother using the fork Clara had provided. She picked up the ham with her bare hands and wolfed it down. Then she broke the cornbread into pieces and used the smaller portions to sop up the yolk from the two fried eggs. She washed it all down with a pitcher of water still cold from the well. When she was done, she felt like a new person.

Her belly was full, her headache was gone, the pain in her chest had subsided to a dull ache, and even though she didn't know what the future would bring, it didn't matter because Clara Summers had kissed her. Technically, she had initiated the kiss, but Clara had been a more than willing participant.

She smiled at the remembered feel of Clara's mouth on hers. Touching. Teasing. Opening for further exploration. She smiled wider when she thought of Clara's body beneath hers. Soft in all the right places, firm in some unexpected ones, and oh-so-responsive to her touch. She wanted to go back for more.

A soft knock on the door dragged her from her reverie.

"Are you decent?" Clara asked as she stuck her head in the room.

"My attire is, but my thoughts certainly aren't. You never told me you were such a good kisser."

Clara looked scandalized.

"Careful. Percy might hear you."

Wilhelmina could hear Percy singing at the top of his lungs. Off-key, but with great enthusiasm. Clara came in, closed the door behind her, and wedged the chair under the doorknob to give them some privacy.

"I brought fresh bandages so I can change your dressing."

"You don't have to think of an excuse to undress me." Wilhelmina pulled the nightshirt over her head and tossed it aside. She sat before Clara wearing nothing but her underwear and the slowly unraveling bandages. "All you have to do is ask."

Clara set the oversized bowl on the nightstand.

"You can't say things like that."

"Why? Because they're true?"

"No, because they're not decent."

"I don't feel decent when I'm with you."

"How do you feel?"

"Wanton."

Wilhelmina pulled Clara into her lap. She kissed her freely and without reservation. Clara kissed her back the same way, though not for long. She pulled away after only a few minutes. Wilhelmina searched her face, desperate to know what was hidden behind Clara's veiled gaze.

"What's wrong?"

"Nothing." Clara rested her forehead against hers. "I could kiss you all day, but we don't have time." She climbed off the bed and began to remove the bandages barely covering Wilhelmina's shoulder and chest. "Enid and Mary are on their way over. Abram told them they didn't have to come today, but they wouldn't hear of it. They'll probably be here any minute. We need to hide you somewhere before they show up."

Wilhelmina was relieved to hear her actions—her kisses— weren't the cause of Clara's distress. The news of the Braggs' impending arrival concerned her, too, though she tried not to show it. Panicking wouldn't do her any good. She needed to keep her head if she wanted to keep from getting caught—and to keep the Summerses from being forced to pay a severe penalty for saving her life.

"Where do you suggest?" she asked as Clara replaced the old bandages with fresh ones. "There isn't enough clearance for me to fit under the bed, and the smokehouse is too popular a destination to provide a good hiding place."

Clara thought for a moment.

"The hayloft," she said at length. "No one goes up there except for the boys, and they already know about you. You'll be safe there as long as you keep quiet."

Wilhelmina dragged her rifle and cartridge box from under the bed. After Clara handed her her uniform, she began to dress.

"I thought the Braggs were your friends."

"They're more than friends. They're practically family."

Wilhelmina buttoned her coat and put on her hat. She felt like she was preparing for battle even though no enemy was in sight.

"If they're that dear to you, can't you trust them?"

"Not with this. Enid has been like a mother to me since Mama died, but she's as pro-Rebel as they come. If she laid eyes on you, all she'd be able to see is your blue uniform, not the person inside it."

"What do you see when you look at me?"

Clara caressed her face.

"I see you, Wil."

Wilhelmina buckled the wide black belt that cinched her coat into place and draped the cartridge box over her uninjured shoulder.

"You must think I'm a fool."

Clara stood on her tiptoes and pressed a kiss to Wilhelmina's cheek.

"I think you're the bravest person I've ever met, man or woman."

Percy banged on the door.

"Stop smooching and come out of there, you two."

Clara moved the chair and opened the door.

"We were doing no such thing."

"Then why is your face so red?" Percy asked.

Clara cleared her throat as she smoothed her skirts.

"You're supposed to be sick in bed, young man, so go change out of your overalls and into your nightclothes. Try to work up a sweat first so Enid will think you have a fever."

"All right then."

Percy ran up and down the hall. He sounded like a herd of horses as his shoes clomped against the floorboards.

"Come with me, Mr. Wil," Abram said. "I'll show you to the hayloft."

Clara made herself busy in the kitchen. Wilhelmina wanted to stay with her, but she forced herself to follow Abram outside.

The farm was small but thriving. Plants of all kinds were growing in the fields. Chickens roamed free while hogs and goats were confined to their pens. Two mules and a pair of dairy cows roamed the gently rolling pasture.

The whitewashed barn smelled of fresh hay and old horse manure. Its interior walls were lined with rows of neatly arranged tools. In a small stable, a horse with a canvas feedbag strapped around its head dined on what Wilhelmina assumed was oats while a small orange cat cleaned itself on top of a bale of hay.

"The horse's name is Slim, but he's getting too fat for us to call him that much longer," Abram said. He jerked a thumb at the cat. "That's Jack. He might not look like much, but he's a real good mouser."

Jack seemed to know his name. Pausing his grooming, he looked at Wilhelmina with the tip of his flat pink tongue stuck between his teeth.

"Look, Mr. Wil. He's poking his tongue out at you. That means he likes you."

"I'll take your word for it," Wilhelmina said as Jack went back to licking his belly.

"Are you all right, Mr. Wil? Percy said you were feeling kind of poorly this morning."

"That was this morning. I'm better now."

He looked at her hard.

"You still don't look so good. The ladder's over there. Do you feel strong enough to climb it? I can give you a boost if you need one."

The handmade ladder looked strong. And tall. A good ten feet at least.

"I'll be fine, though I don't know how I'm going to manage with one hand."

"That's all right. I'll carry your rifle for you." He took her rifle and scampered up to the hayloft and back before she barely noticed he was gone. "Your turn, Mr. Wil. I'll climb up behind you in case you need that helping hand we talked about."

Wilhelmina tucked her left hand into her coat to prevent herself from using her injured arm. The bullet wound didn't hurt as much as it had the night before, but the burn from the cauterization was starting to smart. She hoped that meant it was starting to heal instead of becoming infected. She couldn't afford to give the camp physician any reason to examine her when she finally returned to camp. *If* she returned to camp. She had to make it through the day undetected before she could worry about tomorrow or the day after.

She grabbed the side of the ladder with her right hand and gripped it tight as she used her legs to push herself up. The first few rungs were easy. The middle ones were a bit harder. By the time she neared the top, her calves burned as well as her legs. How had she lost her conditioning so fast? The trauma she had endured must have been harder on her body than she thought because she was panting by the time she collapsed onto a hay bale.

Abram climbed off the ladder and pulled the wooden doors closed.

"When these are open and it's a clear day, you can see for miles from up here. Percy and I play up here all the time. Well, not as often as we'd like. Looking after the farm takes up most of our time. Clara's, too. We're helping out the Braggs at their place until Mr. Joseph gets back, so now we're looking after two places instead of one."

"Sounds like hard work."

"It is, but I like it."

"Do you want to be a farmer when you grow up?"

"There's a feeling you get when you pick something you grew with your own hands. I like it." Abram stuck a long piece of straw between his lips. "Percy and I used to want to be soldiers, but we changed our minds after we saw all those men laid up at the Ogletrees' place and the ones lying dead on the road. After seeing something like that, I think I'll stick to farming. Did you always want to be a soldier when you grew up, Mr. Wil?"

"When I was growing up, I didn't have a chance to plan my future because my parents had already decided it for me. I was supposed to live a certain life and be a certain way. I never thought it was possible for me to be who I am now. For me to be myself. But anything's possible if you put your mind to it."

"Can you stay with us instead of going back to the war?" Abram asked plaintively. "Clara's different with you here."

"Different how?"

"She hasn't lost her temper even once since you showed up, and she hasn't smiled this much since before Mama died. She's happy, and I think it's all because of you." He stood on the ladder and looked at her before he started to descend. "So don't get killed, okay?"

Wilhelmina laid her rifle across her lap and peered through the cracks between the boards as she heard a wagon approach.

"I'll try not to."

❖

Clara shaded her eyes with her hand as she watched Abram tie Enid's horses to the hitching post near the chicken coop.

"We're in for a hot day today."

Though it was only spring, the heat of the midday sun already made it feel like summer.

"I think you might be right," Enid said as Abram offered her a hand to help her down from the wagon. "How's the patient?"

"About as well as can be expected." Clara shoved her hands in her pockets because she didn't know what else to do with them. She told herself to act normal, but she didn't know what that was anymore. "He's sleeping right now."

"Poor thing. He needs all the rest he can get. I don't want to wake him. It seems odd the sickness came over him all of a sudden. He was fine just yesterday. Not even complaining of a sore throat or anything."

Clara hated deceiving Enid after everything they had been through, but she simply couldn't take the risk of telling her about Wil.

"These things happen," she said with a shrug.

"We can look in on him before we go," Mary said.

After Abram helped Mary climb down from the wagon, she held his hand a fraction longer than necessary. Clara wished she could hold Wil's hand like that in public, but she didn't know when—or if—she would ever be able to.

Enid reached into the back of the wagon.

"I brought some ointment you can rub on Percy's chest. It stinks to high heaven, but the fumes will open him up so he can breathe. You might not want to breathe too deep, though. If I was you, I'd slather him up real good and make him sleep in the barn tonight. That way, only the animals will have to put up with the stink."

Clara twisted the lid off the jar and smelled the greasy substance inside. She jerked her head away when she felt her nose hairs curl.

Enid let out a hearty belly laugh.

"I wasn't joshing when I said it was powerful stuff. Go ahead and take it in the house. While you're gone, Mary and I will see how the mustard greens are coming along. We lost part of our crop to boll weevils last year, and I want to make sure the little devils don't strike again."

Clara tried not to let her eyes drift toward the barn as she walked away. She didn't want to draw Enid or Mary's attention to the hayloft. If she did, they might find Wil hiding inside. Then what would she do? Mary's voice stopped her before she got too far.

"There's been a man in your yard." Mary pointed to a set of tracks leading to the barn. "See his footprints?"

"A Yankee tried to rob our smokehouse the other night," Abram said quickly. "He must have left them then."

"These prints look fresh," Mary said. "Like someone made them today. And aren't those your prints beside them?"

Enid grabbed Mary and pulled her to her side.

"Did that Yank come back, Abram? Is he hiding out somewhere on the property? Is that why you and Clara are acting so funny?"

"He can't come back," Abram said. "He's dead. The Federals shot him for deserting."

Abram looked regretful as soon as he said the words, but it was too late to take them back.

Enid narrowed her eyes.

"How do you know?"

Abram turned to Clara to help him find a way out of the corner he had backed himself into.

"We heard a volley of gunshots later that night and assumed it was a firing squad," Clara said. "We haven't seen anyone roaming around here since."

"Just because you haven't seen them doesn't mean they ain't here," Enid said fearfully. "Soldiers are deserting on both sides. There's a steady stream of them passing through town. Some are wearing blue, and some are wearing gray, but they're all as yellow as they come. They're too scared to fight other men so they go around terrorizing innocent women and children instead. I'm going to fetch Jedediah so he and some of the other boys in the Reserves can check your place out. Mine, too, while they're at it. Unhitch the horses for me, Abram. Come with me, Mary. These men haven't seen a woman in months. There's no telling what they might do to you if they saw you."

Enid climbed into the wagon. Mary followed her, but Abram didn't move.

"Abram, what are you waiting for, boy? Get a move on. We don't have a minute to waste."

Abram held the horses' leads, but didn't untie them from the hitching post.

"I'm sorry for spilling the beans," he said, turning to Clara, "but you got to tell her the rest."

"Tell me the rest of what?" Enid slapped the reins against her thigh. The horses flinched as if they felt the blow. "What in tarnation has gotten into you two?"

Clara took a gamble she hoped wouldn't end up costing her everything.

"Come with me. There's someone I want you to meet."

CHAPTER SIXTEEN

Wilhelmina hid behind a hay bale after she peeked through the spaces in the barn wall and saw Clara and Abram approach the barn with a woman and a girl who appeared to be the woman's daughter in tow. When she heard the barn door creak open, she held her breath and tried not to move. Even the slightest rustle could give away her position.

The door slammed shut. Wilhelmina waited for Clara to start telling the women what she needed them to do on the farm or around the house. Instead, Clara called her name.

"Wil?" Clara's voice was tentative. Uncertain.

Wilhelmina didn't answer. Clara had said she didn't think she could trust Enid Bragg with the knowledge she was hiding a Union soldier. Had Clara changed her mind, or was she giving her up in order to save herself and her family?

"Come on down, Wil," Clara said. "It's okay."

Wilhelmina closed her eyes and resigned herself to her fate, whatever it might turn out to be. She stood and approached the ladder. When her face came into view, Mrs. Bragg gasped as if she had seen a ghost. Wilhelmina climbed down the ladder, not knowing what to expect when she reached the ground.

Clara provided the introductions.

"Enid and Mary Bragg, I'd like to present Wil Fredericks. Wil's part of the Union outfit camped out on Pittsburg Landing."

"Pleased to meet you both." Wil extended her hand, but both Mrs. Bragg and Mary backed away from the offering.

"Jedediah was right all along," Mrs. Bragg said sharply. "You are giving aid to the enemy. I defended you, Clara. How could you look me in the face and lie to me after everything our families have been through?"

Clara's eyes misted over, but she didn't back down.

"Wil didn't come to us until two nights ago. I hadn't met him when Jedediah made those accusations about me."

"Mr. Wil's the one who kept that other Yankee from robbing our smokehouse," Abram said. "He was good to us, so we had to be good to him."

Despite Abram's appeal, Mrs. Bragg didn't soften her stance.

"I'll be eternally grateful to him for standing up for you the way he did, and I'm sure you feel beholden to him as well, but that should be the end of it. What's he doing here? Shouldn't he be with his unit? Or is he a deserter, too?"

"Mr. Wil's itching to get back to the war," Abram said. "He just doesn't have it in him yet."

Mrs. Bragg looked Wilhelmina up and down.

"What's stopping him? He looks pretty healthy to me."

"Looks can be deceiving," Clara said. "Wil was one of the soldiers who were in charge of escorting Papa and Solomon to the prison camp. He was there when Papa died and Solomon escaped. Solomon blames Wil and the other men for Papa's death. He tried to seek revenge last night by shooting Wil and leaving him for dead. Abram and Percy found Wil in the woods. I didn't know what else to do so I brought him here and patched him up."

"Why did you go and do a fool thing like that?" Mrs. Bragg put her hands on her hips and defiantly jutted out her chin. "You should have left him where you found him is what you should have done."

"I couldn't do that. Anyone could have come across him. Or perhaps no one would. He could have died out there all alone. Wouldn't you have done the same thing if you were in my position?"

"I most certainly would not. I would have stuck with my own kind, not switch sides. The Federals killed your papa, made a fugitive out of your brother, blinded my Moses, and Lord knows what they might have done to my Joseph since he hasn't written in going on two months now. Why are you protecting the likes of him?"

Clara looked lost. Wilhelmina wanted to help her, but she didn't know how. Enid and Mary Bragg were like family to Clara. She, on the other hand, was still a relative stranger.

"Because I love him."

Wilhelmina thought she must have misunderstood what Clara had said, but the look in Clara's eyes told her she had heard right.

"You love him?" Mrs. Bragg asked incredulously. "Child, you don't even know him. Where is he from? Who are his people? Has he told you anything about himself except his name? He probably has a wife and a passel of children waiting for him at home while he's down here playing you for a fool. Think about what you're doing, Clara."

"I have thought about it," Clara said resolutely. "And I'm standing with Wil."

"Me, too."

Clara left Mrs. Bragg's side and came to stand next to Wilhelmina's. So did Abram. Wilhelmina felt a lump form in her throat. She wondered what she had done to inspire such loyalty, but she was reluctant to question her good fortune for fear that it might come to an abrupt end.

"Wil is one man, not a whole army," Clara said. "I'm helping him, not the Union."

"That's how it starts." Mrs. Bragg grunted her displeasure. "What would your poor mama say if she could see you now?"

"I hope she would say she's proud of me for following my heart and doing what I feel is right instead of what folks expect." Clara's eyes flashed fire, but when she spoke again, her voice was cordial. "I hope you will, too."

Mrs. Bragg was quiet for a moment, something Wilhelmina thought was probably a rare occurrence.

"Of course I'm proud of you, child. I've always admired a woman who sticks up for herself, and you're definitely doing that now. But this? This is a bit much to take."

She took a step forward, gave Wilhelmina an appraising look, and pinched her arm.

"He's handsome, I'll give you that, but he's much too skinny for my taste. He's all bones, knees, and elbows. He'd never be able to keep me warm at night. He's got good manners, though. Someone must have raised him right. What do you think, Mary?"

"I reckon he'll do."

Mary blushed and looked at Abram as if gauging his reaction to what she had said. Wilhelmina didn't see jealousy on Abram's face. She saw sheer joy instead.

"That settles it then." Mrs. Bragg nodded as if she had come to a decision about something, then waved her hand dismissively. "Get back up there before someone sees you, boy. I can't say I approve of you being here, but if you get caught, it won't be on my account."

"Do you mean it?" Clara asked.

"I wouldn't have said it if I didn't."

"Thank you, ma'am," Wilhelmina said.

"Don't thank me," Mrs. Bragg said. "I'm only doing this because Clara vouched for you. If she hadn't, I would have turned you over to the Hardin County Reserves without thinking twice. I still might if you do something that brings harm to anyone on this homestead. And if you break Clara's heart, I'll damn sure make you wish you hadn't."

"I would never dream of raising the ire of a woman as formidable as you, ma'am."

A corner of Mrs. Bragg's mouth quirked into a smile that she quickly suppressed.

"See that you don't. Come on, you lot. Let's get to work. Those fields won't tend themselves."

Clara lingered after Abram, Mary, and Mrs. Bragg left.

"Stay here until it gets dark. I'll come fetch you when it's safe."

"It's safer if I stay out here. For me and for you."

"Safer how?"

Wilhelmina pointed to the hayloft.

"I have a better vantage point up there. I can see who's coming long before they arrive. And if someone does manage to sneak up on me, you would be able to say you didn't know I was here, which you couldn't do if they found me in your bed. It's for the best if I keep myself apart from you, and you know it."

"That doesn't mean I have to like it."

"Neither do I, but the next time I'm in your bed, I want you to be there with me."

"I want that, too," Clara said shyly.

Wilhelmina felt like her body was on fire. Being so close to Clara made the flames jump higher. Burn brighter. She wanted to kiss her. She wanted to touch her. More than anything else, though, she wanted to keep her safe.

"Did you mean what you said to Mrs. Bragg? Do you really love me?"

"Yes, Wil, I do."

Wil wanted to believe her, but she didn't dare. She had dreamed of finding love before, only to be denied. She didn't want to feel that pain again. She didn't know if she would be able to withstand it this time.

She had known Libby all her life. She had been acquainted with Clara for only two days. Yet the feelings Clara stirred in her were deeper than any she had ever experienced.

She didn't want to leave Clara, but how could she stay? How could she consider planning a future with her when the present was so uncertain?

"But Mrs. Bragg's right, Clara. You don't even know me."

"That's where you're wrong. I've known you from the minute I laid eyes on you. I knew right from the start that you were the one. Didn't you feel it, too?"

"Yes," Wil said, "but I didn't want to get my hopes up again only to have them dashed."

"I'm not Libby."

"No, Clara Summers, you most certainly are not."

Wilhelmina drew Clara into her arms. If she had her way, she would never let go, but she suspected there were many more battles to be fought before their war could come to an end.

❖

Clara struck a match and held the burning end to the wick of a kerosene lantern. After the lantern's flame began to glow, she tossed the spent match into the belly of the stove and adjusted the brightness.

"Boys, say your prayers and get ready for bed while I take this bowl of chicken and dumplings out to Wil."

"Why is he sleeping in the barn tonight?" Percy asked. "Doesn't he want to come back in the house?"

Abram pushed his chair away from the table.

"I told you, Percy. It's better this way. If someone tries to sneak up on us again, Mr. Wil will be able to pick them off before they get too close. And if he has to run, it'll be easier for him to get away. He can shimmy down the ladder and disappear into the woods in ten seconds flat."

"But I can't talk to him if he's out there and I'm in here," Percy said with a pout.

"I can pass a message to him if you like," Clara said. "What do you want me to tell him?"

Percy screwed up his face as he pondered the question.

"I know," he said, brightening. "Tell him not to fall out of the hayloft in his sleep and break his fool neck."

"I'll be sure to tell him. Now get to bed, both of you. I'll be back in a little while to tuck you in."

"If Solomon says we're getting too big to cry, aren't we getting too big for you to tuck us in at night?" Abram asked.

Clara disagreed with Solomon's critique of her "soft" treatment of Abram and Percy, but she didn't want to prejudice Abram's opinion one way or the other.

"Since Solomon isn't here, how do you feel about the matter?"

He thought for a minute.

"I guess I don't mind it none."

"Good." Clara was sure he would change his tune in another year or so, but she'd worry about that when the time came. "Look after your brother, and lock this door behind me. I'll knock when I'm ready to come back in."

"All right. Tell Mr. Wil good night for us."

Clara stood on the porch and waited to hear Abram slide the barrier into place before she continued on her way. Her hand trembled slightly as she held the lantern in front of her. She never used to be afraid to walk around the farm in the dark, but that had changed the night she found a strange man standing in the smokehouse. Now every sound she heard gave her pause, whether it was the rustling of the leaves in the wind, the croaking of a bullfrog on a stump, or the roar of the river as the water made its way downstream. Before, they had been nothing more than the sounds of the night. Now they could be harbingers of danger.

The noises were bad enough. The shadows were even worse. Was that figure she spotted out of the corner of her eye a tree or a soldier with a gun? She wanted to go back to feeling safe again, but she didn't know if she ever would.

She picked up her pace. Hot broth from the chicken and dumplings sloshed over the side of the bowl and burned her hand. She didn't mind the pain because it meant she was still alive. So many other poor, unfortunate souls couldn't say the same.

She wondered how many of the soldiers she had tended to at Treetop Farms were still clinging to life and how many had perished from their wounds. Were they still sprawled on their pallets in and around the Ogletrees' house, or had Union troops sent them to prison after the Rebs conceded defeat in the recent battle?

Clara wanted to see for herself, but she didn't dare go back. If the Yankees had stolen Thomas Ogletree's property, she didn't want to give them any ideas about taking hers, too.

She set the lantern down long enough to open the barn door. The ensuing squeak reminded her to find some oil for the hinges. Another thing to worry about later. First things first.

"Wil? I brought your dinner. I have a message from Percy, too. Which would you like first?"

"A kiss from you."

Wil's voice in her ear startled Clara so badly she nearly dropped both her burdens. The spilled chicken and dumplings would have been a nuisance. The dropped lamp, however, could have proven disastrous if the glass had broken and the burning wick had set the dry hay aflame. The barn would have gone up in minutes.

"You nearly scared me half to death, Wil. What are you doing down here in the dark?"

Wil grinned in the soft glow of the lamplight.

"I didn't mean to frighten you. Jack can see a lot better than I can. I was trying to alleviate my boredom by teaching him to play fetch."

"But he's a cat, not a dog."

"I think someone forgot to tell him that."

Wil tossed a roll of twine. Jack ran after it, picked it up with his teeth, then brought it back, and dropped it at Wil's feet.

Clara set the bowl of chicken and dumplings on a hay bale.

"Well, I never. I always said Jack was different. I just didn't know how much."

Wil tossed the twine again and Jack trotted off to retrieve it.

"I suppose that's why he and I get along so well. Is that why you're drawn to me, too? Because I'm different?"

"No, because you're you."

Wil sat on the hay bale and began shoveling food from the bowl so fast most of the broth ended up on her face instead of in her mouth.

"Slow down," Clara said with a laugh. "You're making a mess, and I forgot to bring a napkin."

She wiped the corner of Wil's mouth with her thumb and moved to dry it on her dress, but Wil grabbed her wrist before she could. Slowly, ever so slowly, Wil drew her hand forward. Clara watched almost in disbelief as Wil took her thumb in her mouth and began to lick it clean.

Wil's eyes never left hers. Clara felt lost in her gaze. Lost in the wonderful sensations Wil's tongue was producing as it slid against her skin.

"Wil."

Her voice sounded like it belonged to someone else. A stranger. There was no doubt about who had ownership of her body, though. Her body belonged to Wil Fredericks.

What was the word Wil had used to describe how she made her feel? Wanton. Yes, that was it. The word had scandalized her at the time, but now it seemed all too apt. As Wil took her thumb deeper into her mouth, Clara felt shameless in every sense of the word.

She pulled her hand away and reached for the lantern.

"Did I do something wrong?" Wil asked. "Did I move too fast?"

Clara shined the light in Wil's eyes, which radiated desire as well as concern.

"If you don't finish what you started, I will never speak to you again."

Wil grinned again, then took her hand and led her to the hayloft.

"We can't have that, now can we?"

CHAPTER SEVENTEEN

Moonlight streamed into the hayloft through the cracks in the boards. Wilhelmina wanted to be able to see every inch of Clara when she undressed, but she didn't want her to feel like she was on display. She lowered the flame on the lantern to compensate.

"Have you ever done anything like this before?" Clara asked.

"No, never."

The men in camp talked about sexual relations endlessly while they sat around the fire, but Wilhelmina didn't know which parts of their conversations were true and which were made up.

"I don't know what to do," Clara said with an embarrassed giggle.

"Neither do I," Wilhelmina admitted with a laugh of her own.

The men had assumed—correctly—that she was a virgin, and often teased her about her lack of experience with women. She hadn't minded the teasing, but she regretted not paying closer attention to their idle chatter.

She swallowed hard, then took a step forward, and closed the distance between her and Clara.

"Maybe we can figure it out together."

"I'd like that."

Wilhelmina cradled Clara's face in her hands and kissed her. Gently. As if it was the first time. Because tonight would be the first time for many things. For both of them.

Clara melted against her. Melted into her. Wilhelmina felt the heat build as their bodies touched up and down. They fit so perfectly together. Like they were made for each other. Like they were meant to be.

The kiss continued. Deepened. As their tongues danced a brisk waltz, Wilhelmina wrapped her arms around Clara's waist and pulled her closer. She needed to feel her. Needed to taste her skin.

She kissed the side of Clara's neck. Felt Clara's pulse pounding against her lips. She untied Clara's apron and tossed it aside. Then she unbuttoned Clara's dress, pushed it off her shoulders, and let it fall to the floor. Clara stood before her wearing nothing but her chemise and pantaloons. Wilhelmina lost her breath just looking at her.

"You're even more beautiful than I imagined."

"You're just saying that." Clara folded her arms over her chest and lowered her eyes. "I have dirt under my fingernails. I have calluses on my hands. My clothes are—"

Wilhelmina placed a finger over Clara's lips to stop her recital of her list of perceived faults.

"I don't care about any of those things. You're beautiful, Clara. The most beautiful woman I've ever seen."

Clara wordlessly lifted her arms, and Wilhelmina pulled Clara's chemise over her head. Clara's lustrous red hair tumbled onto her bare shoulders. Her luminous breasts were full and ripe. Wilhelmina took one into her mouth and was rewarded with a soft moan. The moan grew louder when she flicked her tongue against the hard pink nipple.

"Don't stop," Clara said after Wilhelmina pulled away.

"I don't intend to."

Wilhelmina pulled Clara's pantaloons down and watched her step out of them. The hair at the apex of her thighs was the same shade of red as the locks on her head. Wilhelmina slowly dragged her fingers through it. She felt something slick and hard as Clara rocked her hips against her hand.

"More," Clara said in a fierce whisper. "I want more of that."

Wilhelmina pulled Clara tight against her and slipped two fingers inside her wetness. Clara moaned again.

"Oh, yes, Wil."

Wilhelmina leaned against the wall for support as Clara rode her fingers. With her free hand, she gently kneaded the soft, warm flesh of Clara's breasts. Clara's hips moved faster and faster. Wilhelmina matched her pace, pumping her hand in time with Clara's urgent thrusts.

Clara clutched her shoulders, her eyes wild. Wilhelmina watched a myriad of emotions play out on her face. Heard the aching need in her whispered pleas for "More. More. More."

Then Clara's eyes widened. She arched her back, cried out, and sagged against Wilhelmina. As Clara's head lolled on her chest, Wilhelmina felt strong muscles spasming around her fingers, gripping them tightly, and pulling them deeper.

Wilhelmina gently lowered Clara to the ground. Skimmed a hand across her stomach as they lay on a bed of hay. Clara giggled as she pushed Wilhelmina's hand away.

"Stop. That tickles."

Wilhelmina kissed her and looked into her eyes.

"I love you, Clara Summers."

Clara flashed a lazy smile. "I love you, too, Wil Fredericks." She shook her head in wonder. "I never knew anything could feel that good."

"Neither did I."

Watching Clara had nearly been enough. She had almost been able to feel everything Clara was feeling. Almost, but not quite. Her heart pounded in her chest when Clara reached for her. Pulled her to her feet.

"Then let me show you."

❖

Clara's fingers felt clumsy as she unbuttoned Wil's uniform coat. The brass buttons were cool against her skin, providing a stark contrast to the warmth emanating from Wil's body.

Wil's body.

She remembered the first time she had seen Wil undressed. When she had cut away the bindings around Wil's chest and unveiled her secret. Then she had only seen Wil naked from the waist up. When she had bathed her, she had done so with her eyes averted out of respect to Wil's privacy. Now she didn't need to turn away. Her mouth watered in anticipation.

The only other woman she had seen unclothed, aside from herself, was her mama. Near the end when Mama had been too weak to care for herself and Clara had done it for her. But that wasn't the same. The things she had done for Mama were out of love. The things she wanted to do with Wil were out of love, too, but a much different kind.

She took off Wil's coat and laid it aside. Treating it any other way would have felt disrespectful somehow. She touched the bindings covering Wil's breasts but made no effort to remove them. She sought Wil's permission first.

"May I see you? May I touch you?"

Wil's eyes were wet.

"I think I might die if you don't."

Wil's statement offered an unwelcome reminder of how close she had already come to dying—and how close she still might be if she followed through on her vow to return to the front. Clara pushed those thoughts from her mind. The war didn't exist inside these walls. In here, there was no hate, animosity, or rancor. In here, there was only love.

She clasped the strips of cotton and began to unwrap them, winding the excess material around her hand like thread from a loom. She dropped the bindings on top of Wil's coat and placed her hands on the rise of Wil's breasts. Wil's breath hitched when Clara began to touch her. Her shoulders. Her breasts. Her stomach. Her back. Wil's arms were well-defined, and the indentations in her stomach were like the ridges on a washboard. Clara ran her hand across them. Let her fingers sink into the crevices.

"I've never seen a woman like you."

She had strong hands and a strong back from years of working in the fields and around the farm, but she didn't look like this. She didn't feel like this. She unbuttoned Wil's pants and slid them past her narrow hips. Wil stood before her, fully revealed.

"You're—"

Beautiful? Handsome? Neither word seemed to truly fit.

"You're perfect."

She knelt on the hay and invited Wil to do the same. Then she laid Wil on her back and covered her body with her own. The feel of Wil's skin against hers was almost too much to take. She shuddered at the rightness of it.

Wil parted her legs and, following her instincts, Clara slipped one of hers between them. Wil's center was warm and wet against her thigh. Wil groaned deep in her throat and began to move against her.

Clara kissed Wil's mouth. Her throat. Her chest. She wanted to kiss her everywhere. Even—

"Wait. Where are you going?" Wil asked when Clara started to crawl away.

Clara lay between Wil's legs and slipped her shoulders under Wil's thighs.

"I want to kiss you here."

She closed her lips around Wil's most private part. Stroked it with her tongue. Wil let out a high-pitched keening cry that made Slim shuffle nervously in his stall. Clara had never heard such a beautiful sound. She wanted to hear it again. And again. And again.

She lapped Wil with her tongue. Slowly at first, then faster and faster as Wil bucked against her mouth.

Wil tried to speak but produced only garbled sounds. Soft vowels and hard consonants.

When Clara looked into Wil's eyes, she was nearly undone by the need she saw in them.

Wil groaned, stiffened, then stilled. Clara felt Wil's pulse beating against her tongue.

"I like the way you kiss me," Wil said, her voice raspy and pitched even lower than usual.

Clara lay in Wil's arms and rested her head on her chest. Wil's heart was beating faster than a herd of stampeding horses. She closed her eyes as Wil idly stroked her back. She felt lazy, but she couldn't have slept if she tried.

"When are you leaving?" she asked.

Wil's hand paused before resuming its gentle, soothing caresses.

"Tomorrow. Maybe the day after. I can't leave before I get my strength back, or I won't be able to pull my weight in camp. I also can't wait too long, or I might not be able to catch up to my regiment if they pack up and leave for their next encampment."

Clara gently touched the puckered skin on Wil's chest.

"Short of showing them your wound, what will you say to convince your commanding officers you didn't desert?"

Wil shrugged.

"I haven't figured that part out yet. I can't say I was injured because I would have to prove it. I can't say I was captured because I'd have to make up a lie about how I escaped. The only thing I could possibly say for myself is deserters don't return of their own free will."

Clara couldn't imagine the army accepting Wil back without punishment—if they accepted her at all. If she didn't end up in the stockade, she could find herself standing in front of a firing squad. Neither scenario boded well.

Clara held her tighter, wishing she didn't ever have to let go.

"There's nothing I can say to convince you to stay?"

"There's plenty, but please don't try. I know how dangerous it is for me to resume fighting, but I made a commitment when I enlisted and I intend to keep it. I gave up one life in order to live another. The comforts of home. My father's riches. Those things are lost to me now. All I have left is my name. And I won't see it tarnished by a charge that isn't true." Wil tilted Clara's chin so she could look her in the eye. "Three years isn't that long when you think about it."

The past few days had felt like a lifetime for Clara. Three years would seem like an eternity.

"When my enlistment ends, I'm going to come back for you," Wil said. "I'm going to come back for you, and I'm going to marry you."

The idea thrilled and depressed Clara at the same time. Thrilled her because she had never wanted anything more. Depressed her because she knew it could never come to pass.

"Marry me? How?"

"Isn't that what men and women do when they're in love?"

Wil sounded so certain Clara started to think she was touched in the head for doubting her.

"Yes, it is."

"And don't you love me?"

"Yes, I do, but you're not a man, Wil. You're just dressed like one."

"You're the only person who could say different, and we can't be together if you do. No one would accept it. No one would accept us."

It didn't seem fair. Clara finally knew what love was, but she couldn't share her happiness with anyone she knew because they wouldn't be able to understand how she could be in love with a woman. Not just any woman. A Yankee, to boot.

"Imagine it, Clara. We could have a life together if we want. You, me, Abram, and Percy. We could be a family."

The picture Wil painted was so pretty, Clara could see it in her mind. But there was a problem with the wondrous scenario Wil had laid out: Solomon. He would rather see Wil dead than have her become part of the family. And if he knew she was a woman, that would really get his dander up. In his mind, a woman was supposed to be subservient to a man, not equal to him. Yet, during the crucible of war, Wil had proven herself to be the superior soldier. And, in many ways, the better man.

The fantasy running through Clara's mind faded. A nightmarish reality took its place. The way things stood, she couldn't have both Solomon and Wil in her life. Solomon was her brother, but Wil was the woman she loved.

And in order to have one, she would have to lose the other.

CHAPTER EIGHTEEN

The sound of gunfire woke Wilhelmina from a deep sleep. Her first instinct was to reach for Clara to make sure she hadn't been hit. A chill entered her bones when her hand touched only cold hay. Then she remembered Clara had returned to the house hours ago so Percy and Abram wouldn't grow curious about her whereabouts and take it upon themselves to wander out to the barn and see what she was up to. Wilhelmina had helped her dress, then kissed her good night. The second time. Clara's first attempt to leave hadn't been very successful—in stark contrast to the lovemaking that had followed.

Wilhelmina would have preferred waking up to find Clara in her arms instead of her memory, but the next round of gunshots banished those idyllic thoughts from her mind. She picked up her rifle and peeked through the cracks in the boards to see if the soldiers wielding the weapons she heard were wearing blue or gray. The answer, it turned out, was neither.

Clara, Mary, and Mrs. Bragg were shooting at bottles resting on stumps of wood as Abram offered them advice on how to hold, aim, and fire the respective gun in their hands. Clara held Maynard's pistol, Mrs. Bragg gripped a rifle that looked brand-new, and Mary struggled to wield a musket that appeared old enough to have been used in the Revolutionary War.

Percy and a man with long dark hair and a rail-thin frame observed the proceedings. Then it became clear to Wilhelmina that only Percy was watching the women take target practice because the man standing beside him couldn't see. He had his head cocked toward the gunshots as if his ears were his eyes.

After a few minutes, the man tapped Percy on the shoulder and said something Wilhelmina couldn't hear. Using Percy's voice and his cane to guide him, the man made his way toward the barn. He didn't appear to be much older than she was. Four or five years, at the most. Yet he moved not with the sprightliness of a young man, but the care of an old one.

Wilhelmina didn't know if she should hide or remain where she was. The man couldn't see her, but if Clara or Mrs. Bragg had told him about her, he already knew she was there.

Percy sat the man on the hay bale that had served as Wilhelmina's dinner table the night before.

"There you go, Mr. Moses. Sit right there and rest a spell. You'll be safe in here. Jack and Mr. Wil will keep you company while you wait. Don't forget Mr. Wil's our secret. No one can know about him, hear?" He ran for the door without waiting for an answer. "I'm gonna go back and see if Clara will let me have a turn. I want to learn how to shoot, too."

The door slammed shut behind Percy with an air of finality. Wilhelmina looked at Moses, waiting to follow his lead. Did he expect her to carry on a conversation with him, or was he content to sit quietly until the shooting was done?

"Wil, is it?" Moses asked.

"Yes, sir." Wilhelmina climbed down the ladder to introduce herself properly. "Wil Fredericks, sir," she said, shaking his hand.

"Moses Bragg. Pleased to meet you."

His grip was firm. His hand was only slightly larger than Wilhelmina's. He pumped hers once, then let go. His thumb slid across the back of her hand as he released his hold.

"I hope I'm not disturbing you, but I figured it was safer in here than out there," he said, waving his cane in the general direction of the gunfire.

"Do you think they'll get the hang of it?"

Of the three, only Mrs. Bragg had looked comfortable holding a gun. But each shot Wilhelmina watched her take had missed the mark.

"Mary's too afraid to pull the trigger, and Mama can't shoot straight to save her soul. She's nearly as blind as I am without her spectacles, but she refuses to wear them half the time because of vanity."

Wilhelmina watched Moses use his remaining senses to get his bearings.

"If you don't mind my asking, how did you lose your sight?"

"One of your comrades shot me. Same as Solomon did to you. Does that make us even, I wonder?" he asked with an odd smile.

"It might if we were keeping score."

"Surely someone is. Otherwise, how would we be able to tell which side is winning?"

"How indeed?"

After Jack tapped his front paw against her leg, Wilhelmina picked up the ball of twine and tossed it for him to fetch. He ran after the ball, brought it back, and dropped it at her feet.

"To answer your question about our sharpshooters," Moses said as she tossed the ball again, "Clara might have the best chance to hit what she's aiming at. She can be real determined when she wants to be."

"You don't have to convince me of that. I wouldn't be here if she weren't determined."

"You wouldn't be where? Hiding in a barn or walking the earth?"

Wil considered the question, but not for long. The answer was too easy to require serious thought.

"Both. She could have left me to die, but she didn't. She put herself at risk to save me."

"And you plan to do the same for her."

She tried to tell what he was thinking, but she couldn't read his expression.

"What do you mean?"

"Percy says you intend to return to your regiment. Are you planning to go back because you want to return to the fight, or because you want to keep the fight from coming to Clara?"

"Is the reason I wish to return so important?"

"Yes, it is. Clara cares for you. Abram and Percy do, too. How can you risk dying when you have so much to live for?"

Wilhelmina tapped the ball of twine against her leg, then tossed it as hard as she could.

"To paraphrase a friend who's older and wiser than I am," she said as Jack bounded after the tightly wound ball of string, "I want to be able to look them in the eye when I see them again."

"And if you should fall? What would become of them then? Who would protect them? Their father's dead and Solomon's too busy trying to save himself to worry about anyone else. Your fight isn't at the front, Wil. It's right here on this farm. Which would you rather defend, your president's pride or Clara's honor?"

To keep her emotions from spilling over, Wilhelmina knelt and scratched Jack between his ears.

"Leaving is going to be hard enough. You're only making it worse. I'm a soldier. I have to follow orders."

"There's a time to follow orders, and there's a time to follow your heart. Only you can determine which time it is for you. No one else can make the decision for you. Not me. Not Percy or Abram. Not even Clara." Moses paused. "Her voice sounds so different when she talks about you. I've never heard her sound so happy. But there's one thing I must know."

"What might that be?"

He turned to her as if he could see her.

"When do you plan on telling her that you're a woman?"

❖

Abram waved his hands over his head like a railroad signalman guiding a locomotive into the station.

"All right, that's enough for one day."

"Have you taught us everything we need to know?" Enid asked.

"Not hardly. All of you could use a heap more practice, but we're getting low on bullets." He took his rifle from Enid and draped it over his arm. "Save some for those of us who already know what we're doing."

"Don't make me put you over my knee and spank you, Abram Summers. I did it when you were younger, and I can still do it now. My lap is a bit more padded than it used to be, but the effect is still the same."

Enid ruffled Abram's hair before he danced out of reach. Clara enjoyed the moment of levity. Laughter had been in short supply for far too long. It was good to see everyone smiling again. Even over something as serious as target practice.

"How did we do?" she asked as she began to rake the pieces of shattered glass into a pile.

"You didn't do so bad, considering it was your first time holding a gun," Abram said diplomatically.

"But?"

"I wouldn't go around calling myself a sharpshooter if I was you. Not just yet, anyway. Let me give you a few more lessons first."

Clara used a shovel to drop the shards of glass into the trash bin. Now the only reminder of their shooting lesson was the sharp smell of gun smoke in the air.

"We can't all be as good as you and Davy Crockett."

"Is it safe to come out?" Moses asked, poking his head out the barn door.

"As safe as it's going to get. Hang these up for me, Percy." Clara handed Percy the shovel and rake and offered Moses her arm. "Did you and Wil have a good visit?"

She peeked into the barn before Percy slammed the door shut, but she didn't see Wil, who must have already returned to her hiding place.

"Our conversation was most illuminating. He's a good man."

"I'm glad you think so."

Moses tugged on her arm to get her to stop walking. Percy ran ahead to join Abram, Enid, and Mary at the well.

"He may be a good man, but are you sure he's the right man for you?" Moses asked after Percy was out of earshot. "There are things you don't know about him."

"You sound like Enid. Trust me, Moses. I know everything I need to know about Wil."

"Then do you know he's…not like most men?"

Clara's blood ran cold. Was Moses saying what she thought he was saying? Did he know the truth about Wil? Would he keep her secret and accept her for who she was, or would he turn his back on her? On both of them?

"Yes, Moses, I do."

"And you love him anyway."

The words sounded more like a statement than a question. Like Moses needed to hear them said to convince himself that they were true. Clara watched realization wash over his face and slowly sink into his body. He staggered backward as if he had received a mighty blow, then he planted his feet and turned toward her.

She expected him to be reproachful. Judgmental. Clara wasn't in the mood for either. But when Moses spoke, his voice was filled with tenderness, not contempt.

"Who else knows?" he asked. "I know Mama doesn't, or your ears would still be ringing. Mine, too, for that matter. Do Abram and Percy suspect?"

"No, they have no idea, and I don't have the heart to tell them. Wil's the best man they've ever known. How do I tell them she isn't one? They've already lost Mama and Papa. I can't take Wil from them, too."

"So no one else knows?"

"Aside from me and Wil, the only ones who know her true sex are you and two of Wil's friends from Philadelphia, though one can no longer be considered a friend. I know this is difficult for you to hear, Moses, but Wil makes me happy. That's all I've ever wanted. Nothing more and nothing less. She trusted her heart to someone in the past and she ended up getting betrayed. Please tell me you won't do the same. I don't care what you say about me, but—"

"I'm going to tell you a story."

Moses's voice was so quiet Clara was almost afraid to hear what he had to say.

"When I was in the army, I made friends with a man named Lawrence Thibodeaux. Lawrence was from Louisiana. A true Cajun, through and through. The men in the unit called him Two Times, because his accent was so thick he had to say everything twice before we could understand him. He was bigger than an oak tree, and he could lick any man dumb enough to stand in front of him. You wanted him on your side in a fight because you knew there was no way you could lose with him in your corner."

Clara waited for Moses to get to the point of his slow-spun yarn.

"Lawrence always carried a letter with him. It had been folded and unfolded so many times, the paper was starting to fall apart. He used to read it whenever he started pining for home. For most of us, that meant every other day or so. We teased him all the time about that letter, but he wouldn't tell anyone what was in it or who wrote it. He just said it was from his 'special friend' back home."

Clara thought of the letter Wil carried. The one Libby had written to tell her she had decided their friendship must come to an end. The man in Moses's story had obviously sought comfort from his letter. Wil, in contrast, had found only heartache.

"He was my tentmate," Moses said, "so I got it in my head one night that I was going to steal the letter from him while he was sleeping and read it to the rest of the boys while we were sitting around the campfire the next morning."

"Did you?"

"Yes," Moses said sadly, "but I wish I hadn't."

"What happened?"

"Lawrence's face turned three shades of red when I pulled out the letter and read the first line. I had never seen him so mad. Turns out he was more embarrassed than angry. He tried his best to get to me, but four men grabbed him, held him back, and egged me to go on. He fought them as hard as he could, but he couldn't throw them off. So I kept reading. It was a love letter, sure enough. Filled with sentiments not meant to be shared with an audience. I'll be honest. I got a little envious reading those words. So did the men hearing them. We all wanted someone to be writing them to us instead of someone else. But when I got to the end of the letter, the name written at the bottom of the page was a man's instead of a woman's. All the loud talk dried up like a riverbed during a drought. You could have heard a pin drop after that. The men in our regiment never looked at Lawrence the same way again after that, and he was killed by a Union scout before I could work up the nerve to apologize for what I did and let him know it didn't matter one whit to me who he loved as long as that person made him happy. I didn't get the chance to tell him that, so I'm going to make sure I take the time to tell you. Wil's secret is safe with me, Clara. And so is yours."

Clara couldn't think of a way to express her immense gratitude, so she wrapped her arms around Moses's neck, hugged him tight, and said the only words that came to mind.

"Thank you."

Wilhelmina waited anxiously for Clara and Moses to finish their whispered conversation. She couldn't hear what they were saying. It drove her crazy to be left unawares when so much was at stake. What had she done wrong? How had Moses managed to see through her ruse when sighted men had looked right past her?

She had tried to tell him he was mistaken, but he hadn't believed her.

"Your voice is a close approximation of the real thing," he had said. "And the palms of your hands are callused enough to pass muster, but I've never felt such soft skin on a man. Even one who's never worked a day in his life. Surely Clara would have noticed something like that when she—"

His face had grown ashen. Her heart had sunk as she watched him put the pieces of the puzzle together in his mind.

"She had to undress you so she could tend to your wound. She had to see you for who you really were. Yet she still continues to harbor you. To claim she cares for you. Are her feelings for you real, or all part of an act?"

Wilhelmina had thought of the tender moments she and Clara had shared. Of the promises they had made. They had certainly felt real to her. She had wanted to tell Moses how much she loved Clara and how much Clara seemed to love her, but the choice wasn't hers to make.

"I'm afraid you'll have to ask her."

And that's exactly what Moses had set out to do. She had watched helplessly as Moses had drawn Clara away from the others. She had watched as Clara's eyes searched his face. Then she had seen what she hadn't hoped to see. Fear. Not of an enemy bearing down with a gun in his hand. Fear of discovery.

Would Clara deny everything they had meant to each other—everything they could still be—in order to keep her own secrets safe?

Wilhelmina didn't want to consider the possibility. How could she get this close to everything she had ever wanted, only to watch it slip away?

Then the unimaginable happened.

Clara smiled.

Not just any ordinary smile. A bright, shining smile that lit up not just her face but the whole sky.

"Thank you," Clara said, hugging Moses to her. "Thank you."

Clara led Moses to the well, where everyone was taking turns drinking their fill from a ladle filled with cool water. Then she began to walk back toward the barn. Wilhelmina wanted to meet her halfway, but forced herself to remain in her hiding place.

"Moses knows," Clara said after she closed the barn door behind her. "He knows the truth about you—about us—and he doesn't care. He promised to guard our secret as closely as if it were his own."

Wilhelmina climbed down the ladder and opened her arms wide as Clara launched herself into them.

How could this be? How could these poor, simple farm folk accept her without reservation when her friends and family members—blessed with all of life's advantages—had refused to do the same?

It wasn't what you owned that made you rich, she realized. It was who you were inside. In that respect, the Summerses and the Braggs were wealthy beyond measure.

Wilhelmina's tears mingled with Clara's as they kissed.

"I have chores to finish," Clara said, pulling away, "but I'll come back tonight when we can be alone."

"Hurry."

Wilhelmina was already counting the minutes. Though she and Clara had much to celebrate this day, their time together was quickly running out.

CHAPTER NINETEEN

Clara couldn't believe her good fortune. She had been so worried about how people would react if they found out she had fallen in love with a woman. How could they possibly understand, she had asked herself, when even she was still coming to terms with the idea?

But the truth couldn't be denied. She was in love with Wilhelmina Fredericks. She wanted to spend the rest of her days with her. Make a life with her. Grow old with her.

She hadn't expected anyone except Wil to share her joy. Then Moses had surprised her by giving her his blessing. Did she think everyone else in town would feel the same way if given a chance to express their opinions on the matter? Of course not, but at least she and Wil had one person on their side. One was better than none at all.

Her heart was so light she felt like bursting into song. She refrained somehow and concentrated on the fried chicken and mashed potatoes she was making so she wouldn't torment herself with visions of what was to follow after supper. Sneaking out to the barn after the boys went to bed so she could be with Wil in that way again. Would they always have to sneak around in order to be together? Or could Wil's crazy scheme of getting married actually come to pass?

Clara smiled when she pictured the two of them standing before the justice of the peace and saying, "I do." Her smile faded, however, when she pictured Wil saying good-bye. Because Wil was determined to return to the fight. And by this time tomorrow, she might already be gone.

A knock on the door drew Clara from her reverie. The knock was firm, but not as forceful as Jedediah's. When he banged on the door, it sounded like he was trying to knock it down with his bare hands. Enid never bothered knocking. She used to barge right in. Lately, though, she had taken to announcing her presence so she wouldn't be mistaken for a marauding Yankee.

This visitor, Clara could tell, was somebody new.

"See who it is, Abram. This chicken is bound to burn if I take my eye off it too long."

Abram drew the curtain aside and peeked out the front window. He jumped back and started waving his hand frantically at Percy. "Bring me the rifle. There's a Yankee standing on our porch."

Percy stood on a chair and took the rifle down from its perch above the mantle.

"That window ain't been cleaned in a while," Clara said, taking the chicken off the heat. "Are you sure it isn't Wil?"

"I'm positive. Wil's a young man. This one's older than dirt."

Abram checked to make sure the rifle was loaded, then raised it to his shoulder and threw the door open.

"Careful where you point that thing, son," the soldier on the porch said, raising his hands. "It might go off when you least expect it."

"I know how to handle a gun, mister," Abram said. "My rifle only goes off when I want it to, and I only hit what I'm aiming at. Right now, I'm aiming at you."

"So I see."

Clara joined them in the doorway.

"How can we help you, mister?"

The man took off his cap and slowly lowered his hands.

"I don't mean to disturb you, ma'am, but I'm looking for a friend of mine who went missing after the battle yesterday. His name's Wil Fredericks, and I think he might have wandered onto your farm a few days ago looking for provisions. This place looks exactly as he described it, and if you don't mind my saying, so do you."

Clara looked around, but the man appeared to have come alone. Was he really a friend of Wil's like he said, or was he someone else entirely? Perhaps someone in charge of rounding up deserters and taking them in to be shot.

"What are you looking for him for?"

"I don't know if he's dead or alive, and it would do my heart good to know one way or the other. Have you seen him in the last few days? Has he been back by this way?"

The man wrung his hat in his hands. He looked more like a worried father than a hardened killer. Clara thought she might be able to trust him, but she needed to know for sure.

"What's your name, mister?"

"Weekley. Erwin Weekley. Wil and I serve together in the Seventy-seventh Pennsylvania. I have his things here if you don't believe me."

He held up a dusty haversack. When Clara peered inside, she spied a Bible, several sheets of writing paper, and assorted underthings. When she straightened, the man's name finally registered with her.

"Your name's Weekley, you said?" she asked, motioning for Abram to lower his gun.

"Yes. Do you know me?"

"Not personally, but I do know of you. You're the one our brother Solomon is looking for. He holds you partly responsible for Papa's death. If he finds you, he aims to kill you. You and Wil both."

"So you have seen Wil. Where is he? Is he all right?"

"If you head to the barn over yonder, Mr. Weekley, you can ask him yourself."

❖

Wilhelmina couldn't believe her eyes. She rushed to shake Erwin's hand.

"It *is* you. I saw you dart out of the woods and head toward the house, but I thought my mind was playing tricks on me after being cooped up for so long."

"It is so good to see you, son. When you didn't return to camp, Billy and I thought you had perished."

Erwin clapped her on the shoulder as if he were greeting a long-lost friend.

"From the looks of things," he said after she staggered from the blow, "you nearly did. Have a seat, son, and tell me what happened."

She rubbed her shoulder, trying in vain to lessen the throbbing ache Erwin's enthusiastic greeting had caused. Giving up on the lost cause, she sat on a hay bale and told him everything that had happened since they were separated on the second day of the pitched battle in and around Pittsburg Landing.

"That's some story," Erwin said when she was done.

"I was planning on coming back tomorrow, but now that you're here, I might as well leave tonight. You can help me convince Doc Gibson I'm fit to fight. I doubt he'll take my word for it, but he's apt to be more agreeable if I have you to vouch for me."

Erwin looked at Clara's, Abram's, and Percy's forlorn faces.

"No need to rush, son. Tomorrow is as good a time as any. It will give you a chance to say your good-byes first."

One night wasn't nearly long enough to tell Clara all the things she needed to say, but it would have to do.

"I'll come back for you first thing in the morning," Erwin said. "In the meantime, was that fried chicken I smelled back at the house?"

"Would you like to join us for dinner, Mr. Weekley?" Clara asked.

"I wouldn't want to impose."

"Nonsense. Any friend of Wil's is a friend of ours. I'll let you two talk. I'll send Percy to fetch you when everything's ready. Come on, boys. Let's leave them to it."

"Thank you kindly, ma'am." He turned to Wilhelmina after Clara, Percy, and Abram returned to the house. "She is as pretty as a picture, Wil."

"I think so, too," Wilhelmina said proudly. "I've made up my mind. I'm not going back to Philadelphia once the war is over. I'm going to come back here when all is said and done."

"This is a particularly lovely part of the country, even if both sides are doing their dead level best to blow it to kingdom come. What will you do once you've fulfilled your duty? Try your hand at farming?"

"I thought I might. I may need Clara and the boys to teach me a few things, but I've always been a pretty good study. I'll let you in on a little secret, Mr. Weekley."

She leaned forward, slightly nervous as she prepared to share her news with him. She wanted his approval—desperately so—but she didn't know if she would receive it.

"I've asked Clara for her hand and she's said yes."

Erwin looked momentarily surprised.

"I guess that means congratulations are in order. You certainly move fast once you set your mind to it, don't you, son? I can certainly vouch for that. I asked my wife to marry me before the end of our first date. She exhibited enough patience to wait for a few more outings took place before she said yes, but I like to think she made up her mind that first night."

Wilhelmina thought of the first night she had met Clara. When she had looked into her eyes and known she had met someone she wanted to be in her life for the rest of her life.

"It doesn't take long once you know something's meant to be."

Clara's feet felt leaden as she made the short trek from the house to the barn. She had made this journey many times over the years. Tonight, though, she felt like she was taking a trip to the gallows. The first time she had followed this path to see Wil, it had marked the beginning. Her journey tonight felt like the end.

She had told herself to be strong. She had told herself not to let her feelings show so she wouldn't make Wil feel bad about leaving. But she felt her resolve weaken as soon as she opened the barn door and found Wil and Jack playing one last game of fetch.

She set the lantern down and turned away so Wil wouldn't see the tears in her eyes.

"What's wrong?"

Wil let the ball of twine fall from her hand, came over to her, and slipped her arms around her waist. Clara leaned against her, seeking solace in her strength.

"I thought we would have more time."

"We will. When I come back, we'll have all the time in the world."

"But what if you don't come back?"

Clara didn't want to imagine such a thing, but she had to face facts. They both did.

Wil had already been shot once, but she had managed to survive. She might not be as fortunate if it happened again.

"You can't get rid of me that easily." Wil took Clara by her shoulders and turned her to face her. "I'm coming back for you, and I won't let anyone or anything stand in my way. I promise."

Most promises were made to be broken, but Clara hoped this one was meant to be kept.

"Will you wait for me?"

"Of course, Wil. Do you even have to ask?"

"Maybe I just wanted to hear you say it."

Wil flashed her familiar lopsided grin. The one that made Clara's heart flutter and her stomach turn somersaults. Lord, she was going to miss that grin.

Wil pulled her toward the hayloft. Clara allowed herself to be led.

After they climbed the ladder, they undressed each other and made love. Slowly at first, then with an increasing sense of urgency. Of desperation.

Clara tried to commit every kiss, every touch, every caress to memory. Because once the sun rose and Erwin returned to escort Wil back to their regiment, memories would be all she had to sustain her.

"Stay with me tonight," Wil said afterward as Clara lay limp and sated in her arms.

Clara started to protest. What would Abram and Percy say if they discovered she had spent the night with Wil? But if this was the last night she and Wil would ever spend together, she didn't want to spend a moment of it apart.

She closed her eyes and held on tight. Held on for dear life. Held on because she couldn't force herself to let go.

"I wouldn't dream of being anywhere else."

CHAPTER TWENTY

While Clara fastened her dress, Wilhelmina buttoned her uniform coat and tugged her hat into place. They dressed without speaking because there were no words left to say besides good-bye, and Wilhelmina didn't know if she could manage it. After she cinched her belt around her waist, she reached for Clara's hand and laced their fingers together. The connection they had formed was so powerful she doubted anything could break it, but time and distance were about to put it to the test.

Wilhelmina knew she shouldn't let this moment pass without remarking on it, but she lacked the eloquence to express her feelings. She couldn't quote from classic literature like Erwin. All she could do was speak from the heart.

"Clara—"

Clara squeezed her hand and let go.

"Mr. Weekley will be here soon," Clara said, turning away. "I'll make you some breakfast before you go. And the boys will be wanting a chance to say their fare-thee-wells."

"Clara—"

Wilhelmina reached for her, but Clara pressed her hands against her chest to hold her at bay.

"Don't, Wil," Clara said with tears in her eyes. "Don't say you love me. I already know. And don't say you'll come back because we both know it's a promise you might not be able to keep. Just—" She gripped Wilhelmina's coat, holding the dark blue wool tight in her fists. "Just stay safe. And don't forget about me."

"No chance of that."

Wilhelmina kissed her. Like it was the first time. Like it was the last time. Because once she abandoned the refuge she had found on this farm, in this drafty barn—and in Clara's arms—she might not be able to find her way back to it.

"Stay here," Clara said after she climbed down the ladder. "I'll be back."

So will I, Wilhelmina thought, though she didn't dare say it out loud. Doing so under these circumstances would feel like inviting disaster.

She grabbed her rifle and looped her cartridge box over her shoulder.

"I guess this is it, Jack." She bent to scratch him between his ears as he leaned against her legs. "Take care of yourself, okay? And don't forget everything I taught you."

As if he understood her words, Jack picked up the ball of twine and dropped it at her feet.

"Last time," she said sadly. "Let's make it a good one."

She tossed the ball of twine and watched him run after it. When he brought it back, he held it in his teeth instead of letting go. Then he batted the air with his paw as if waving good-bye.

"I'm going to miss you, too," she said, giving his head a final scratch.

"Are you sure you can't stay, Mr. Wil?"

Wilhelmina turned to find Abram and Percy standing behind her. Their faces were puffy from sleep—and unshed tears.

"Yes, I'm sure, Abram. I gave my word and I intend to keep it."

"But don't you love us no more?" Percy asked.

Wilhelmina bent so she could look him in the eye.

"I love you, Abram, and Clara more than I can say. Don't ever forget that."

"We won't, Mr. Wil," Abram said, putting an arm around Percy's shoulder. "I'll make sure he understands." He held out his hand. "Be careful now, you hear?"

"I will."

Wilhelmina shook Abram's hand. She could tell he would become a good man one day, and she was grateful she was able to see a glimpse now in case she didn't get the chance later.

Erwin showed up as Wilhelmina was finishing a plate of biscuits, sausage, and scrambled eggs.

"Are you ready, son?"

Wilhelmina finished the rest of her coffee, wiped her mouth with the back of her hand, and rose from her seat.

"Yes, sir, I think I am."

She let her eyes linger on Abram's and Percy's faces, taking them in one by one. She saved Clara for last, basking in her beauty. Reflecting on the memories they had made—and fervently wishing they would be lucky enough to make more.

"Wait," Clara said. "Don't go."

Wilhelmina's heart was already heavy. Hearing Clara's plea made it grow extra weight.

"Clara—"

"I'm not trying to stop you," Clara said, a panicked expression creeping across her face. "I think I hear someone coming."

After Clara fell silent, Wilhelmina strained to hear what had caught her attention. The faint sound of hoofbeats gradually grew louder.

Abram ran to the door and peeked out.

"It's Jed. And he's dragging Solomon behind him."

Wilhelmina moved closer to the door but made sure to remain out of sight. She saw a man with dark brown hair riding a chestnut stallion. The horse was moving at a canter. Not very fast, but too fast for the man trailing behind it to keep up.

Solomon, his wrists bound by a rope attached to the pommel of the horse's saddle, coughed and spat as he was dragged face-first through the dirt.

"I'll kill him."

Abram grabbed for Wilhelmina's rifle, but she lifted it over her head and held it out of reach.

"You'll do no such thing," Clara said. "Let me handle this."

"What do you intend to do?" Wilhelmina asked.

"I don't know how I'm going to finish, but I'm going to start by asking Jedediah what he wants."

❖

Clara walked out of the barn with Abram and Percy trailing behind her. She could feel Wil's eyes on her, watching her from the shadows.

She didn't know what was about to happen, but she felt like her whole life had been building to this moment. Now that the moment had finally arrived, she knew nothing would ever be the same.

She wished she had the pistol Wil had given her, but she had left it in the house. She had left it behind because being with Wil made her feel safe. Even if she had the pistol on her, she didn't know if she would be able to use it on Jedediah. He had been a thorn in her side for years, but she couldn't compel herself to bring harm to him or anyone else.

After Jedediah directed his horse to stop, Solomon groaned and rolled onto his back. His face was scratched and bruised. His clothes were covered in dust. Clara wanted to go to him, but the strange look on Jedediah's face convinced her to remain where she was.

Jedediah looked nearly as bedraggled as Solomon. He had always prided himself on his appearance, but his eyes were red, his clothes were unkempt, and his face unshaven.

How the mighty had fallen.

"What are you doing, Jedediah?" Clara asked. "Why do you have Solomon trussed up like that?"

"I caught him trying to steal a couple of chickens from our coop. I could have shot him, but I refrained because I thought you might be agreeable to a trade."

"What kind of trade?" Clara asked warily.

"I want to exchange his freedom for your land. My father has chosen to give up rather than fight. He has decided to remain in Corinth with Mother rather than return to Shiloh."

"Why don't you join them? There's nothing left for you here."

"I don't want to live in Mississippi. Tennessee is my home. Always has been. Always will be. My father is too old to make another fortune, but I'm still young enough to make mine." He looked around the farm. "This place isn't much, but it will get me started. All you need to do is find the deed and sign it over to me. In return, I'll hand your brother over to you instead of the Rebs he deserted from or the Yankees who have stolen my family's land. So which is it to be? Your father's land or your brother's life?"

"Don't do it, Clara," Solomon said. "Papa wouldn't want you to. Let this piece of shit turn me in. I ain't afraid to die."

According to Solomon, Papa had given his last breath to keep him safe. Now it was Clara's turn to do something similar.

"I can't give you what ain't mine, Jedediah. Papa's dead, and our land's already been claimed. Same as yours."

Jedediah looked doubtful. Clara had expected him to take her at her word. She should have known he would require more.

"Claimed by who?" he asked. "I don't see any Yankees around here."

"Then I suppose you haven't looked hard enough."

Clara turned at the sound of Wil's voice. She saw Wil and Mr. Weekley standing outside the barn with their rifles aimed at Jedediah's chest. She felt so proud seeing the determined look on Wil's face—and the frightened one on Jedediah's. He was so used to pushing people around. Now someone was finally pushing back. Not just someone. Wil.

"You're trespassing on private property, Jedediah. My property. I'm well within my rights to shoot you," Wil said, moving closer. "Untie that man, ride off, and don't come back."

"Or what?" Jedediah asked. "What happens if I don't do what you say?"

"I won't leave it up to someone else to kill you. I'll do it myself."

"You're just a boy. I could tear you apart with my bare hands."

"That scrawny son of a bitch is tougher than he looks," Solomon said. "I shot him square in the chest and he's still standing here breathing. Do you really think you can do better, Jed?"

Jedediah fell silent as he considered his options. The Reserves had scattered, the Rebs were gone, and Yankee troops were everywhere. He had been beaten, even if he wasn't willing to admit defeat.

Several long minutes later, he untied the rope attached to his saddle and dug his heels into his horse's side. Then he rode off without a word.

"Do you think we've seen the last of him?" Abram asked.

Wil shouldered her rifle.

"I think I'd better stick around to make sure."

Clara looked at her, unable to convince herself that what Wil had said was true. She had finally come to terms with Wil leaving. Now there was a possibility she might stay?

"Do you really mean it, Mr. Wil?" Percy asked. "You're not going to leave us after all?"

"No, Percy, I'm not. If Clara will have me, that is."

When Wil looked at her, Clara was nearly undone by what she saw. Wil's eyes glowed with love. For Abram. For Percy. And for her.

"I think we already know the answer to that question," Percy said.

"You know who these men are, don't you, Clara?" Solomon asked as Abram helped him to his feet. "They're the ones who killed Papa."

"They're also the men who just helped save your life," Clara said. "By my reckoning, that makes you square, doesn't it?"

"That depends." Solomon rubbed his wrists where the rope had scraped them raw. "You still planning to take me in, Fredericks?"

"No," Wil said, "I'm not, but I am planning to marry your sister. Is that all right by you?"

"I don't know if I cotton to the idea of having a Yankee for a brother-in-law," Solomon said, making Clara wonder if she and Wil were about to fall victim to the last obstacle in their path after clearing all the others. "But from what I've seen, you're a heap better man than the one that just rode out of here with his tail between his legs."

"So what does that mean?"

Clara needed to hear him say it straight out, not hint around it. "If you want him, I ain't gonna stand in your way." Solomon rubbed his chin. Dirt and leaves fell from his shaggy beard. "Some folks in town might not like it, but other people's opinions of this family ain't mattered to us before. Why should we let it start making a difference now?"

"Thank you, Solomon," Clara said.

"For what?"

"For not making me choose between my family and my heart."

"Seems to me you already did. And, for what it's worth, I think you made the right choice."

"So do I."

"I'd better be getting back to camp," Mr. Weekley said as reveille sounded in the distance. He paused to shake Wil's hand. "This is where we part ways, son, though I hope we will be allowed to renew our acquaintance after the hostilities conclude."

"I hope so, too, sir. You're welcome to pay us a visit anytime."

Mr. Weekley started to walk away, but Solomon called out to him before he got very far.

"Hold up, Weekley. I'm going with you."

"After everything that has transpired," Mr. Weekley said, "I'm more than willing to look the other way."

"I can't keep running on this bum leg of mine," Solomon said. "The Federals are bound to catch up to me sooner or later. I might as well do this on my terms. Take me in. I'm ready to serve my time."

"Are you sure, Solomon?" Clara asked.

"You don't need me to look after you and the boys no more." He looked from her to Wil and back again. "You've got someone else to do it for you."

"No," Wil said, wrapping her arm around Clara's waist. "We've got each other."

"Don't worry," Mr. Weekley said. "I'll look after him as best I can."

Though Clara was sad to see Solomon go, she was glad he was able to find redemption before he left. When he finally made it back home, he would be whole in body as well as in spirit.

After Solomon and Mr. Weekley disappeared into the woods, Clara turned to Wil, the enemy soldier who had invaded her heart.

"Why did you change your mind and decide to stay?"

Wil laid her weapon aside for the last time and took her into her arms.

"Because I would rather die by your side than live without you."

Clara closed her eyes as Wil kissed her. Though the nation was still divided, their hearts were united. The war continued all around them, but their battle was over. Love had won.

EPILOGUE

June 1866
Shiloh, Tennessee

Wil Fredericks woke before the sun rose. She loved this time of day. This odd mixture of morning and night. When the house was quiet, save for the sound of her wife sleeping in her arms.

Clara's left hand rested on Wil's chest, which had been freed of its usual bindings so she could doze in comfort—and Clara could touch her with no restrictions impeding her path. Wil twirled the gold band on the ring finger of Clara's hand. The ring had once adorned Clara's mother's hand. Now it rested on hers. Wil had bought it back from Mr. Stallings at the general store four years ago, and, when she slipped it on Clara's finger later that same day, she had resolved to do everything in her power to make sure Clara and the ring were never parted again.

Farm life wasn't easy. The work was hard—backbreaking at times—but Wil was happy to do it because she had her family by her side to share the load. Her wife, her brothers-in-law, and the Braggs, who treated her as one of their own. Just as they did with the Summerses.

Today wasn't a workday, though. Today was special. Because today Abram and Mary Bragg were to be married. Not standing alone before a justice of the peace like Wil and Clara had when they had exchanged vows, but surrounded by family and friends.

Joseph Bragg had returned from the war older and grayer, but essentially unharmed. He would give Mary away today, and Moses would walk Enid down the aisle while Nancy, his pregnant wife of three years, would look on beaming with pride. Clara would serve as Mary's matron of honor, and Wil, Percy, and Solomon would stand up for Abram. Because that's what families did. They stood up for each other even when they occasionally found themselves at odds.

So much had changed since Wil had marched into this small town four years prior. The dirt roads heading into and out of town were filled with carpetbaggers traveling from the North to the South so they could seek their fortunes during the reconstruction, as well as grieving relatives in search of the final resting places of their fallen sons, husbands, brothers, and fathers.

One thing remained unchanged, however: the love Wil felt for the woman who had been able to look past her disguise and see her for who she really was.

"Wake up, Clara. Today is going to be a beautiful day."

About the Author

Yolanda Wallace is not a professional writer, but she plays one in her spare time. Her love of travel and adventure has helped her pen ten globe-spanning novels, including the Lambda Award-winning *Month of Sundays*. Her short stories have appeared in multiple anthologies including *Romantic Interludes 2: Secrets* and *Women of the Dark Streets*. She and her partner live in beautiful coastal Georgia, where they are parents to two children of the four-legged variety.

Books Available from Bold Strokes Books

Divided Nation, United Hearts by Yolanda Wallace. In a nation torn in two by a most uncivil war, can love conquer the divide? (978-1-62639-847-4)

Fury's Bridge by Brcy Willows. What if your life depended on someone who didn't believe in your existence? (978-1-62639-841-2)

Lightning Strikes by Cass Sellars. When Parker Duncan and Sydney Hyatt's one-night stand turns to more, both women must fight demons past and present to cling to the relationship neither of them thought she wanted. (978-1-62639-956-3)

Love in Disaster by Charlotte Greene. A professor and a celebrity chef are drawn together by chance, but can their attraction survive a natural disaster? (978-1-62639-885-6)

Secret Hearts by Radclyffe. Can two women from different worlds find common ground while fighting their secret desires? (978-1-62639-932-7)

Sins of Our Fathers by A. Rose Mathieu. Solving gruesome murder cases is only one of Elizabeth Campbell's challenges; another is her growing attraction to the female detective who is hell-bent on keeping her client in prison. (978-1-62639-873-3)

The Sniper's Kiss by Justine Saracen. The power of a kiss: it can swell your heart with splendor, declare abject submission, and sometimes blow your brains out. (978-1-62639-839-9)

Troop 18 by Jessica L. Webb. Charged with uncovering the destructive secret that a troop of RCMP cadets has been hiding, Andy must put aside her worries about Kate and uncover the conspiracy before it's too late. (978-1-62639-934-1)

Worthy of Trust and Confidence by Kara A. McLeod. FBI Special Agent Ryan O'Connor is about to discover the hard way that when you can only handle one type of answer to a question, it really is better not to ask. (978-1-62639-889-4)

Amounting to Nothing by Karis Walsh. When mounted police officer Billie Mitchell steps in to save beautiful murder witness Merissa Karr, worlds collide on the rough city streets of Tacoma, Washington. (978-1-62639-728-6)

Becoming You by Michelle Grubb. Airlie Porter has a secret. A deep, dark, destructive secret that threatens to engulf her if she can't find the courage to face who she really is and who she really wants to be with. (978-1-62639-811-5)

Birthright by Missouri Vaun. When spies bring news that a swordswoman imprisoned in a neighboring kingdom bears the Royal mark, Princess Kathryn sets out to rescue Aiden, true heir to the Belstaff throne. (978-1-62639-485-8)

Crescent City Confidential by Aurora Rey. When romance and danger are in the air, writer Sam Torres learns the Big Easy is anything but. (978-1-62639-764-4)

Love Down Under by MJ Williamz. Wylie loves Amarina, but if Amarina isn't out, can their relationship last? (978-1-62639-726-2)

Privacy Glass by Missouri Vaun. Things heat up when Nash Wiley commandeers a limo and her best friend for a late drive out to the beach: Champagne on ice, seat belts optional, and privacy glass a must. (978-1-62639-705-7)

The Impasse by Franci McMahon. A horse packing excursion into the Montana Wilderness becomes an adventure of terrifying proportions for Miles and ten women on an outfitter led trip. (978-1-62639-781-1)

The Right Kind of Wrong by PJ Trebelhorn. Bartender Quinn Burke is happy with her life as a playgirl until she realizes she can't fight her feelings any longer for her best friend, bookstore owner Grace Everett. (978-1-62639-771-2)

Wishing on a Dream by Julie Cannon. Can two women change everything for the chance at love? (978-1-62639-762-0)

A Quiet Death by Cari Hunter. When the body of a young Pakistani girl is found out on the moors, the investigation leaves Detective Sanne Jensen facing an ordeal she may not survive. (978-1-62639-815-3)

Buried Heart by Laydin Michaels. When Drew Chambliss meets Cicely Jones, her buried past finds its way to the surface—will they survive its discovery or will their chance at love turn to dust? (978-1-62639-801-6)

Escape: Exodus Book Three by Gun Brooke. Aboard the Exodus ship *Pathfinder*, President Thea Tylio still holds Caya Lindemay, a clairvoyant changer, in protective custody, which has devastating consequences endangering their relationship and the entire Exodus mission. (978-1-62639-635-7)

Genuine Gold by Ann Aptaker. New York, 1952. Outlaw Cantor Gold is thrown back into her honky-tonk Coney Island past, where crime and passion simmer in a neon glare. (978-1-62639-730-9)

Into Thin Air by Jeannie Levig. When her girlfriend disappears, Hannah Lewis discovers her world isn't as orderly as she thought it was. (978-1-62639-722-4)

Night Voice by CF Frizzell. When talk show host Sable finally acknowledges her risqué radio relationship with a mysterious caller, she welcomes a *real* relationship with local tradeswoman Riley Burke. (978-1-62639-813-9)

Raging at the Stars by Lesley Davis. When the unbelievable theories start revealing themselves as truths, can you trust in the ones who have conspired against you from the start? (978-1-62639-720-0)

She Wolf by Sheri Lewis Wohl. When the hunter becomes the hunted, more than love might be lost. (978-1-62639-741-5)

Smothered and Covered by Missouri Vaun. The last person Nash Wiley expects to bump into over a two a.m. breakfast at Waffle House is her college crush, decked out in a curve-hugging law enforcement uniform. (978-1-62639-704-0)

The Butterfly Whisperer by Lisa Moreau. Reunited after ten years, can Jordan and Sophie heal the past and rediscover love or will differing desires keep them apart? (978-1-62639-791-0)

The Devil's Due by Ali Vali. Cain and Emma Casey are awaiting the birth of their third child, but as always in Cain's world, there are new and old enemies to face in post Katrina-ravaged New Orleans. (978-1-62639-591-6)

Widows of the Sun-Moon by Barbara Ann Wright. With immortality now out of their grasp, the gods of Calamity fight amongst themselves, egged on by the mad goddess they thought they'd left behind. (978-1-62639-777-4)

18 Months by Samantha Boyette. Alissa Reeves has only had two girlfriends and they've both gone missing. Now it's up to her to find out why. (978-1-62639-804-7)

Arrested Hearts by Holly Stratimore. A reckless cop with a secret death wish and a health nut who is afraid to die might be a perfect combination for love. (978-1-62639-809-2)

Capturing Jessica by Jane Hardee. Hyperrealist sculptor Michael tries desperately to conceal the love she holds for best friend, Jess, unaware Jess's feelings for her are changing. (978-1-62639-836-8)

Counting to Zero by AJ Quinn. NSA agent Emma Thorpe and computer hacker Paxton James must learn to trust each other as they work to stop a threat clock that's rapidly counting down to zero. (978-1-62639-783-5)

Courageous Love by KC Richardson. Two women fight a devastating disease, and their own demons, while trying to fall in love. (978-1-62639-797-2)

Pathogen by Jessica L. Webb. Can Dr. Kate Morrison navigate a deadly virus and the threat of bioterrorism, as well as her new relationship with Sergeant Andy Wyles and her own troubled past? (978-1-62639-833-7)

Rainbow Gap by Lee Lynch. Jaudon Vickers and Berry Garland, polar opposites, dream and love in this tale of lesbian lives set in Central Florida against the tapestry of societal change and the Vietnam War. (978-1-62639-799-6)

Steel and Promise by Alexa Black. Lady Nivrai's cruel desires and modified body make most of the galaxy fear her, but courtesan Cailyn Derys soon discovers the real monsters are the ones without the claws. (978-1-62639-805-4)

Swelter by D. Jackson Leigh. Teal Giovanni's mistake shines an unwanted spotlight on a small Texas ranch where August Reese is secluded until she can testify against a powerful drug kingpin. (978-1-62639-795-8)

Without Justice by Carsen Taite. Cade Kelly and Emily Sinclair must battle each other in the pursuit of justice, but can they fight their undeniable attraction outside the walls of the courtroom? (978-1-62639-560-2)